Maeve Kelly was born in Dundalk, County Louth, in 1930. After qualifying as a nurse in London, she worked in Oxford and Ireland, where for many years she lived and farmed in County Clare. She broadcasts on RTE, is a frequent guest speaker at writers' and women's conferences, gives readings and runs writers' workshops throughout Ireland. She won a Hennessy Literary Award in 1972. She has published two collections of short stories, *A Life of Her Own* (Poolbeg Press, 1976) and *Orange Horses* (Michael Joseph, 1990; Blackstaff Press, 1991), a collection of poetry, *Resolution* (Blackstaff Press, 1986), and a second novel, *Florrie's Girls* (Michael Joseph, 1989; Blackstaff Press, 1991). Maeve Kelly lives in Limerick.

NECESSARY -TREASONS-

MAEVE KELLY

THE
BLACKSTAFF PRESS
BELFAST

For the women and men in my life, but especially for my husband Gerard, my son Joseph, my daughter Oonagh, and, last but by no means least, for my mother Ellen. This book should also be dedicated to my sisters and brothers, whose influence on my life has been considerable, but especially to Seamus and Brian, who gave me extra insights into the human experience.

First published in hardback in 1985 by
Michael Joseph Limited
27 Wrights Lane, London W8 5TZ

First published in paperback in 1986 by
Methuen and Company Limited

This edition published in 1991 by
The Blackstaff Press Limited
3 Galway Park, Dundonald, Belfast BT16 0AN, Northern Ireland
with the assistance of
The Arts Council of Northern Ireland

Printed by The Guernsey Press Company Limited

British Library Cataloguing in Publication Data
Kelly, Maeve, 1930–
Necessary treasons.
I. Title
823.914 [F]
ISBN 0-85640-479-9

1

On a winter's afternoon, Eve Gleeson picked shells along a beach in west Clare. She paused occasionally to straighten up and admire the house in which she was spending the weekend. In solitary splendour it commanded the view of the bay and the broad sweep of the estuary where it widened to meet the Atlantic Ocean. Behind the house conifers climbed the hill, their dark green a velvety background to the pink brick façade glowing in pale sunlight.

Earlier Eve had watched a flight of geese arrowing in to their feeding ground. Something about their wild freedom tempted her out of the house, in spite of the near freezing temperatures. The sisters who were her hosts exclaimed in horror and almost in unison at the notion. Their brother Hugh, her 'unofficial' fiancé, intervened with his customary tact on her behalf, suggesting that she might pick shells for them.

'Well,' they relented. 'Perhaps. But she must make herself up warm. We can't have her catching pneumonia. It's such a responsibility having guests.' They had a habit of talking about her to Hugh as if she wasn't there. She had been amused at first but was now beginning to find it less comical. Hastily putting on muffler, woollen cap, gloves and two pairs of socks, she fled.

The shells were as fragile and delicately coloured as the pictures the sisters made from them. Varnished and mounted on black velvet, they were transformed into stylised floral designs or glued on pots containing rooted cuttings from rare Himalayan or South American plants.

5

'So useful for presents,' Bridget had told her. 'We have a great many cousins who are always getting married and having babies and we like to send the parents something. Babies only need food and love. And we can't provide that for them, can we?'

She agreed because she was expected to, hoping there was no implied insult. Should she have said something like 'But of course you have plenty of love to give' or 'I'm sure you would feed them if you could'?

The sound of sea water crunching on stones reminded her that the tide was coming in. Further up the estuary a lone curlew called, intensifying the solitude. What a wonderful, peaceful place it was. Hugh was lucky.

Hugh's grandfather, who had inherited the house in 1876, had the typical Victorian interest in botany and on some of his travels as a young man had acquired the basis of his collection of plants. Many specimen shrubs had died but a few survived. Their long Latin names meant nothing to Eve. Honora was the expert in this respect but did not flaunt her knowledge. That would have been vulgar. Their grandfather designed the terraced garden behind the house, which had long since been abandoned by the sisters, who now concentrated mainly on herbaceous borders and shrubberies and rockeries.

The first owner of the house, built in the late seventeenth century, was a Dutch merchant, one of those who left traces of their presence in the Dutch gables scattered here and there in the city of Limerick and in parts of Clare. The builder was himself a Dutchman. ROTHERY FECIT was inscribed over the doorway to the stableyard. The Rothery family produced craftsmen and builders during the seventeenth and eighteenth centuries. Their solid but elegant houses stood the test of time. The merchant acquired the land and the original tower house at a time when the native owners were everywhere being dispossessed. It was a convenient situation for a man who imported French wines and textiles and other luxuries from the continent. The new landowners were eager purchasers as they set about consolidating their gains by displays of wealth and

6

power. The recently dispossessed may have chafed, but for the most part they smouldered in silence.

Eve considered the name of the Creaghs' house singularly unimaginative. 'Tower Hill' had no touch of poetry about it and certainly none of the sisters' quirky eccentricity. But, she reflected, it suited Hugh; and at the thought, she sighed. The tower was like him: straight, reliable, functional. She glanced in its direction but from the beach all she could see was a hint of grey stone behind the stunted branches of a Dutch elm blackened by disease.

'A funny coincidence,' Florence had remarked at breakfast, commenting on the name. 'Let's hope it doesn't spread into the panelling in the front hall.'

They had a simple pride in the antiquity of the house. It had, according to family tradition, been bought by their ancestors 'after many vicissitudes'.

'That's what it says in one of the papers upstairs,' Honora told Eve. 'Hugh knows more about it than I do. He spends a lot of time sorting out those things up in the attic. It's quite damp and unhealthy but he will persist. They are interesting papers, but who cares about that sort of thing nowadays? And you never know what might come from it. Skeletons in the cupboard. Leave well enough alone, I always say.'

In fact Hugh was at that very moment in the attic. 'Rummaging,' Ruth said. He had offered to go with Eve to the beach, but since he had already mentioned a little wistfully that he would like to look for some missing letters she said, 'Don't be silly, Hugh. You don't have to chaperone me. I'd quite like the walk on my own.' This was partly true and partly to provide him with the excuse he needed.

He had apparently led the sisters to believe that marriage was in the offing. They seized on the notion with excitement. 'What a babe,' they exclaimed when they saw her. 'So young. So vulnerable. So brave. Marriage is a serious business. Are you sure you are ready? A doctor must be very responsible. Our dear Hugh is a busy man. With grave responsibilities. Very grave. Life and death, you know. In the hollow of his hand. Can you imagine it? All those precious lives relying on his wisdom.' The fussing confused her.

It would have been rude to have said she hadn't agreed to anything. It would have spoiled their pleasure. It might even have humiliated them a little, since they appeared to think so much of their brother – although there were small comments and gestures which sometimes seemed to give the lie to their expressed approval. But perhaps she was just misinterpreting their signals. Standing behind them, Hugh grinned sheepishly. When she blurted out, 'I am not a complete fool,' she was alarmed by their response. The wilting, the hurt withdrawal, the acts of contrition, the endless references to the remark were excessive punishment for a moment of tactlessness.

'My dear, we do all know, for Hugh has told us often, how clever you are. All those exams. None of us ever had brains like that. Our poor dear parents had to provide for our education out of their own pockets. Lucky for us they had the means. Otherwise we should have remained uneducated and even sillier than we are. We do admire you. It must be wonderful to be so clever. Of course we gave up everything to look after them. So perhaps we paid them back a little. One can never repay one's parents of course. Not fully. Not for all that care and attention. Wonderful parents we had, wonderful.'

She was demolished. It was hard to know who said what or if they all spoke together. There were only four sisters, yet there seemed to be hundreds of fluttering hands and high sweet voices and smoky-blue eyes and cloudy-grey hair. They were, she was amazed to see, all remarkably beautiful. Hugh was attractive in a heavy way, but the sisters, so many years older than he, were stunning. And they were so quick. The eyes, like the hands, were everywhere, darting around doors, flying across the dinner table, peering into saucepans, whisking a chocolate mousse, 'dear Hugh's favourite', brushing suddenly discovered cobwebs from corners, 'this house is so old, much too old', or trilling up and down the piano or, most surprising of all, the piano accordion.

That was Ruth. The house was full of movement but never noisy except when Ruth played the piano accordion. Then everyone scattered to their rooms, locking their doors to keep out the brash vulgar sound. 'Sorry, dears, sorry,' Ruth would call, between bouts. 'I do apologise. But it's no fun if it's not loud. It's my one little weakness. Bear with me, please, bear with me.'

There was no escape, not even in the bathroom with both taps on, nor in the sitting room with radio volume turned to maximum. The tiny Ruth balanced the monstrous instrument on her knees as if determined to control its powerful masculine energy. Sousa's marches were rendered with ferocity. Battalions of soldiers marched through the hall, spitting from the corners of their mouths, shifting heavy rucksacks and guns.

Protest was useless. Hugh laughed at Eve's baffled face. 'You'll get used to them. But they are fascinating, aren't they? And I did warn you.'

'The reality is much stranger than the imagined. Are they –' She almost said 'quite normal' but a wary flicker in his expression told her to take care. 'Always like this?'

'They lead very isolated lives. After all, they haven't much contact with other people. Their friends have died off or are living abroad, or simply find the journey here too much. I've a feeling you'll bring new ideas to them. I know they like you.'

It seemed so. Their effusive greetings could hardly be affected. But then there were all those odd little remarks. Nudgings almost. Were they just signals to her to remember her place or pathetic efforts to hold on to their own? And who would want to oust four ageing sisters from their niche in the mountain? It would be like robbing a nest of its precious occupants.

Eve had met Hugh's sisters only twice before this weekend visit. From the start they had exchanged the quick looks she was beginning to be familiar with, eyes flickering signals of alarm or suspicion. In an effort to reassure them, in case they were suffering pangs of sisterly jealousy, she deliberately tried to be casual with Hugh and he reacted without too much surprise. Perhaps their relationship *was* casual, she thought. Perhaps that was what was so good about it.

It was a shock to discover that he had such unusual sisters. When she had first met him he had the solitary look of a man unencumbered by relationships. It had given him an impregnable air. He was standing alone, in the corner of a drawing room, removed from the chatter of a housewarming party. All around him people swirled and gossiped. He is like a tree, she thought, he is just like a tree. He will drop his leaves at the appropriate time but he will always be a tree. Then he turned his head and she saw that he was uncomfortable. Someone made a joke near him and the laughter around the joker seemed to remind him of his isolation, for he moved, as if on impulse, to a group across the room, where he began to talk. They listened with polite interest. Later in the evening as they passed plates of food to one another at the buffet table he remarked, 'I haven't seen you before, have I? I seem to know most people here.'

'My name is Eve Gleeson. I've lived here all my life, apart from university in Cork.'

'Well.' He sighed. 'I suppose I'm a bit out of touch. I'm Hugh Creagh. I've lived here or around here most of my life too. Well, I was born in Clare of course. But Clare and Limerick have always been very close. Until we got the ferry. That links us with Kerry now. It makes a difference.'

'You're Dr Creagh,' she said. 'I seem to remember my mother attended you at one time. But years ago, I think.'

'Really?' he said and suddenly turned away from her.

What have I done, she thought. Have I insulted him? But after all he is rude. Fancy turning his back like that. And she forgot about him.

Their second meeting had begun as badly as their first had ended. She had collected some newly framed prints when she saw him standing glaring at her Mini, which she had parked with not an inch to spare between his Granada and a large van.

'Sorry, sorry. I was only a minute. I'll move it. Now.'

'I didn't think anyone could get in front of me,' he said and relaxed at her apology. 'I should have remembered the Mini. Can I help you with those?' pointing to the pictures she was pushing on to the back seat.

'No. No. Thanks just the same,' she cried, wishing he would go away.

10

'We met at that party,' he said.

'Yes. I remember. We exchanged a few words.'

'I wasn't in very good form that night,' he said. 'I can't have been much company.'

She smiled blankly and sat behind the wheel while he towered over both her and the car.

'Have you time for a drink of something or other?'

'No. I'm afraid I haven't. But thanks for asking me.'

He had a funny stiff way of turning, as if afflicted by sudden discomfort. He sat into his car as she nosed out of his way. Through her rear mirror she caught a glimpse of his face, heavy and sad. A melancholy man, she thought. I can do without that. Then she stopped the car and called back to him. 'Yes, I think after all I have the time. I'd love a cup of tea and a cream bun.' His face lightened by the merest shade and he heaved himself out of his seat.

He guided her through the foyer of Cruises Hotel, a hand tipping her elbow. He is steering me, she thought. How funny. They sat near a window in the lounge overlooking the street. Outside, the world hustled. Inside, commercial travellers and countrywomen in town for a day's shopping sipped their tea and munched their sandwiches and cream buns. The tea was good, the cream on the cakes fresh.

'You're enjoying that,' he said, leaning back in his chair and watching her with approval. She licked the cream off her fingers, watching for his reaction. 'You like cream,' he said.

'I don't particularly.' She shook her head to emphasise the denial. 'I feel a little hungry today. That's all. But you seem to enjoy watching people eat.'

'I like to see people happy. That's what I noticed about you at that party. You looked so serene and happy. And your hair. I noticed your hair. Botticelli.'

'I suppose you see a lot of misery,' she replied, trying to deflect what was suspiciously like a compliment.

'I can't say I do. No more than you do. Aren't you a remedial teacher?'

'How do you know that?'

'I asked.'

11

She turned away from his intent blue eyes. 'This is my first job. And the children seem quite happy. There are problems, though.'

'I'm sure you're very good with them.'

'I'm sure you're a very good doctor.'

'We seem to be playing a kind of chess.'

She sipped her coffee and he said, 'You have beautiful eyebrows,' and then looked down at his empty cup.

She had the strangest feeling of tenderness for him. His lashes were dark and thick. 'You have very nice eyelashes. I'm sure your women friends must envy you.'

'I don't have any women friends. I live quite alone. I visit my sisters in Clare occasionally. Well. Every other weekend, I suppose. It varies. Sometimes they come to see me.'

What am I doing talking to this strange man about eyelashes and eyebrows and sisters, Eve thought.

'I mention your eyebrows,' he said, 'because it is the one thing I remember my mother remarking about my sisters, who are quite good-looking. Probably they were beautiful when they were young. But all mother ever said was, "Ruth has beautiful eyebrows." And so she had, smooth and dark under her bright hair. Two beautiful shining curves. Your hair is darker. You're more chestnut, I think.'

There was a silence then, which grew heavier the longer it was left uncured. At last Eve blurted out what seemed like a stone thrown to shatter some dangerous conspiracy: 'Well, I'm not a blonde.'

'Nor dumb,' he said with a smile which illuminated his sober features.

'I don't know why blondes should always be called dumb or be even considered especially attractive,' Eve said. 'I suppose it was all those film stars putting peroxide in their hair that started the rot.'

'I think it has a longer tradition than that. My brother Donogh was blond, and athletic and clever too.'

'A lot of people think looks are important. I don't.'

'You don't have to,' Hugh said firmly. 'If you weren't so good-looking you would think it was important. But you

12

ought to
be aware o...

What am ...
go,' leaping to ...
the room, throu...
He watched while ...
called, 'May I phone ...
and waved cheerfully t...

A few days later a lar...
were chrysanthemums the c...
them said, 'The nearest I cou...

'How funny and old-fashion...
she went to the looking-glass an...   ...rs
next to her hair. Her amused, sher...   ...kled
with glee and mockery. 'You are bein...   ...leeson,'
she said. 'This is called wooing.' She dan...   ...the room,
singing, 'A-wooing we will go, a-wooing we...   go. Hey ho the
merry oh, a-wooing we will go.' Later in the evening he
telephoned and invited her to the theatre the following week.
She could not refuse.

When the occasion arrived she insisted on paying for herself.
He was genuinely shocked. 'You're my guest,' he protested. 'I
cannot allow such a thing.'

'Well, I'm sorry,' Eve said. 'I always pay my own way. I've
got into the habit of it. I don't like being paid for.'

'You're my guest,' he repeated. 'Don't you understand?'

He was silent for the duration of the play, a comedy.
Eventually Eve's laughter had a heartless sound to her own
ears. They both sat as mute islands in a great sea of mirth.
When the play was over he drove her to her flat. She offered
him a drink or a cup of coffee. To her dismay and surprise, he
thanked her and said he would appreciate one very much.

'It's just like you,' he said, looking around the room while
she brewed the coffee.

'I love it,' she responded. 'It's only a bed-sitter but it's my
very own.'

'I like your colour scheme,' he said.

'It's functional but full of light,' she answered. 'I can stack

board. I take off the legs
...ke my batik?' It hung on the
...e golden rays pointed to a tumble
...ting from earth's dark cavern.
... of Persephone,' she said. 'Don't you see?'
... Of course,' he said. 'It's a happy interpretation.'
...sed to scare me, that story. I hated it. That dark king and
the poor mother searching for her daughter.'

'Well. Spring triumphs in the end. Joy conquers grief.
Resurrection.'

A few days later they passed each other in the street. She was
with a man she had once thought she loved. Hugh saluted them
both gravely. It was obvious he was angry or disappointed.

'Who was that?' her companion asked in exaggerated
disbelief. 'Is he real? Did you see him? He practically bowed.'

'He's just polite, that's all. Ever heard of good manners?'

The row that followed was not really over Hugh, she realised
later. It was a repeat performance of other rows with other
would-be lovers – those ephemeral young men of her recent
past. Each complained of her attitude, some accusing her of
indifference, others of prudery. She made excuses and gave
explanations but her honesty was not appreciated. She had not
fallen in love with them and she was not able to pretend for the
sake of a sexual experience. Her contemporaries took risks in
their relationships and suffered the consequences. I don't want
to leap into bed with people I hardly know, she said. I've seen
too many disasters. She didn't want to end up like the girl she
knew at university who was pregnant in her second year, who
missed lectures during her pregnancy, and failed her finals
because the infant had whooping cough and measles in her last
term. Friends, including Eve, had tried to help but in the end
they had their own work to do. Eve saw her weep for herself
and then kiss the child with a passion of guilt simply because
she had wept. I should be happy, she cried. I deserve to be
happy. I should be a good mother. But I'm not. I'm not.

It was a relief to find in Hugh the qualities she missed in
younger men – reason, patience and, above all, integrity. He
was occasionally moody but he made no demands. He was

sometimes possessive, especially when she had made arrangements to meet her women friends and he felt some urgent need to see her. He made few amorous advances. She felt safe with him and could relax in his company.

They often had lunch together, either in a restaurant or in her apartment. He flattered her gently. She knew that she was blossoming under his admiring gaze and was amused to find herself in romantic settings with candlelight and flowers.

'It's a bit wasted on me,' she told him. 'Tables for two and compliments over coffee?'

'I don't notice it doing you any harm. I mean everything I say to you. I hope you believe that. Why shouldn't I tell you you have beautiful hair and brilliant eyes?'

'So have you, and I don't keep telling you.'

'What do you mean?' he asked in surprise.

'You have beautiful hair and brilliant eyes,' she teased. 'There you are, you're blushing.'

'I give up,' he laughed.

'I think ours is an old-fashioned courtship,' she said one day as they were lunching in her apartment. 'Very verbal. Shouldn't you sing under my window some night?'

'If I could sing I would,' he said. 'I don't have any talents. Except that I think I might be good at sculpting if I tried. I'm sure it's fascinating and fulfilling.'

'Your head would make a marvellous bronze. I can just see it on a stand in some elegant drawing room.'

'I'm not sure that I wish for such a fate,' he said.

'Some people's features seem chiselled. Yours are sculpted.'

'I don't know what the difference can be. I suppose it's a compliment. You keep pinching my lines.'

'Why should you not be flattered? You are beautiful. I hadn't realised it until lately?'

'At least I'm growing on you. That's a good sign.'

It was early afternoon on a black November day. Outside in the streets the population of Limerick went about its business, trying to penetrate the thick mist, neither rain nor fog but wetting and choking, that enveloped the city.

'It's an oasis of light in here,' Hugh said. 'I wish I could stay all afternoon with you.' He got up as he spoke and reached for his coat. She helped him put it on.

'I wish you could stay too,' she said.

'When you look like that,' he said, 'I could – I could – '

'What could you do?'

'You know what I could do,' Hugh said smiling at her. 'You know how I feel about you.'

'I suppose I do. But you never show it very much.'

'That's because I respect you. If I thought all that restraint was wasted, I'd kick myself from here to Timbuctoo.'

'Hugh,' she said and shook her head with a touch of hopelessness.

She had moved away from him and was standing under her batik. He smiled again, looking at the picture and then at her and said, 'Do you know what an ironic choice of yours that batik is?' Her answer was apparently superfluous for he turned quickly with one of his quick, decisive movements. 'I have a patient waiting. Goodbye, darling Eve. Be good, sweet maid, and let who will be clever. See you tomorrow.'

She rushed to embrace him. She reached up and kissed him on the mouth. He sighed deeply and held her close, his lips responding to hers. Then he said, 'I've got to go. I have to go,' releasing her arms gently and regretfully.

When he had left she paced the room several times, then sat on her divan, hands between her knees, rocking to and fro. A momentous opportunity had been lost. She had a strange, wild desire for him, something she had never felt before. Years and years ago, she thought, I remember *something* like this. She and a girl friend were playacting in her bedroom, pretending to be lovers in some romantic film. They had kissed in imitation of the cinema scene. Both had pulled apart in amazement at the strength of the sudden shared sensation. Eve was elated by the experience, which seemed to fill her body with a tumult, half fearful, half eager. She then began to listen to the hints and dire warnings of sin and the pleasures of the flesh, which until that moment had been the meaningless utterances of priests on the pulpit or in the confessional.

Remembering the incident, Eve smiled to herself as ruefully

16

as Hugh had done earlier. It was dangerous territory. But surely Hugh must know it better than she? Surely he must have had experience of such things? He was noncommittal about his previous affairs. One or two, that's all, nothing very serious, he said, and left it at that. Or I didn't meet the right woman. I had other things to occupy me. She did not wish to probe into his past in case there were secret hurts. But he did not seem bitter. And his relationship with his family was healthy and normal. He was amused by them and tolerant but, clearly, he loved them. She knew it to be another compliment to her when she was brought to meet them. She hesitated before accepting his invitation for the weekend. For Hugh, such an invitation had significance. For her, it was a movement forward into something from which she might find it hard to retreat. But she was intrigued and curious and he would have been disappointed at a refusal.

2

The sound of a car travelling along the road above the beach interrupted Eve's thoughts. It skidded into the gateway and shrieked up the drive, scattering gravel as it went. Eve winced for the tyres. That must be Eleanor. There had been raised eyebrows and innuendoes about her driving. The sisters' references were sad and apologetic. They constantly reminded themselves to be charitable. 'No. We mustn't say any more. Eleanor is a fine character. A bit unstable, but bursting with brains.' Eve's imagination took flight, picturing grey matter oozing between the fissures of a female skull. The sisters made many references to cleverness. She was not quite sure what they meant.

She crossed the road and followed the skid marks through the gates. At Easter the first tourists would travel this way but between October and March not more than five or six cars passed in a day. Although they were only seven miles from the nearest town, the mountain and encroaching sea cut them off on a peninsula. The road led to the sand dunes and the beach, in summer the haunt of townspeople and holidaymakers from farther afield. The sisters gardened then, said Hugh, frantically trying to keep at bay the lush weeds of June and July. The soil, enriched by many years' application of seaweed and farmyard manure brought in by the cartload, seemed to grow everything in abundance. Azaleas and rhododendrons flourished, as might be expected from the slightly peaty soil, but so did exotic lilies and rare alpines and even the plants normally associated with limestone.

18

Gardening was a serious business with them. As with their other activities, they directed all their enthusiasm towards the work in hand. The result was to be seen not only in the two acres around the house but in their stooped backs and broken nails, their flushed faces and soil-encrusted skin. By July they had won the battle and began to straighten up. By August they were enjoying the fruits of their labour with easier minds. In September they closed the house to visitors and took a well-earned rest. As the beaches emptied, they ventured into the water themselves, taking advantage of the few warm days left.

Hugh admired their stamina. He told Eve they were heroic in a strange way. Eve's first impression was that they fed off one another, each strengthening the other's personality or eccentricity in a disconcerting bond of loyalty. They rushed to defend one another from the slightest hint of censure. Indeed, thinking about them as she picked the shells, she could only see them as a collective and had to make an effort to separate them.

When Eve reached the top of the drive, Eleanor was standing by the hall door staring at her. She wore a mustard-coloured rough-tweed coat and her feet were planted on the ground as if she had just climbed Mount Everest and was about to stick the flag in.

'I haven't knocked,' she said briskly. 'I suppose you're Hugh's fiancée. Congratulations. I'm Eleanor Creagh, Hugh's ex-sister-in-law, as I'm sure you have heard. How do you do.'

Eve was about to say, 'We are not officially engaged,' when it struck her how foolish it would sound. Instead she said, 'Perhaps we should try the back door. But they usually keep it locked.'

'Don't I know it. They're afraid someone will burst in on their poteen sessions or their sex orgies. They know we're here of course. Couldn't avoid it. I make enough noise to rouse a home for deaf mutes.'

Eve stared at the open MG. 'I suppose a motorcycle would be too expensive.' She couldn't understand why she had said it.

'Not afraid of a little weather, are you?' Eleanor asked brusquely. 'Can't say it bothers me. No. It's the insurance

19

angle. Safety helmets and all that. A nuisance. I like to keep my hair on when I'm driving.' She pulled off a brown wig and handed it to Eve.

'It seems a very good idea.' Eve handed it back. Eleanor smoothed down her cropped grey-brown hair and put the wig on again.

'They hate it, of course. "How can you be so vulgar, Eleanor?"' She mimicked their shocked tones exactly. 'I expect they've taught you to hate me already. I know the tricks. Nothing in the open. But enough of the truth to help you build a picture, which, I may say, is totally false. I'm much worse than even they know.' She laughed harshly and banged the door with her fist, yelling, 'We've arrived,' as she did so. 'Are you going to leave us out here all night?' She dropped her voice to a melodramatic whisper. 'They probably want to give you pneumonia. I expect they're planning to get rid of you already. Fancy stealing dear Hugh away. Tut-tut.' She stood back and glared at the door for a moment, apparently assessing its volume and weight, then charged forward to attack it again just as it was pulled in and Ruth stood there smiling.

'Why, Eleanor, how nice. How very nice. Were we expecting you? Welcome, welcome, welcome. Did you knock? I'm afraid the bell isn't working. And Eve. Oh, you poor creature you. Just look at you. Frozen to the marrow. Come in. Come in, pet. Come in.'

Eleanor kissed Ruth on the cheek. 'It's lovely to be here again. Ages since I saw you all. You are looking wonderful, Ruth. Fit as a fiddle. Or should I say accordion. You must play me a tune tonight. I'm sure, Miss, Miss – ' She paused delicately and said to Eve, 'I didn't get your name. We didn't have time for formal introductions,' she explained to Ruth. 'We just met on your doorstep.'

'Oh, oh,' Ruth cried, clapping her hands together like a child. 'I must do the honours then, mustn't I? It's such fun introducing people, don't you think? One never knows what the outcome might be. And there we are, little Ruthy, playing God, and throwing down the dice.'

'I know exactly what you mean, Ruth. Don't let us deprive you of your moment of triumph. We're waiting. Roll the dice. Pull out the pin and let the future explode.'

Eve started to say, 'As a matter of fact we did – '

'Nod at each other, no more,' Eleanor interrupted savagely. But Ruth had drawn back and was looking warily at them. 'There isn't much point, is there? You know she's Hugh's fiancée, don't you? Well, not quite, I suppose – his girlfriend. But I think there's an understanding, isn't there? And she must know you're Eleanor. Who else could you be?' Eleanor guffawed. 'A perfect introduction. Hallo, Miss almost-fiancée, girlfriend. Glad to meet you. Am I in my usual room, Ruth, or have I been evicted yet?'

'You know we always keep Donogh's room for you,' Ruth called up the stairs after her. 'No one else is ever allowed to sleep there.' Was that a barb, a poisoned arrow, shot after the retreating back? The sweet smoky eyes were hooded for a second before they lifted to beam into Eve's. 'Now, pet, come and have supper. We shan't wait for Eleanor. She is never on time.'

Hugh had heard Eleanor's banging on the front door and ignored it. Then he heard her determined steps to the landing below him and the clanking of the lavatory chain. Honora gave her fruity call, 'Hugh-oo. Su-up-per,' and below in the hall Florence boomed the dinner gong. The musty smell of the attic clung to his clothes and hands. He met Eleanor as she left the bathroom.

'Been cobwebbing again?' she asked. He pushed his hand defensively over his head. 'Very becoming.' She grinned. 'Little Eve will be impressed. Find any family papers pertaining to my present state? Any twentieth-century missives from Donogh?'

'You know we have all tried everything possible.'

'Wish you'd try fixing the lav. chain. Haven't you got any plumbers in west Clare or are they all too busy piping Phil the Fluther's Ball?'

'Eleanor, you are the only one in the whole world who cannot pull a lavatory chain properly. A little kindness, that's all it needs. A gentle touch. Every time you come we have the same problem.'

'You might install modern plumbing. But then life's full of these little ups and downs. I suppose we must just suffer on. You, dear Hugh-oo, had better hurry up and wash your hands or they'll be sending out a search party.' The dinner gong sounded twice down in the hall. 'See,' she said and laughed at the repressed fury on his face.

The fire in the drawing room was lit. The mixture of peat and logs burned brightly. Eve held her hands out to the warmth, smiling at the flames.

'You look nice tonight, dear,' Ruth said. 'I'm sure Hugh must be very proud of you.'

'Why?' Eve asked. 'Because I look nice tonight?'

She regretted it instantly. It was more caustic than she had intended. Already tears of hurt and puzzlement were brimming over in Ruth's eyes and Eve would be reduced to remorse for the rest of the evening.

'I'm glad you think so,' Eve added in haste. 'I bought this dress especially for the weekend.' Banality might avert tragedy.

For a moment it seemed as if she were too late. She waited for withdrawal or a dismissive remark, but the gesture was accepted, for Ruth said, after a pause during which Eve hung perilously between forgiveness and condemnation, 'That was thoughtful of you. I always say it is a great compliment when people dress up, especially for us. I am afraid we are rather old-fashioned, both in manner and in dress.' Eve could not be sure if the last sentence hid a reprimand, but, even if it did, she deserved it.

Later, at supper, in the relaxed and warm atmosphere, she felt happier. Hugh sat opposite her at the table. She rested her eyes on his face, drawing from it comfort and reassurance. In this house she felt vulnerable. Only when she was near him did she feel less at risk. Once during the evening, he was surprised to find her stroking his sleeve, and for a horrifying moment she thought he was embarrassed and would look furtively around to see if they were observed. It seemed then as if their whole future was threatened. Her ability to love him depended on a

22

single glance. She almost cried with relief when he smiled at her and touched her fingers with his own. Watching him now across the table, her confidence was restored completely. This was Hugh's home and it must be full of loving memories which would one day include her own.

'Open the windows and let's hear the sea.' Bridget was at the head of the table pouring coffee when Eleanor rapped out the request like a commanding officer.

'I didn't know you could hear it from this distance,' Eve said.

'If the wind is right and the tide is coming in, you can hear it quite clearly,' Hugh told her. 'But it's very cold for open windows. Do you think we should, Eleanor?'

'You know how hard it is to get the heat up again,' Bridget warned.

'I forgot about that. Ah well, we can go outside and listen.' She looked around the table invitingly. 'No takers? What a lot of old maids you are.'

'We hear the sea every day,' Honora remarked. 'It is no novelty for us. But if you are going outside, make yourself up warm. You might catch cold and pass it on to your patients. Perhaps even to us. Not that we matter, although indeed at our age colds can be quite dangerous.'

'I'll go with you.' Eve suddenly needed to express some kind of sisterhood with Eleanor. 'There is something fascinating about the sea on a winter's night. An untamed beast. At home in its jungle. Summer seas have all the spirit knocked out of them. It seems a little indecent to have people disporting themselves on beaches as if they don't recognise that power.'

Hugh looked at her in astonishment.

'What a funny thing to say,' Honora said.

'I know just what she means.' Florence, nun-like, had kept her head down, listening. 'It's positively disgusting the way people flaunt themselves. Brazen, that's what they are.'

Bridget intervened tactfully. 'Eve didn't quite mean that, I think, but we understand your feelings. Our privacy goes in the summer.' She turned to Eve. 'We sometimes find it hard to get used to it. When we were children, no one ever came here, apart from the people we invited to stay, of course. It was almost a private beach then.'

'People knew their place then,' Florence burst out. 'They wouldn't dare walk across our gardens. But now they keep coming up to the house and asking for things in the most impertinent manner. Water to make their tea, or a "grain of salt", as they put it, for their sandwiches, or even to use the phone because the baby is sick and they want free advice from our poor doctor who is run off his feet. We dread the summer. Simply dread it. But now I won't let them use the phone. I pretend it's out of order. Why should I? They made their beds, let them lie on them. They got married and they had their babies. Let them look after them and buy their own salt for their sandwiches.'

'It is certainly rather inconsiderate of them,' said Eve.

'If you knew. If you only knew.' Florence turned to her in relief.

'Well, I'm sure she doesn't want to hear all our sad stories,' Honora interrupted. 'While they are having their little breath of air we will help Rosie clear up. A woman's work is never done.'

'A well-timed interruption,' Eleanor said outside. 'You just escaped in the middle of one of Flo's tirades.'

'I sympathise with her. It is horrible to be taken advantage of.'

'Oh indeed?' Eleanor's tone made Eve wince. 'We are a sensitive soul. What a furore over nothing. A few simple requests now and again. There may have been one mother one day with a sick baby, or one unfortunate man who couldn't swallow his sandwiches without lacerating his stomach in the process and hadn't the wit or wherewithal to boil some sea water and get his own sea salt.'

'When you put it like that, it does seem a bit silly. But she was so upset.'

'You'll learn,' Eleanor said nonchalantly.

I don't want to learn, Eve thought. I don't want to discover their hidden meanings, the truth behind the hints.

'The trouble is,' Eleanor went on, 'when you marry one,

24

you marry all. It's the family mafia. I expect it's the same everywhere. Otherwise why all those mother-in-law jokes?'

'That doesn't prove anything. There are rape jokes as well.'

'Yes, my child. But they are all part of the same sexist world and the family is part of that. Anyway, I don't feel like going into all that just now. It's too cold.' She pushed her hands deep into her pockets. Behind the clouds the moon moved palely and the sea showed black and shining, fringed with white.

'Three rows of breakers,' Eleanor murmured. 'A lovely storm beach. What wouldn't I give to be down there.'

'I suppose it is too cold,' Eve said agreeably.

'You complain a lot about the weather, don't you?' Eleanor jerked her head as if shaking off an irritating fly. 'It's the wrong month. September is best for bass. February is a useless kind of month.'

'It's the first of the Irish spring.'

'Trust us to start in the middle of winter.'

'But don't you think there are little stirrings in February? It's getting brighter. I always start marking on the calendar now so that I can celebrate when I can put the light off for tea. And even in town you can hear the birds growing active.'

Eleanor did not reply and Eve felt foolish. Perhaps she should not have disagreed. So many people disagreed just for the sake of argument. She didn't want Eleanor to think she was like that. There was something admirable about Eleanor, a kind of grim strength. She didn't want to lose a potential friend, perhaps even an ally. Yet it would not do to align herself too openly with her. Just in case. She pushed away the unworthy thought and tried to make amends.

'Of course you are right, really. It isn't very spring-like out here. It was freezing down on the beach.'

'Always stick to your guns,' Eleanor advised harshly. 'That's another thing you'd better learn in this house. Never retract. Never apologise. They'll have your guts for garters.'

She plodded towards the garden steps. Eve watched her descend and follow the paths between the blank flowerbeds and the shrubbery until she was swallowed up by dark shapes.

Eve hurried into the house. Opening the door into the

25

dining room, she asked, 'Hugh, would you like a walk?'

The room was empty; the table, which had reverted to a vast mahogany stand for a centrepiece of dried flowers, shone in the firelight. In the corner the standard lamp glowed against the wall on which hung family photographs. Curious, she went to examine them and then felt guilty, as if she were prying in private closets. Hugh on his graduation day was recognisable in a big silver frame. An unknown little girl in a stiff pose glowered from an oval frame. In the corner there was a wedding group. Again Hugh was there, this time as best man. And the bride, caught forever in a look of trustful love as she gazed at her husband, was a slender, smiling Eleanor. 'Oh,' Eve said aloud in dismay. Before she ran from the room she took one furtive glance at the groom. He was not in the least like Hugh. She had such a sense of relief at suddenly averted disaster that her heart pounded.

Hugh was reading by the drawing-room fire. He looked at home, his feet on the pouffe, his pipe lighting. Ruth and Bridget sat opposite him, Bridget knitting what appeared to be a muffler, Ruth darning socks.

'Hugh,' Eve said again. 'Would you care for a quick walk?'

The fact that she had already issued the invitation to an empty room made it sound to Eve inane. Bridget and Ruth appeared to share her opinion, for they both put down their work and stared at her, one in horror, the other with quiet disapproval.

'What a cracky thing,' Ruth said. 'On a night like this. Some people are quite cracky.'

She bent her head to pick up a thread. Bridget frowned and said more gently, 'Hugh looks so comfy there in his armchair it seems a pity to disturb him.'

Eve looked at him for response. His pipe had half slipped out of his mouth, the book had fallen on his chest, and he gave a first little rising snore.

'There you are,' Ruth said. 'There's your answer. Now that settles it. Take the pipe from his mouth like a good child and come and sit beside us. We haven't had a little chat by ourselves yet.'

Bridget leaned forward and added conspiratorially, 'We must get to know one another better.'

It would have been churlish to refuse. But she prayed silently, Oh God, save me from whatever I need to be saved from.

They questioned her delicately about her work.

'I don't know how you people do it,' Bridget said. 'You're so brave. I could never face poor little children in that condition. I'm such a coward.'

'We're a very sensitive family,' Ruth explained. 'All of us are the same. We cannot bear suffering. It's a dreadful disadvantage. We're so useless. Perhaps if we went out into the world we'd get hard and be able to do things.'

Eve was confused. When Ruth said, 'We're so useless,' her reaction was one of sympathy. One might reassure and say, nonsense, of course not, and quite truthfully be able to point out the many marvellous and useful things they were doing. But then the almost sanctimonious self-justification destroyed sympathy. 'It's nothing to do with hardness,' she protested weakly.

'Oh, but you must be very hard. A very good thing too. Nurses must too or they simply wouldn't be able to do their work.'

'They must surely be very bad nurses if they become hard, as you say,' Eve replied. She wondered if their definition of the word was the usual one.

'I should certainly hate to be nursed by someone who was feeling my pain,' Bridget said briskly. 'It would make it all the more difficult to bear, having to think about their feelings instead of being able to wallow in one's own misery. Nurses ought not to have any feelings. It would be wrong of them.'

'I dare say if she was a good nurse she would be careful not to let you know how she felt, and a remedial teacher wouldn't be much use if she was a great drooling slob weeping all over her pupils.'

'My dear,' Bridget said. 'You sound angry. I hope we haven't offended you?'

'That's the last thing we want,' Ruth agreed. 'If you and

Hugh are right for each other, then it is only right that we should love you too.'

The heat from the fire made her dizzy. She glanced towards Hugh, still snoring softly. With a great effort she got up and said, 'I'll join Eleanor for a few moments.'

'What do you want to do that for?' they asked. 'You'll freeze outside.'

'I'd like a little fresh air,' she excused herself feebly.

'Are you all right, dear?' They stared at her with a strange mixture of alarm, solicitude and – could it possibly be? – some form of calculation. She rushed from the room to the front door, carelessly letting it bang after her.

I hope that wakes him, she thought, and I'll probably get pneumonia out here. She inhaled the icy air with relish.

Eleanor's voice came from the darkness. 'Lesson number two. You can't win. You are young, pretty, clever and sane. It is no contest.'

'I don't know what you mean,' Eve said. 'I just found that room overpoweringly stuffy.'

'Suffocating,' Eleanor said.

3

Hugh was innocently unaware of the effect his sleeping form and mild snoring had on Eve. He usually slept after dinner at Tower Hill, probably as a result of the strong sea air. It had nothing to do with age, he told Ruth, when in a cantankerous moment she made some remark about crabbed age and youth not being able to live together. He was, he pointed out, in the prime of life, and he had plenty to offer Eve.

'She doesn't seem to have any qualms,' he said.

'Well, of course we all know she's very lucky,' Ruth said. 'I was only thinking of you.'

Her comment angered him, especially when she added insult to injury by saying, 'You'll be forty-five next birthday.' He managed to restrain himself from reminding her that she was over ten years older. That would have led to a family argument, the others joining in and no doubt changing sides with gusto. It could go on for days. Just when it was dying someone would breathe a kiss of life into it: 'Remember when you said last week ... '

Yet his approaching birthday affected him as no other had. In previous years, birthdays had merely been marks on a calendar, occasions for receiving cards from each sister, usually handpainted or with pressed flowers encased in cellophane or plastic. Sometimes a knitted object accompanied a card, an egg cosy with a tiny tassel, a tea cosy in the shape of a thatched cottage, a cover for a hot-water bottle, a pair of mitts. This last came from Florence.

'Doctors' hands are always like icebergs,' she wrote,

29

although she had never been to a doctor in her life. 'Rude health, I have rude health,' she boasted. They all agreed. Hugh told Eve that they must be as strong as horses to survive the winters in their draughty house. Now and again they 'came down with a cold' and coughed for weeks, being nursed, each one in turn, by the others. One year they were all ill together with Asian flu but wouldn't let Hugh examine them or call another doctor.

'A waste of time and money,' they said. 'We are indestructible.'

Yet they were all getting older, Hugh included. Lately he had begun to take stock of himself – not for any particular reason or even because Ruth's remark had irked him. He simply noticed that there were unconnected events which seemed to be re-shaping his life and which were responsible for what he could only call 'flashes of insight'. It was an emotive and even emotional term for him to use. He knew that he would never be regarded by his family and colleagues as an imaginative man. Patient, reliable: those were the words used to describe him. His sisters occasionally signalled to each other that he was dull, but they would never express it aloud and never admit it to outsiders.

Why was it, then, that he had a curious sensation at times that he was standing outside himself, witnessing changes which were unheralded and often uncomfortable. At forty he had assumed he would remain a bachelor. He had almost resigned himself to the prospect of a retirement in Tower Hill and had expected a gentle downward slide towards that event. Change and development were the marks of youth, not of middle age. Yet here he was experiencing disturbances which forced him to examine and analyse where he had formerly accepted and justified.

The experience of love astounded him. He was alarmed by the speed with which it altered his perception of time and even his own place in that time. It was a kind of insane ecstasy, throwing him into a turmoil which he dared not show. Concealment required discipline and restraint, leading him to make retreats from the present. Searching through the papers

30

in the attic became a consolation. The past was safe and dead with his ancestors. The future lay with Eve, and it beckoned tantalisingly. In the meantime the normal incidents of the workaday world were to be endured as the pricks and insults of unwelcome intruders.

At times he was overwhelmed by a depression so black and all-enveloping that he could scarcely think or speak. These moods usually followed some new perception, one of his 'insights'. He had never been in tune with nature, as was his poet friend Adrian. He scarcely understood the meaning of the term. Yet last autumn he had been filled with melancholy at the sight of a sycamore tree denuded after a storm. And on a particular frosty morning in Tower Hill when windowpanes were engraved with ice, he experienced deep nostalgia at the memory of the boy who used to trace designs with his fingers on the same windows many years before. Now he noticed houses, landscaped and settled, on what had been yesterday's pastures and wild moorland. Once, in the middle of a consultation with a patient, he realised that the man had been born in the very year Hugh had proudly put up his brass plate announcing surgery hours. These insignificant and inevitable marks of passing time became signposts of great meaning. In the city a crowd of teenagers jostling across a footpath, refusing to give way to his seniority, brought to mind an image of himself at fifteen, stolid, polite and mature. The recollection provoked pain and discontent. What had he done with his youth? What was left for him to do?

He began to ponder on the mediocrity of his life. It was all-pervasive, stifling every energetic impulse. One evening he passed an old woman wrapped in a bundle of newspapers lying inside the railings of the Dominican church. She was curled in on herself foetus-like, heedless of the world around her, protected from the cold by layers of newsprint announcing battles and murders. He envied her independence of spirit in choosing the pavement before the hostel. Eve, when he told her, simply said, 'Poor creature,' which he thought callous, and then added that Eleanor was an eccentric also. He could hardly call her 'mediocre'.

'Oh, Eleanor,' he said impatiently. 'Eleanor is different.' He wondered why Eve laughed.

The ruined towers and castles dotted throughout Clare and Limerick did not escape his critical eye. Nowhere was there a building which could be said to stretch the ingenuity of his countrymen. No great vision had found release in stone, expressing the majesty of human endeavour. There were fine houses, but where was the 'citadel', the magic monument to extravagant desires? When he went on a trip to New Grange with Adrian, he remarked that this ancient tomb with its glittering façades of white stone was closer to what he sought.

'Proper order,' Adrian said. 'This challenges death. This is no mere defence. The Celts threw spears at the ocean. The Romans built walls to keep it out. That's the crucial difference between races and temperaments, between the individual with a mystical respect for life and the huckster who bargains with death.'

Before Christmas Hugh had suggested to his sisters that they reconstruct the tower beside the house. He would pay the bill. They dismissed the idea. 'We couldn't let you throw away your hard-earned money. Wait till we're gone and you can do what you like with it.'

He had fantasies of working with stonemasons, cutting and hauling rock, shaping great stairs and vaulted ceilings. They were surprised to see him on one visit chiselling hopelessly but fiercely at a piece of stone. He ignored their knowing looks and kind remarks about the love bug getting him. He paced the base of the tower and examined the thickness of the crumbling walls and dreamed of a great edifice with dungeons and secret passageways and enormous kitchens and huge stone fireplaces, with carved heads on the corners of the mantelpiece.

It was a relief to the sisters when he directed his attention to the family papers, although at first they mounted a faint resistance to what they appeared to regard as an intrusion. One evening Honora asked him to go up to her room and fetch her watch from her dressing box. A letter slipped out from a pocket in the lid and he read it. When he asked her about it, she said crossly, 'I wish people wouldn't go poking their noses in my private papers.'

'You sent me up. I wasn't poking. But what is it all about? Where did you get it?'

'It's ancient history.' She tried to brush aside his question by ripping a row of stitches in her knitting and then concentrating on picking them up. The television sound was turned down and the screen showed a newsreader mouthing something from the corner of the room.

'Aren't you listening to the news?' he asked.

'It's always bad news,' Ruth said. 'Why should we make ourselves miserable? More bombings and cars being blown up and people being assassinated in front of their children.'

'At least get the weather report,' Hugh said.

'They are just old papers,' Honora said, having picked up the stitches.

'You mean there are more? Why have I never seen them?'

Bridget interrupted firmly, 'They are her inheritance from grandmother. They aren't worth anything.'

'How is it you never mentioned them?'

'Why should we?' Ruth joined in. 'They were left to Honora. It's nobody's business but hers. All we got was the use of the house and the land for our lifetime. And the movables. So Honora got the letters because of her name. Everything else is entailed to you and Donogh.'

'It was an awkward will,' Hugh agreed. 'But I never knew you cared.'

'Suppose we wanted to sell the house? Suppose we wanted to live somewhere else? Fiji or the Canaries. Somewhere warm. Just because we stayed at home out of a sense of duty doesn't mean we didn't have ambitions.'

'What has all this got to do with the letter?'

'Nothing. You brought it up. The papers are Honora's to do with as she likes. Why should she mention them?'

'Well,' Hugh agreed, backing down, 'it's just that I find the whole thing interesting.'

'There are heaps of them in the lumber room,' Honora said.

'I haven't read them all, but you can go through them if you like.'

'That's kind of you,' Hugh said. 'I'll be careful.'

'Don't worry about them,' Honora called after him as he left the room. 'Bits of paper. But mind the dust. It might make you sneeze and come out in a rash again.'

'That was Donogh, I think,' Florence said from the corner, where she had been staring at the television screen trying to lip-read. 'Donogh always came out in a rash. Dust and strawberries.'

'Turn up the weather,' Ruth said. 'Not that they ever tell us anything we don't know.'

'It's amusing watching them make fools of themselves with all their charts and numbers.' Honora was leaning over to turn up the sound as she spoke and then changed her mind. 'We don't want to hear it.'

'Rain spreading from the west,' Florence lip-read.

'If they rang us up, we could tell them that rain has fizzled out,' Ruth said.

'Drizzled out you mean,' Bridget said, and they all smiled except Florence, who was still busy lip-reading.

Hugh replaced the letter in Honora's dressing box, which had belonged to their grandmother. There she had kept her lotions and perfumes and a necklet, a strong gold chain with one large ruby suspended. His sister wore it occasionally, since it was a family tradition that whoever bore the name Honora was allowed to have it. It had never been willed to anyone. His sisters had inherited their mother's jewels, which they liked and occasionally wore. No one cared for Honora's necklet. It was heavy and the ruby not a good colour and rather crudely cut. They had had it valued once but the jeweller had dismissed it as being of antique value only, the gold just worth its weight. They were angry with him when he suggested they give it to a museum.

'Have it lie in some musty box? What fools we'd be. Give it to the country? What did the country ever do for us?'

Hugh was glad they had kept it. He wondered if he should ask Honora to give it to Eve but decided against the idea. She

34

would probably refuse. She might even be offended at being asked. And Eve would probably not appreciate it. Perhaps Eleanor was the one who should have it, but that, he knew, was out of the question. His sisters had never forgiven her for driving Donogh away from his home.

He had read the letter again before putting it back. It was short, composed with a firm hand and showing the strong down-strokes of a quill pen. On the top was written *Letter from Honora Creagh to Pierce Creagh, gent.* It began abruptly:

I make haste to tell you all is lost. My husband and my sons dead, murdered. I grieve that Limerick ever was. This necklet I here send and my 2 mares I hope my servant will bring safe. My husband wished you give this Thomas Hickey shelter if you be safe. My sons were hanged, each face to face, by that O'Brien whose word you know. These fields we loved are bare, our cattle slaughtered, our castle lies in ruins. My leg being wounded I now lie in Turlagh's house and die in faith of Christ.
Signed,
Honora Creagh

'These fields we loved are bare.' The sentence hovered in the air about him as he repeated it aloud after closing the lumber-room door behind him. Through the small arched window a glimmer of yellow wintry sun brightened for a moment the dark room. He stared out at the sea, slate grey with a streak of light painted along its meeting place with the sky. He tried to picture the fields beyond the dark conifers of the plantation near the house. They were hemmed in by stone walls, with a mixture of fuchsia and hawthorn hedge and invasive gorse creeping everywhere. Were those the fields referred to in the letter?

He switched on the light and looked around him. Books, paintings, moth-eaten rugs were stacked or rolled against the wall. A pile of obsolete kitchen equipment lay in a jumble near a corner. A meat mincer and a coffee grinder seemed to embrace, their iron handles linking each other where they lay rustily on an enormous cracked serving plate. The large white china cups of his childhood had been retired here, the gold shamrocks still glistening beneath the rims. He supposed the sisters hadn't had the heart to throw them out. His rocking horse, Donogh's Hornby train, dolls, a doll's house, a ragged teddy bear, leather handbags in profusion, hundreds of pairs of shoes, fishing rods in their cloth covers and two tin trunks, unlocked, were part of the collection. He opened the nearest trunk. Inside lay a mass of papers, some rolled neatly and tied with twine, others thrown in higgledy-piggledy fashion, yellowed, fraying and a few quite obviously beyond rescue. Tentatively he unrolled a paper in good condition. On it was written, *A letter from Daniel Viscount Clare to Donat O'Brien, Esq., Ennistymon, preserved at Dromoland and copied by Peter Creagh.* Like the other letter it began without salutation:

You are to remove all the Protestants from Clare Castle and keep them confined in Pierce Creagh's house with a guard of your militia men and townsmen, except George Stamer, whom you are to leave at Clare Castle with a guard I order for him, Mr Purdon, and Thomas Hickman, who are both to remain under the charge of Hugh Sweeny at Clare Castle along with George Stamer. And herein fail not without delay to confine Bindon, Hewitt, and such other townsmen as are in the county, though you have not them in the list returned from Dublin, as Colpoys, young Lee, young Vandeleur, Smith, and all such, especially when you hear of an invader. Take every one of them that are young (Sir or Mr) and let the common sort lie in the prison, and the rest strictly guarded, or rather put into some strong castle with a grate to be locked on the outside, like Ballybannon. The old people need not be so strictly used, but leave not a young Protestant in the county without strait confinement for which this will be your warrant.

Signed,
(Clare)

Hugh knew little of the history of sixteenth-century Clare and Limerick. A few dates – the Treaty of Limerick, 1691; the siege by Cromwell's forces, 1651 – were the memory aids that pointed to its turbulent past. But here in his own home he had come upon a witness which brought the dull facts of learned

36

history to life. The measured, practical tone of the letter recalled the vain attempt of James to restore power to his Catholic allies. The other letter, perhaps written after the earlier siege (neither of the letters was dated), spoke with the voice of the common people. The suffering behind the woman's words could only be guessed at. Hugh was not concerned with that. He was intrigued to find a link between himself and the period which had seen the death of Gaelic Ireland.

His sisters had no such need to resurrect ancestral memories. Totally preoccupied as they were with sewing, cooking, gardening, writing letters to friends and distant cousins, making jams, talking to each other, their house was a kingdom in itself, their world encompassed by its walls. He envied them their activities, the dexterity of their fingers, their nimble ways with shells and wool. He envied their inconsequential conversation even when it irritated him. Like butterflies they flew from topic to topic, sipping at ideas he was forced by his nature to ponder. Brilliant or shallow, he could never decide which, they were certainly far removed from the Honora Creagh who wrote that her sons had been hanged face to face.

He stayed in the lumber room for hours, worrying his sisters, who came tapping at the door with an ancient electric fire, for which of course there was no socket. Bridget brought him a rug and draped it around his shoulders as he sat hunched over the tin trunk. He hardly responded when she said, 'You'll get your death.'

Honora brought him hot lemon and whiskey because it might ward off the cold he was bound to catch. He knew he must cut a ridiculous figure, enveloped in a plaid rug, his fingers purple and numbed, his nose red and icy, as he pored over countless pieces of paper.

For the most part they were a confused heap of bills and receipts, details of land lettings, accounts of timber sold, wages paid, general farm accounts dealing with the purchase of cattle and the planting of crops. Some referred to other farms long since sold in hard times. There were estimates for the grinding of corn in an old water mill. It seemed sinful that all that

37

struggle should have gone for nothing, to end like this in a sterile house with four women gossiping to keep each other company. If only Donogh had stayed, things might have been different. The worst thing Hugh had ever done was to introduce him to Eleanor.

One other letter came to light before he closed the trunk and he went to bed meditating on it. It was enclosed in a small packet on which was written *Pierce Creagh to his brother Andrew* and, in large flowery handwriting, *This letter I copied from my grandmother's copy, who copied it from her grandfather's copy.* There was no date and no address:

> *I pray you have a care lest you be drawn too much into this quarrel. Take lesson from the past. We are not long settled. We can not dare so much. Neither let your son make too hasty marriage. Who knows which way the wind will blow. Word reaches me the English throne is not safe. Let Peter marry neither old English nor Irish. Dame Margaret has a young cousin who may suit for reasons I will tell when we next meet. I pray it may be Easter. This James may not be true to us. My fields had no plough before March, the season being so wet and rough, which may not yield too well. My beeves do fair. My English hath improved much. I pray you practise yours. Give shelter to my servants two nights only. My gift is for your quarter rent. Use it for that purpose* AND FOR NO OTHER.

The last four words were heavily printed for emphasis. With uprisings all about, Hugh could guess at the other purpose for which a gift of money might be used.

Later, when he lay in bed, his feet burning on the hot bottle his sisters had thoughtfully provided, he went over all he had read. He wondered what Adrian, who appeared to have no sense of family, would make of it. His poetry was his key to immortality, his mark on the cave wall. 'Adrian was here, that's all.' That was fine for someone who had no proof of the ancestral struggle, no house filled with the reproachful reminders of the dead who seemed to be pleading directly to Hugh to make sense of their suffering.

Eve might understand his feelings but he wasn't sure if he could confide completely in her. She would be sympathetic, but he wanted more. Empathy, perhaps. Comprehension without the stumbling-block of words. There were many differences between them. Not just age, which he felt could easily be surmounted. Her recent interest in what she called 'women's rights' seemed to him an outrageous waste of time when there were so many real issues of injustice to be fought. He could concede that women were sometimes at a disadvantage but their power was at times quite frightening. Perhaps it was just as well they did not realise what they had. At the thought he smiled a little and fell asleep.

4

It was raining when Hugh and Eve drove back to Limerick early on the Monday morning.

'We didn't get much of a chance to talk,' Eve commented rather sadly as they discussed the house, the sisters and Eleanor. 'Your sisters have very strong personalities.'

'If I called them domineering you'd jump down my throat,' Hugh teased.

'I didn't say they were domineering. I didn't mean that, I meant – strong.'

'They're not milk and water people,' Hugh said proudly.

She drew away from him to stare down at the great curve of the Shannon only partly visible in the rain. Hugh had turned off the main road through Cratloe, which climbed high above the city. The dust from the cement factory hung like a pall over the countryside. Hugh said in gloomy tones, 'I don't know how we breathe.' He had been equally morbid at the sight of the alumina plant further down the estuary. 'Progress,' he muttered, as they passed, 'the ugly obscenity of progress.'

'You've got Monday morning blues in a big way,' Eve said.

For her sake he tried to be cheerful but his thoughts kept returning to the letters in the attic. A world of cruelty and violence lay behind them. He could only guess at the despair and rage of those who struggled to survive while the people who had dispossessed them grew prosperous. A scattered population with few common bonds must have felt helpless in the face of an organised enemy. If people had been able to come together to bury their differences, forget their personal greed, how different would the result have been. Too much individualism produced anarchy. With that kind of society conquest was inevitable. Separation and isolation helped to finish the job.

Eve asked him to drop her off at the printer's.

'Not more posters?' he asked.

'Yes, Hugh. More posters and more leaflets.'

'More litter.'

'We have to keep in touch with other women. Leaflets and posters get the message across.'

'What message is it this time?'

'Oh, nothing much, Hugh. You're not really interested.'

'I'm always interested in everything you do. I just don't see the point in it all.'

'You see,' she said and got out of the car laughing at him.

He watched her stepping over a collection of sweet papers and plastic bottles brought together by a gust of wind. She jabbed a finger mockingly at the mess and ran to the printer's shop. He regretted his gloom on the journey but she would understand it, he was certain. He had intended asking her to go with him to a jeweller's shop, where they could select an engagement ring. It was time to put a seal on their relationship. His sisters had made peculiar comments over the weekend about 'regularising' affairs, as if there was something irregular in his love for Eve.

When he had mentioned an engagement ring to her before, she looked amazed at the idea. But she knew how he felt about her. She knew that marriage was the logical outcome for a man of his standing and substance. He wanted to put down real roots. He wanted to father a son. He would call him Pierce after that other Pierce who had survived the upheavals of his time.

He debated with himself in this way to get rid of the few qualms he had about choosing a ring without her knowledge. A gift of a jewel should be a surprise, not a basement bargain selected together. There was much to be said for the strategy of fait accompli and in any case her taste in jewellery was not as sophisticated as his own. The size of the ring would not matter.

It could be altered or exchanged. The surprise element was all-important.

She had often said that she did not care much for fripperies, as she put it, but this was different. A precious stone of great value could not be treated lightly. The deliberate act of choosing the ring had to be seen as a statement of his power as a husband. In accepting the ring she would also accept that fact. But supposing she rejected it?

It was sometimes hard to know how she would react. A perfectly normal remark occasionally brought a surprising response. When he told her he liked her to look beautiful, meaning it as a compliment, he was amazed and hurt when she drew away from him and said, 'I have my own ideas.' What could she have meant? He puzzled over this but could not bring himself to question her about it. At times she erected a barrier between them, a barrier of indifference, which in someone else he would have thought ill mannered, but in her seemed just part of her quirky, naive independence. It was, he felt, a childish way of showing spirit and he found that endearing.

He had not fallen in love with her at first sight. There had been no sudden descent into that pit of crazy human emotions. But the turmoil he experienced was as intense as if it had been a sudden rapturous revelation. No one, he believed, could know Eve as he knew her, in her most intimate thoughts. He was occasionally wounded by her but he accepted his pain as being part of the process of love. She never hurt him wilfully. Pain, after all, was evidence of life. It was merely the obverse of joy. And he had known much joy since he met Eve. For that he was grateful. He did not show his gratitude to her. It would have demeaned both of them. Love between man and woman was as natural as breathing. Lack of it was a perverse distortion of universal law. Having met Eve, having experienced the pleasure of watching her rush up the steps of his house towards him, or flinging her funny canvas bag over her shoulder as she ran with her delicate long steps towards some task or other, he began to believe that its absence would be worse than death. To have gone through life without knowing such pleasure was

42

never to have been truly born. To deny it when opportunity offered was to turn his back on life.

In the early weeks and months of his discovery of Eve – and he did feel it to be a discovery, one reached at the end of a long and tedious journey in which there had been many false trails and wrong turnings – he often longed to confide in someone but there was no one he could trust with such a secret. His sisters would have made too much of a fuss. His closest friend, Adrian, was too much of a raw cynic about women. Mention of Eve would have brought some damaging, tart response. Hugh wryly recognised his own wish to protect Eve, and though he fought against it because he knew she would not like it, calling it control or possessiveness, he silently reached out to protect her from the faintest smear. Even an innuendo or a generalised joke against women would have tarnished her, and with her his new, bright, glowing treasure of love.

To Eve, he presented his usual, grave, in-control self. Only his sisters caught glimpses of something else, and they who had known him since infancy simply remarked, 'You can't beat nature.' They overheard him carrying on a monologue about Eve in front of the shaving mirror as he cut away his stubble of beard. His routine de-whiskering was interrupted by ejaculations. Oh my God. My God. Eve ... Eve ... Eve ... Her name would burst from his throat as if forced out under pressure.

'Father always went on like that,' Ruth said to the other sisters. 'Hugh gets more like him every day. It's like a reincarnation. The way he walks and holds himself.'

'Oh, don't,' Honora cried. 'You give me the creeps of the heart, as poor Donogh used to say. Remember when he was a little boy how he always said that.'

'Remember how father used to shout for mother the minute he came into the house. "Where's your mother?" he'd say, and then, "Anna, Anna, Anna," until she had to cry out from wherever she was, "Yes, Tom, I'm here."'

'They were always in love,' Honora said. 'But they were so alike. How could Hugh feel like that over this child? She's hardly more than a baby.'

43

'Who knows?' Bridget said charitably. 'It's not for us to question.'

At midday Hugh left the hospital and walked to the jeweller's shop. Choosing the jewel was a pleasure in its own right. As a boy he had collected semi-precious stones and had polished them himself. He had dreamed then of being a goldsmith or a silversmith. Ambition turned dreams to ashes and he had wanted success and respect. One made one's choices very early on. He contemplated the tray before him.

'The diamond is always popular,' the shop assistant said. 'Ladies never seem to tire of diamonds. But perhaps you should bring the good lady with you.'

Shop jargon, Hugh thought with rancour. Interrupting your thoughts. Couldn't they even invent a new one? Lovely day. Lovely weather. Nice between the showers.

'I can come back again,' he said sternly, 'if you feel I am taking up too much of your time.'

'Oh no, indeed. It's just that it is a difficult thing to choose.'

'I do not agree,' Hugh said. 'I shall certainly know what I want when I see it.'

The assistant hastily produced another tray. 'Some fine examples of modern setting, if I may say so.'

'If you feel you must,' Hugh said even more testily. 'Have you an amethyst?'

'I'm not sure. We don't keep a large stock of amethysts.'

Hugh clamped his tweed cap firmly on his head, said, 'Good day,' and stalked out. The insufferable inanity of the fellow. You would think he was buying a tie. No style, no sense of the occasion. And the grovelling language. Hugh kicked a plastic sweet bag out of the way and watched it swirl on its journey, caught up in another gust of wind.

Leaving the shop, his earlier anticipation reduced to irritation, he was glad he had arranged to meet Adrian for lunch. A solitary meal in a hotel with the aimless conversation of regular customers would add to his bad humour.

Adrian, standing at the bar, greeted him bluntly. 'By the look on your face you need a large whiskey. Is life that bad?'

'I didn't know it showed. Minor irritations, that's all.'

'They're the ones that do the damage,' Adrian said and ordered for him.

'Middle-aged blues,' Hugh said. 'I think I'll opt out and join the irresponsible young.'

'Perhaps you should.' Adrian smiled. 'I think you missed out on youth. You let Donogh have all the fun.'

'It didn't do him much good,' Hugh said.

'Ever hear from him?'

'No. A Christmas card some years ago. Postmarked Scotland.'

'Does Eleanor know?'

'We never discuss Donogh.'

'I'm meeting her later.'

Hugh wasn't interested. 'Apart from that, what else are you doing? Working hard like the rest of us or being a dilettante?'

'I work hard at being a dilettante.' Adrian grinned. 'No point in us all dying of coronaries. Think of all that experience wasted. And these young fellows waiting to take our places. All they do is prescribe pills. The whole business has gone to hell. I swear to God I don't believe one of these young men could deliver a baby or take out an appendix.'

'I'd sooner see a good midwife deliver a baby any day. They have the natural feel for it. It isn't a man's job at all. And I'm not sure that I'd let you near me with a knife. Not even for an appendix.'

'Coward.' Adrian laughed. 'All you need is a good anaesthetist. Any plumber could do the rest.'

'Anaesthetics. Now there's a trade. At one time I had thought of it. I wonder, am I too late?'

'You must be crazy. Think of their mortality rate. I wouldn't have their job for anything. And they never get paid enough. You fellows are the ones who make all the money. You and the butcher boys and women's-diseases men.'

'Have another.'

'Just a beer will do.'

'Written anything lately?' Hugh asked while he waited to order.

'Mm.' The mumble hid a complacent smile.

45

'Well, what was it? Another story of island life? Potato picking in Scotland?'

'Do you know what it is,' Adrian said calmly. 'I get sick of you lot and your bloody smart talk. You're too lazy to learn the language your ancestors were tortured for and you have the gall to make snide remarks about the rest of us who are trying to do something about it.'

'Do something? What are you doing? Here we are in the last lap of the twentieth century and people can't even communicate in their mother tongue, not to mind a dead language that no one gives a shit for.'

'A shit. That's fine Anglo-Saxon for you. If you were any kind of an honest fellow, you would use the invective of the Gael. You don't know what you've lost, Hugh. That's the tragedy of it. Even swearing in Irish would be more satisfying.'

'My ancestors didn't speak much of it, judging by the records they left behind them.'

'Of course they did. Notice how stilted their English is. Some cute lawyer did the job for them. Not that it did most of them any good. They were sold out in the end.'

'Yes, I know,' Hugh said wearily. 'The girls to Barbadoes. It's ancient history.'

'Language.' Adrian was off on his hobby horse. 'Language. None of us can communicate in English because we still don't think that way. Right down in your gut, that's where language begins, and in the rocks and the seas that shape you – and they shape you more than your mother's womb shaped you. The mealy-mouthed vowels of English are a huckster's jargon. Trade and commerce. I can tell you the French don't like their language being taken over by trade and commerce English. Neither do the Scandinavians. In no time at all we'll be mongrels. Mongrels. Barking our asses off over nothing. Here, give me another beer. This kind of talk always makes me thirsty.'

Hugh declined the offer of a drink. Mongrels. Was that what it was all about? The loss of language the first erosion of culture? There were no new gods like the old ones.

'Anyway, it's all Willie Shakespeare's fault.'

Hugh shook his head despairingly. 'You're not still at that.'

'Me and James Joyce.'

'Oh, spare me Dublinese Ulysses.'

'You don't know what's good for you, boyo. If Willie Shakespeare hadn't been such a rag-bag of everyone else's ideas, just at a time when English rapacity was yielding fruits from new colonies ...'

He snorted, like a horse, Hugh thought uncharitably.

'Colonies. Slave trading. More hypocrisy. That loquacious plunderer of words was born in the right time at the right place. The biggest this-is-your-life man to hit planet earth, before or since.'

'You're just jealous. And you can't ignore the sonnets.'

'Jealous! He should have been smothered at birth. Potted history in the plays and potted sentimentality in the sonnets. He was a homo, you know, a homo.'

'Aren't they all,' Hugh said wearily. 'Who the hell cares?'

'Disgusting perverts,' Adrian said. And they laughed. 'Do you feel better now?'

Hugh did feel better. 'All right,' he admitted. 'It worked. Why don't you come to town more often? Leave that shack you live in for a few days.'

'It may be a shack to you. Home sweet home to me. It's cut stone, you know, hand hewn. The conservationists don't think much of it, but only for me the cows would have had it.'

'Some mad farmer probably threw it together in a fit of megalomania.'

'It's pretty old. The windows are original. Might be one of your ould lad's. A great place to write me poems.'

He looked at Hugh with a whimsical grin, not quite concealing his slightly triumphant air of achievement.

'As long as you don't get pneumonia while you're writing them. Have you got rid of the draughts yet? Did you ever plaster the inside?'

'I have wall hangings, as you well know.'

'Moth-eaten carpets,' Hugh said derisively. 'What other people throw out into their dustbins.'

'You'd be amazed at what people throw out. I got a grand

pair of fire-irons a few weeks ago. Just because there was no brass on them. Women are a holy terror on brass these times. With all their complaints about housework you think they'd leave the brass to fellows like me who have time to polish it. Never could understand women. You and I have had a lucky escape.'

It did not seem the appropriate time to tell him about Eve or his hunt in the jeweller's shop.

'What about your poems? Have any published lately?'

With a flourish Adrian drew out a book from his inside pocket.

'The old rabbit-in-the-hat trick. And hardback,' Hugh said admiringly.

'Don't mind about the hardback,' Adrian said. 'We true-blue natives don't have to stoop to paperback like the rest of you English-using suckers. After all, we are preserving the culture of the nation. The least they could do is cover the stuff properly, protect it from the elements and sticky fingers in libraries. But it's what's inside that counts. You know what they say. Never judge the book by the cover. Do you want a read? I made concessions to you and your kind. Each poem has the English translation beside it. Not literal of course. But you wouldn't need that, and I reckon anyone who takes the trouble to buy the book won't need it either.'

Hugh turned a few pages idly. The phrases leaped out at him with an urgency that startled him and filled him with a painful feeling, almost a sense of loss. Or was it despair? Or rage at his own limited understanding?

'I'm sure they're very good. Can I buy a copy in town?'

'You can have this one, with my compliments.'

'No, no. I must buy one. It's only right. I think it is a great thing to do. You must be very proud.'

'In a way. But I don't give myself the chance of having a fall so I nip the pride in the bud.'

Tuirseach, uaigneach, suarach, imní, mullóg. The words lit his life with a new radiance suffused with melancholy. It was true. Their lives, their very souls, were wrapped up for ever in these words now embalmed on the page. He could feel the rain in the

48

soft consonants and the splendour of the wild hills in their board, embracing vowels. Was it fancy to attach so much to sound, to mere utterance? And the rain was not the sleety grey spitting of this town, but the aristocratic drenching of disdainful nature bringing life or inevitable death to everything it touched. He felt the tears spring to his eyes in sudden happiness and sadness. 'Thank God for you, Adrian,' he said. 'Thank God for you.'

It was odd, he thought later, how Adrian had accepted the tribute as if it were his due. They had smilingly embraced each other before parting, with the familiarity and dignity a friendship of such long standing deserved. Yet he had not told him about Eve. Some other time. Adrian would understand. He would not accuse him of being secretive. And he would have to admire Eve, and perhaps envy Hugh a little, in spite of his professed misogyny, which Hugh suspected was a pose, perhaps a cover-up for old rejections.

Hugh walked briskly across the bridge to visit his hospital patients. The rain had cleared temporarily and he enjoyed the short walk. It gave him the chance to reflect further on his conversation with Adrian. He would buy a good dictionary, he decided, and take up Irish again. He ought to be able to read his friend's work without having to rely on a translation.

The hospital, which was a mere ten minutes' walk from his house, was a second home to him. He had inherited house and practice from his mother's brother. The house, a fine late Victorian villa, had been his uncle's pride but the practice was the great achievement of his life. He had come in from the 'back of beyond', he boasted, to challenge the established professional men of Limerick – a different creed, a different breed, he said. But I learned their ways. I could bow and scrape with the best of them.

Hugh had always liked his uncle and had known, even as a small boy, that he would inherit. Donogh had been too much of a playboy for the old man, who had reformed in late middle age after a lifetime's hard drinking. As the rural population moved into the growing city, his country connections stood him in good stead. He kept a hunter in stables and rode with County Limerick Hounds. His jovial manner and knowledge of horses made him popular with the 'county crowd', as he called them mockingly. Hugh's father had once referred to him as 'that lackey' because he saw him hold open a door in a town hotel for one of his ex-patients. His tact or sycophancy paid off. He died wealthy and respected. His money was left to the hospital; the great silver cups he had won at point-to-points and hunt races went to Donogh, who promptly sold them to a dealer. Hugh rescued one from an antique shop. The rest were probably melted down, his name, the names of his loved horses wiped out for ever. Loyalty to the old man's memory prompted Hugh to give the single surviving memento of his hunting and racing days pride of place on the sideboard in his drawing room.

His memory lived on in the hospital and, although Hugh could never live up to the legend he had created, progress through the hospital had been cushioned for him. He inherited not only the practice and the house, but hospital beds for his patients and the respect due to one who was following in a family tradition. In the cosy world of a small hospital he filled with dignity the niche made for him by his uncle. He would not leave behind sagas of escapades on the hunting field, or the gleefully remembered ripostes of a man who was witty even while he removed portions of the human anatomy. But none of that worried Hugh. Until recently he had never even considered what he might or might not leave behind. His clinics for private and public patients, his daily rounds of his hospital inmates, his weekly sessions in the operating theatre where he performed minor surgery had occupied him fully. Three years ago, two years ago, he would have counted himself the happiest of men. If he had met Eve then, he would have believed himself to be at the pinnacle of his life.

Was it the mere fact of his age that aroused these feelings of gloom and hopelessness? Was he suffering from some chemical imbalance? He could not bring himself to consult another physician. Was he cursed by those damned letters in the attic? The idea was ridiculous. No, he decided. He had simply reached a crossroads. He was a textbook case for a midlife crisis. He had fallen in love too late. It was a phase he was going through and he would get over it. He would grit his teeth and suffer it through.

5

While Hugh was choosing the ring, his unsuspecting bride-to-be was arguing at the other end of town with a printer. She had ordered posters for the women's political meeting and the printer had got the colours wrong.

'Green's a lovely colour, miss,' he was protesting.

'I asked for red. It has to be eye-catching.'

'Take it from me, miss, it doesn't matter a damn what colour you put on them. If people are interested, they'll read; if not, they'll pass by.'

'I wonder you have a business at all, with that attitude.'

They argued back and forth. 'I ordered red. I won't pay you for these. If you don't do them, I'll take the order elsewhere. Apart from everything else, you are putting me to a great deal of inconvenience. Our meeting is in three days' time. You were supposed to have the posters ready two days ago.'

'What's a nice little girl like you doing getting mixed up in this sort of thing?' he tried.

'There are other printers,' she said, 'and if you don't do these and do them properly I'll see to it that not one women's organisation will have a raffle ticket or an invitation to a charity function or a poster printed with you.'

He capitulated. She left, flushed and justified.

She met Eleanor on the way to the Desmond. She was not exactly frightened of Eleanor – intimidated, rather. Her recent victory over the printer gave her courage. To Eleanor's open surprise she suggested they have a drink together.

'Oh,' Eleanor said. 'Are you taking a rest from do-gooding?'

Eve ignored her and they went through the swing doors in tandem. 'What will you have?'

'I'll just have a glass of water,' Eleanor said with a pious expression. 'I never drink during working hours.'

'Orange juice?' Eve asked desperately. 'Lime? Lemonade? Sure you wouldn't like a mineral?'

'I never touch the stuff.' Eleanor patted her middle significantly. 'Gas. Acid. Traumatic for the innards. Water will do fine.'

'Would you like some ice in it? A slice of lemon?'

'One thing I will say about this town,' Eleanor commented, 'the water tastes good. Just as it is, please. No tarting up. No disguises necessary.'

'I never knew you were such a puritan.' Eve's patience had wilted.

Gotcha, Eleanor thought. Got a little response there. 'I wouldn't say I'm a puritan. I'm just normal.'

'What's everyone else then, if you're normal?'

'I'm not sure if that's an insult, but I can tell you without any razzmatazz elaboration: everyone else is abnormal. And where do you fit in?'

'Me?' she laughed. 'I haven't thought about me much.'

'Liar,' Eleanor said. 'I bet you think of nothing else. You in relation to someone else. Or something else. At the moment someone else. Dear Hugh, I suspect.'

'I wish you wouldn't call him that. He is a dear. And I'm very fond of him.'

'Any lusht there?' Eleanor deliberately slurred the syllable.

To her surprise again, Eve looked at her calmly and said, 'Yes, as a matter of fact. Are you nosey enough to want time, date, details?' But she flushed while she said it.

'I'm sorry, I didn't mean to be so rude. I have no right. Please forgive me.'

'You aren't rude. You're just you.'

Today was full of surprises, Eleanor thought. 'I must be losing my touch. Provocation is my hobby. Anything to shift this damn country off its arse and get rid of some of the

53

complacency. Even, maybe, some of the great, all-pervading apathy.'

'You aren't the first one to try that. Why do you imagine you'll survive when all the others have gone down? This country is a big mouth and it swallows people whole. I thought you knew that.'

Eleanor observed the grimness of Eve's face with interest. This was something to ponder over. Little Miss Greatheart had a pain in her gut too. 'It must be the weather,' she said. 'It has to be the weather. There's a little green man up there in one of the satellites adding poison to the clouds. I knew that weather guy had a funny leer on his face last night on the box. What's eating you? I thought there were orange blossoms in the air, wedding bells, white lace and happy ever after in your horoscope. What's happened? Got your birth planets crossed?'

'Nothing. It's nothing. I'm just edgy. You don't know me well enough to be able to guess what my dreams are.'

'True. You're dead right. And here's to you.' She lifted the glass of water and felt suddenly foolish. Flamboyantly overacting. A middle-aged hippy. 'When's the engagement announcement?'

'There is nothing settled.'

'What a pity. I could do with a family reunion. I haven't had a real fight for ages.'

'It's just a game to you. To all of you.'

'Well, I don't know about them. But a weekend at Tower Hill gives me a new zest for living. Does me the world of good. I sharpen my teeth on them. But then I'm not married to one of them. At least not now. It will be different for you.'

'It seems to me you're married to them all. You keep going back.'

'I think it's the house. A seventeenth-century house is something to marvel at. Especially a family house like that. I don't know how it escaped. Perhaps it was too ugly for anyone to bother with. Half a fortress, with all those steps. Now it's so inaccessible not even a speculator would be bothered with it. I think that's why I like it. It's a survivor. They are all survivors.'

Eve said hesitantly, 'Your husband? Was he like them?'

54

'Yes.'

'Is he dead? I don't wish to pry if you don't want to talk about it. But you know the way they hint at things. They make you feel stupid not knowing.'

'It's no secret. We're separated.'

'Oh, I'm sorry.'

'Don't be. He was a tough man to live with.'

'You had no children?'

'Yes, as a matter of fact. I had one. I don't wish to talk about it.'

She pushed the glass away from her so violently that it almost went over the edge.

'I'm sorry,' Eve said again. 'It's just that I'd like to know everything about them, and that includes you.'

'You're right. You should be forewarned. Remember, when you marry one, you marry them all. Especially when you marry Hugh. None of this cosy little nuclear family act. This is a big extended family. Very prolific grandparents. There are hordes of cousins out there all breeding away for good old Mother Ireland. Doing their bit for Mother Church too. You mustn't miss a christening, or a wedding, or a twenty-first anniversary, or they will be mortally wounded. No Creaghs, oddly enough. The male side seems to be dying out. I expect they want Hugh to do something about it now that Donogh has failed. At least, as far as I know, he hasn't produced a male heir.'

The child was a daughter, Eve thought, unless it had died. Perhaps that was the tragedy behind Eleanor's fierceness.

Eleanor's remark about the need to produce a male heir left Eve with a sense of danger, as if a burden was already about to be settled on her shoulders. To justify their presence in the lounge bar and to make up for Eleanor's insistence on water, she had ordered a small whiskey for herself. It was beginning to work on her empty stomach.

'I think I'll have something to eat here,' she said. 'Have you time to join me?'

Eleanor was already regretting having revealed so much of her personal life. She made a move to go.

'Hugh is very independent-minded,' Eve remarked. 'He would never be dictated to by his family.'

Eleanor adjusted the strap of her handbag.

'He can be very obstinate,' Eve added.

Eleanor gave her peculiar donkey-like laugh. 'Oh yes, obstinate. Donogh was obstinate too. You always had to dangle the carrot in front of him. Sometimes you run out of carrots.'

'Donogh doesn't sound much like Hugh. Hugh is considerate.'

'Don't let that fool you.'

'Don't you like Hugh?'

'Not particularly. But what does that matter? You're the one who's marrying him. Good luck to you.'

She left. Their goodbyes were the briefest of civil exchanges. She went quickly through the swing doors, out into the street as if going into permanent exile. She could be knocked down by a lorry, Eve thought morbidly. I may never see her again. The bar chatter seemed callous, the soft lighting deceitfully seductive. Beside her two women sipped their coffee and cream. She wondered if they had overheard the conversation, wondered if it would provide a subject for idle gossip. Eleanor was a well-known figure with her clinic for the tinkers and the occasional abusive letters to the local press. Self-consciously, noting the curious stares of the coffee drinkers, she rushed to the exit, tripping on the doorstep and dropping her bag. She was aware of smiles of pity and mockery as she gathered her belongings, raincoat, library books and handbag, and fled back to work.

The wind whipping up from the side streets cowed pedestrians at each street corner. April is the cruellest month, Adrian quoted to himself, savouring the words in his mouth as if they had a physical flavour. April is the cruellest month. He watched sardonically as a woman's hat went sailing across the traffic followed by a plastic bag. The traffic crunched through everything relentlessly, a collective gargantua devouring all before it. Ape, he thought. Prrilll. Krooo. Ell. Cruel April. The pavements were slippery with rain. Just in time he sidestepped to avoid a dog's turd and concentrated on the Eliot lines, clutching at survival and sanity. Breeding lilacs out of the dead land. Stirring dull roots with spring rain. He wished he had written that. Winter kept us warm, he mused, covering earth in forgetful snow. Should it be forgetting snow?

His patients said that Adrian hibernated in winter, only venturing out like the squirrel when the days lengthened. If some real emergency brought him to visit the sick during the dark days of the year, he showed his discontent, shifting uneasily by chair or bedside. They winced from his cold, clumsy hands palpating abdomen or tapping in an old-fashioned way at breastbone and rib while he listened to the mysterious sounds of disease. Relatives made faces behind his back and were glad they had a real doctor in Peter Barrett, who used the technology of medicine with aplomb but managed to hold on to the cheery optimism of the ideal GP. Adrian's women patients, who hoped his long and gloomy look hid a sensitive nature, would have settled for relief and encouragement if they could not get a cure. Adrian understood their fears yet could not allay them. He envied Eleanor her brisk manner, rollercoasting through the ups and downs of illness, scolding, admonishing, making her crude jokes, revitalising the feeble. Her patients left her surgery grinning, strengthened in their battle for life. Why was he going to see Eleanor, he asked himself, as he leaped across at a traffic junction. Did he think they could retrieve what they had lost years ago, when they were carefree students together? Why did he bother contacting her two or three times each year? They were not the same people any more. All had changed, changed utterly. He used to read his poems aloud to her during their last term. She would lie sprawled across a bench in St Stephen's Green, listening intently, her long, bare legs carelessly seductive. And then Donogh would come running, blond hair flopping over his forehead, that tennis racquet always in his hand. He would throw imaginary balls in the air and, with a graceful upward movement of his arms, mime one of his superb serves. Eleanor would be instantly up, eyes alight with welcome, Adrian's

57

poems cast aside and forgotten. There had never been anyone quite like her. It was nothing to Eleanor to cycle forty miles to a favourite picnic spot. No one had the same zest and energy or joie de vivre. Did he want to show off his book, to make some excuse as to why he had not invited her to the launching? A few years earlier, when he had given her something to read and comment on, all she picked out was the word 'nobility', and all she said was, 'When I hear the word nobility I reach for the puke bowl.' Yet it was that bitterness which drew him back to her every time, as if he hoped that by association some of the iron in her soul might enter his – without the disadvantage of the painful experience.

In January he had telephoned her, suggesting they might meet in the spring.

'Why not now?' she asked. 'Why not today? Why not tomorrow? I might be dead by spring. You might be finally petrified in your museum, a fine monument to yourself.'

'You know I hate travelling in winter,' he replied. Too bad, she had said, and put down the phone. He had sent her a postcard with a view of the local pier and two fishing boats, and wrote on the back, *See you in the spring*. She did not reply.

Adrian drove through the main street and turned at St Mary's Cathedral. A little further on was the Protestant grave-yard where his grandmother was buried. He had promised his father that he would maintain an annual commemoration there.

'The Church,' his father had said, 'separated in death those whom they could not divide in life.'

So in a little green oasis, practically in the heart of the old town, with a chieftain's view of the river, his grandmother lay with her Protestant cousins, while the man she married, loved and bore children for lay at the other side of the city with his Catholic family. His grandmother had the best view of Limerick. There were moments, after all, when the city was quite lovely. Adrian admired the glimpses of the towers built to support huge cannon reaching down to the river's edge. The stone balustrades of the principal bridge were imposing too.

Where the river flowed high and deep to become the long curving estuary, the effect was of elegance tinged with hints of a noble past. A famous actor had once described it in his melancholy tones as a lonely and beautiful widow. Perhaps, thought Adrian, he wasn't so far off the mark. There was something bereft about it, as if it could never quite understand its loss. The aged cathedral with its romanesque arches hugged the remains of the city walls. Here and there other fragments of the old walls straggled behind back streets, buttressed to withstand the attacks which had destroyed the city and the spirit within it. Of all the places in Ireland, Limerick, and indeed the whole of Thomond – which in the old days stretched back to Hugh's house on the Shannon mouth, embracing virtually all of Clare – suffered as much from dissension within as from attacks from without. In a way Limerick epitomised that lack of unity and ability to compromise which had brought about the final destruction of Gaelic Ireland. Hugh, of course, would say that the same spirit still lived on in Limerick and in Ireland. Adrian had to agree that his native city had turned in on itself, become ever more insular and incestuous, lived and died licking its wounds. Other towns throughout the world had arisen again after worse defeats. Why should this one have lost its soul? Old tribal jealousies, resistance to change, all played their part. But was it more than that? Had the taste of defeat been so bitter that the people had lost the stomach for fight? The broken Treaty of Limerick and the ensuing penal laws left an indelible mark on each new generation. Bad government, poverty and famine compounded despair. Long memories and ancient history were impossible burdens. After all the fighting and the little uprisings, the wish for peace and a quiet life might very well have led to stagnation and apathy. Adrian sometimes fancifully compared the destruction of the spirit of the city (though in his more realistic moments he asked himself if such a spirit had ever come truly alive) with the death of the Inca civilisation. Limerick was the last frontier of Gaelic Ireland. There was no hope of recovering that Ireland. Yet tantalising reminders were still there, in the language, in stone carvings, even in the faces of the population, who might have been the living models of those round-eyed, thin-mouthed images immortalised on abbey and church walls and on Celtic crosses. At times it seemed to Adrian that he walked through a doomed city, peopled by ghosts who had managed to acquire the outward habits and clothing of a modern age but who fretted constantly while they searched for their lost souls.

He was always glad when he left Limerick, and he rushed back to his tower with as much speed as possible, although his conscience pricked him because he used the city as a large warehouse, a place to purchase material goods. He had no feeling of affection for it. The clouds billowing up the estuary blocked out sunlight, excluding signs of the immense universe around. Nothing much happened in Limerick. No one was doing anything important or going anywhere in particular. But then, he thought, where in Ireland could you go? Ireland was the place you came back to, to die.

You could not enjoy a vital, purposeful existence here. Hemmed in by the implacable sea, you pondered on the meaning of life and became a poet or a priest. What country could afford such luxury? Too many poets, too many priests.

'Too many rogues and charlatans,' Eleanor retorted much later. 'And don't give me history. History is crap. Men invented history and God at the same time because they were too lazy to draw the water and hew the wood, and the hunting was poor, and they had to have some excuse for their idle ways or the missus wouldn't let them leap into the hay with her. I thought you had more sense.'

But that was after he had called to see her and caught her in a weak moment. He found her in the clinic starting the afternoon session. The waiting room was full. The receptionist brought him into Eleanor's surgery, a tiny room with a couch, washbasin, desk and the other recognisable paraphernalia of their trade.

'I won't keep you,' he said by way of apology for interrupting her work. 'I should have telephoned you. But I know you hate the phone.'

'A damnable invention,' she said but she smiled. 'It's nice to see you again.'

'I thought it would be.'

She frowned at his little joke. It appeared she was in no mood for the facetious. She did not ask him to sit down, but stood there, not looking at him, fidgeting slightly with the stethoscope. For the first time since he had known her, even allowing for the times she had come to him for help after some bad beatings from Donogh, he saw that she was a little pathetic. Unguarded, the expression of near defeat was easy to recognise.

'What's wrong?' he asked and was sorry the minute he had spoken.

'Nothing,' she said and turned away. To his embarrassment she sat down at the desk, put her hands over her face and began to weep. The tears trickled through her fingers and down the backs of her hands while he watched helpless, stunned to find himself in this situation. He could call on no resources from within himself, no past experience, to cope with it. His stomach churned. 'What is it?' he tried again.

'Oh Christ. If I knew what it was, I wouldn't be crying.'

The need to make some sort of response saved her. She stopped crying and groped in a drawer for a paper tissue. When she had blown her nose, she lifted her head and looked at him challengingly through red-rimmed eyes. 'A pretty kettle of fish,' she said. 'How am I going to face my patients?'

'Splash your face with cold water,' he suggested.

'Oh. You know about tears?' she said, but went to the basin.

'You need a holiday I suppose,' he said helpfully. 'Overwork, too many patients. Why don't you take one?'

'I'll tell you why,' she answered. 'I know of no one I like well enough to bring with me. Unless you'd like to come of course.'

She wasn't joking. Once they had liked one another. The intervening years of bitterness hadn't quite killed off that affection. It should have been stronger than love. He had, he suddenly remembered, been really fond of her.

'Yes,' he said. 'Why not? You're busy now. I'll take you out to dinner and we can discuss it.'

'No. You haven't seen my house. Meet me here at half past five and I'll drive you there and then I'll cook you dinner.'

She turned away and started putting her hair into place.

The moment Adrian sat back in his own car he regretted his impulse. He was as mad as she was even to contemplate a holiday together. They would more than likely drive each other totally insane after a few days. And it looked as if she had problems. But they were nothing to do with him. Whatever nightmare of loneliness and despair she was battling with now was something she would have to deal with herself. He had come to terms with his own solitude a long time ago and he would have imagined Eleanor had done the same. It was surprising to discover that she hadn't. Again, that was none of his business. In any case, as he well knew, there was no help to be got from anyone. He supposed she needed a little support; and perhaps the holiday might be a good idea. She had always been good company. He remembered a wonderful camping holiday they had had in Greece when they were both students. Before Donogh. He had not gone abroad since, spending all his holidays in the Gaeltacht. It would be nice to see Italy. The grand tour. It would be like putting the clock back. But then Eleanor had become something of a queer fish lately; there were some things that could never be changed.

While he mused, he had a nagging sense of guilt, barely scratching its way into his consciousness, that he was being shallow and even cruel, as if she had no real feelings, as if she were of no importance as a person. Hugh treated her that way in spite of the touch of fear he showed now and again. There were others too who treated her as a figure of fun, partly because they were afraid of her – or at least afraid of what she might say. That plain searching look she gave you made you wonder if you had anything to hide, and made you want to hide whatever it was she saw. He didn't mind it. She was, he supposed, in her own way, on the same quest as himself; the quest for some kind of truth, some kind of purpose, in this troubled life.

6

'One thing about dear Hugh,' Honora said, 'his bad humours are short-lived. Little flurries. Little April showers. He was always the same, even as a child.'

The sisters were in the kitchen, where Bridget was making almond pastry. The others watched as she crumbled the margarine and flour between her fingertips. Florence sat at one end of the kitchen table soaking almonds in boiling water and then popping the skins off with relish.

'He has got very secretive lately. I don't know what has come over him,' Ruth said. 'Take this business about him being asked to go on the council. It was only by chance we heard. If Eve hadn't let it slip.'

'I think he thought we were prying,' Bridget said.

'As if we'd be bothered,' Ruth grumbled. 'We just like to know what's happening. I like to know what goes on and if I don't ask will anyone tell me?'

'Nobody ever tells me anything,' Florence said. 'And you don't hear me complaining.'

'Oh well, of course you were always perfect,' Ruth said, going out and banging the door.

'Huffy, huffy,' Florence said. 'She never grew out of that, did she? And you always said she would. I don't believe we ever grow out of anything. I think we are just the same now as we were when we were infants. We just grow old. We learn a few useless bits of information about life which we hardly ever use, and then we die.'

Honora rattled the scuttle vigorously and said, 'We're

running out of anthracite. Whose turn is it?'

'Can't Rosie do it?' Florence asked.

'Can't you do it?' Bridget said pointedly and Florence left with the scuttle, saying as she went, 'I have to do everything in this house.'

'I wish the summer would hurry up and come,' Honora said. 'I wonder, will there be a wedding?'

Bridget said, 'They seem to be in love.'

'She is a funny little thing, isn't she?' Honora remarked. 'Would you say she was a little common? Just a little?'

'For goodness sake, don't let Hugh hear you,' Bridget said in dismay.

'Well, there's no harm in thinking it,' Honora said. 'I know Hugh doesn't like her picture in the paper with the women's libbers. You'd never think it to look at her, would you?'

'Never think what?' Bridget asked as she began to chop the almonds.

'They have lost all respect. They bring us all down. It's horrible. All this talk of battered wives. I expect they look for it. They probably won't cook their husband's meal for him and he gives them a little tip.'

'You never know,' Bridget said reflectively. 'Remember poor Mamie d'Arcy? Her husband killed her with the shovel because they got into an argument about something.'

'Women shouldn't argue,' Honora said.

'I don't think Eve is like that. She is very quiet and refined,' Bridget said. 'Could you hand me the castor sugar?'

'And that clinic they run,' Honora continued. 'Isn't it a nerve calling it a clinic? They aren't doctors, are they?'

'Politicians have clinics,' Bridget remarked, rolling out the pastry dough.

'That's true,' Honora admitted. 'But how could Eve give advice to anyone? What would she know?'

'Perhaps she has learned from her work.'

'You don't learn much from work,' Honora said. 'She hasn't lived long enough to learn much from life. At our age we have learned a lot. About people. Well, a certain amount.'

Bridget smiled at her sister. 'You aren't very consistent.'

'I don't want to be consistent,' Honora replied. 'It's much too boring.' They both laughed.

If they had asked Eve why she joined the 'women's libbers' she would scarcely have been able to tell them. And she would certainly have rejected claim to the title. She had gone to a meeting which had been advertised around the town with flamboyant shop posters under the title WOMEN IN A CHANGING WORLD. Afterwards she met a group from the audience who had come into the hotel lounge bar to discuss the speakers and what they had to say. There was an air of excitement about them which made her think of a soda siphon, the fizzy water bursting out under pressure. But she had no sense of identification with them. They were all married and much older than she.

It was probably curiosity which prompted her to join them in an arranged meeting at one of their houses. There, brought in like specimens from a strange subculture, were some deserted wives. The meeting had been organised by Ann Collins, a tall rangy redhead of great energy, who introduced everyone as if they were at a party, and produced tea and biscuits – which enhanced that impression. One by one, the women who had been deserted told of the difficulties they had when left on their own with children, how little money they had, how lonely and worthless they felt, how bitter and betrayed. One woman began to sob. Eve had never heard or seen anyone cry with such abandon. The women from the group were embarrassed and shocked, witness to a despair they had never encountered, saying feebly, 'Oh, don't upset yourself,' until Ann suddenly rushed over and put her arms around the woman, rocking her as if she were a child. Then someone else dashed out to get more tea, the woman apologised, dried her eyes and left.

'Oh, what tears. What tears,' Ann said after she had gone, and then suggested they do something practical.

'*We* can't weep,' she said. 'There's a demo for Civil Legal Aid out at Plassy tomorrow. Some European politicians are going to be there. I think we should be there too. Some young solicitors I know are organising it. Let's give them support.'

65

No one was free. She looked at Eve, who hesitated and then said that she might manage a few hours in the afternoon. 'I've been putting in extra hours, so I think I'll be OK.'

That was Eve's first demonstration. She waved her placard at the bemused politicians, who seemed discomfited by the unexpected attention. The stewards were irritated. And that was all. She left feeling deflated and with the suspicion that the young solicitors would soon be immersed in their own practices and would not have the energy or commitment to do any more.

It all seemed futile and she said as much to Ann Collins. 'It's hard to know the rights and wrongs of family quarrels. And there are no guidelines. Family law is practically non-existent apparently.'

'Don't listen to them,' Ann said. 'Professionals always pretend their jobs are impossibly difficult. Otherwise they wouldn't be able to charge so much. You can't take sides in this business, you know. Either you're with us or against us.'

'I'm not with or against anyone,' Eve said.

'Then why are you here today?'

'No one else offered.'

Ann laughed out loud. 'You're right. But remember, we are outsiders. When you fight for a cause, you're on the opposite side.'

She leaned over. 'You're a *pressure group*,' she said dramatically. 'That's the dirty word today. Last year it was pseudo-intellectuals. Next year, liberal something or other. Destroying the stability of the state. Uprooting family life.'

'You're married?'

'Yes, happily. And yes, I have children. Three. Two girls and a boy. As far as I know, they are reasonably well adjusted, but then I'm lucky. I married the right man.'

'Perhaps he married the right woman,' Eve said.

'Oh well, who knows?' Ann grinned.

Her cheerful reasonableness lured Eve into the fold. It was hard to refuse to share some of the burden of work which suddenly became a part of their lives. From that first meeting they got the use of a room in the social services centre, placed advertisements in the paper saying that they were willing to help and advise women in distress and began to read up on welfare payments and the state of the law in relation to women.

Every other Wednesday they sat in a small room, hardly bigger than a cubicle, and heard the stories of the women who came to them for help. At times the complaints seemed monotonously repetitive and Eve wondered why the women seemed unable to help themselves. Until, that is, she learned how unskilled they were, unable to find work to support themselves; and even when they did, who would mind their children? Now and again, frustrated rage burst out, sometimes in a great rush of words which could hardly be checked by murmurings of sympathy or discreet questions. At such times Eve herself felt infected by the same rage and frustration, especially since there was so little practical help they could give. Where could they go, the women with children who were kicked out of their homes in the middle of the night by a violent husband? Where could they get accommodation they could afford, the women with children who had been suddenly abandoned by the traditional breadwinner? Whether deserted or married, it seemed the result was the same: pain and grief. If marriage was not the problem, what was? Was there some fatal flaw in the female sex which led them to destroy themselves for the sake of the stronger male? Were they victims of their own masochism? The necessary sacrifices on the primitive altar of reproduction? Yet, and yet, she thought, I was quite happy on my own until Hugh came a-wooing. I have never wanted to be tied to any man. Would these women have been content to have casual relations with men (if that were tolerated) so that they could come and go as they please, bear their children happily and live on their own when it suited them? But always there was money, money, or the lack of it. Without fail, it came back to that.

'If society wants children, and it does, then society must pay for them,' Ann told her firmly. 'But it's cheaper to keep a woman tied to a man, economically dependent while he goes out to work for the great capitalist system.'

'So that's what it is.' Eve laughed. 'Another capitalist plot.'
She didn't know why she laughed. It wasn't in the least funny.
To hide her confusion she went to the filing cabinet and
pretended to tidy up the files. Everything was becoming so
confusing that she found herself beginning to dither. Rockets
were going off inside her head, zooming in all directions. She
had begun to read some of the feminist writings. She had to
clarify for herself these new ideas which came at her with such
terrifying speed. When she read Simone de Beauvoir's *The
Second Sex* it was with the joy of one who has discovered the
Messiah. As her male contemporaries read James Joyce for his
gritty re-affirmation of life's incongruities, so she saw *The
Second Sex* as a kind of bible for its clear and rational
exposition of the confused world she inhabited. There were
other books and other preachers, Ann and Eleanor unwittingly
among them.

Occasionally, Eve thought longingly of the convent life. She
would like to bury herself where rules brought certainty. But
was that the answer? An order of women worshipping a male
god, dictated to by a male bishop, the handmaidens in a church
that gave them little opportunity for developing or even for
contributing. Supposing she ended up like Eleanor, disillusioned and agnostic? She was amazed and disturbed to
discover herself flirting with such ideas while knowing that
Hugh was anticipating a lifelong partnership with her and that
she had not discouraged him in his expectation. It was some
consolation for her to know that Ann, in spite of her never-
failing good sense, suffered from the same ambivalence. Ann
admitted that some nights after a bad session she felt she hated
the kind and loving man she had married. 'I don't even want to
make love with him,' she confessed. 'He says I'm turning into a
lesbian.'

Eve looked embarrassed and Ann leaned over and patted
her hand. 'Sorry.' She smiled. 'I keep forgetting you're so
sensitive. Most people your age wouldn't turn a hair.'

'People seem to be matronising me a lot lately,' Eve said
sharply, but Ann didn't seem to hear.

'Our group is getting smaller. Do you notice?' she asked

Eve. 'Middle-class women have no stamina. I'm middle class myself, God knows, but I think I'm not that bad. Look at the excuses they give for not coming to a meeting or helping us out. They have to play golf, or drive the children to dancing classes or music lessons, or they have to entertain their husband's business acquaintances, or whatever. All of that is more important than what we are trying to do here. That's what's really wrong, you know. Women are oppressed as much by the selfishness of their own sex as by the prejudice and jealousy of the other.'

'I think our meetings are quite good,' Eve said. 'And people do have their own lives to lead and their own domestic problems.'

'I know, I know.' Ann nodded. 'Anyway, who wants to argue all the time? I find I'm becoming a bore. My family are starting to say, "Oh, not that again," and my husband gets up and leaves the room. And why *should* we have to argue and fight for grown women, who, if there were any justice at all, would need no protection. It's all so degrading. The very titles – deserted wives, battered wives – are insulting. The word lesbian is insulting, because of the implication of abnormality. It seems to me perfectly reasonable that we should love each other, even if we are the same sex.'

'But it's not normal to be lesbian,' Eve said.

'You mean it's not average, not majority,' Ann retorted. 'That's what makes the difference. Majority rules OK. I suppose the truth is we are programmed to get results. The act of love should at least have the potential to produce something, a poem, a child, a painting.' She got up, rattling her car keys, and said, 'Sometimes I think we are like a battalion of soldiers who have had our first taste of combat. Girls are too protected in their teens. We aren't toughened for life the way boys are. Yet look what happens the first time we have a baby. Talk about being thrown in at the deep end. Nothing in our education prepares us for that. We should all be conscripted at fifteen.'

'You make it sound like a war.'

'It is a kind of war. Aren't we watching our comrades going

down all around us? Battered, raped, defeated. The enemy is our friend or belongs to our friend's club. We don't know who to hate – and we have to hate for a while or we wouldn't bother doing anything about anything. We annoy everyone around us who doesn't feel the same. It gets so confusing it would drive anyone crazy.'

That, Eve reflected, seemed to be the nub of the matter – confusion. It permeated discussions and committee meetings. They went around in circles arguing and agreeing as if caught in a treadmill. They seemed to be challenging assumptions and power structures without quite understanding the implications. Politically naive, fearful of radical change, they wished for miracles. Only two or three had the support of their husbands. The others were either deserted or separated or attended the meeting without telling their husbands.

'John was furious when he heard what I was doing,' a woman confessed one night. 'He doesn't want me getting tied up with criminal types.'

'She means the husbands are criminal types. And some of them are,' Ann told Eve. 'Her husband is a very successful businessman who hasn't too many scruples about making large profits. But there you are. He supports the church charities and he is a model of rectitude in other ways. She isn't much loss. You could never get her to do anything. She was always too busy. Did you ever notice that the people who are always complaining of being too busy never seem to do anything constructive?'

Eve did not respond.

'You think I'm being catty? You're right. Miaou. Miaou.'

'Poor cats,' Eve smiled.

'True, true,' Ann said. 'Why should we malign the creatures by comparing them to men? By all accounts they are very intelligent creatures.'

'But smelly,' Eve said.

'Aren't we all?' Ann asked rhetorically. 'Have you ever noticed how we all love our own smells but think everyone else's disgusting?'

'I can't say I've noticed.'

'Perhaps you don't smell.'

'Perhaps I'm too young and sensitive,' Eve said and they laughed.

They often laughed. Hugh rarely laughed when he was with her and you could hardly call Eleanor's scornful whinny a laugh.

Being part of the group was an education in itself. Eve began to make guesses about the staying power of the new members. When one woman said she would do anything but she could not listen to the sad stories because she was too sensitive, Eve expected her to leave after a few months. But she stayed on, making suggestions, sounding reasonable and intelligent, though she was somehow never around for the dirty jumble sales they organised to raise money, and certainly never around when there was a confrontation with the Health Board. One of the most surprising things was the nervous tension shown by the women at the first meetings with officialdom. Even Ann Collins was scared. 'They frighten the hell out of me,' she confided. 'They sit there with their grave faces and their office suits and they dole out economic facts and figures to us as if we were mentally deficient. Which in a way, I suppose, we are. Did you see how respectably dressed we all are at meetings with them? Down to our pearls. Next time, by God, next time I'll wear my jeans.'

Eve mentioned none of this to Hugh. His response to her earlier comments about her involvement showed little sympathy. 'If you feel you need to be a member of a club, why don't you join the Countrywomen's Association? I believe they do very useful work.'

He was so bourgeois it was unbearable. How could she possibly be in love with him? When one evening he presented her with the engagement ring her instinct was to refuse it. But the look on his face destroyed that possibility immediately. She had to accept it gratefully, as indeed she was grateful for the gift, for his care in choosing it, even for his love. Nonetheless she said, 'I wish you hadn't.'

He didn't want to listen to any more protests. They went with maidenly blushes and had to be ignored. 'Darling

71

Hugh,' she said and kissed him. 'Why do you make such a big deal out of everything?'

'Don't you want it? Don't you love me?'

She closed her eyes while she answered, 'Of course I do. Of course, of course I do.'

'Aren't you protesting a lot?' he asked, frowning.

She found herself in the tangle a lie makes. It would never unravel, never get to the clean end where she might discover for herself that she really did love him. But could she say she did not love him? That would be even more untrue. They had never made physical love. Once or twice it seemed as if they might, but Hugh always backed off, leaving her uncertain and with the feeling that his attitude to lovemaking was much less spontaneous than her own. But she respected his wish for restraint. It was a change from having to evade the amorous attentions of younger, lustier suitors. The danger was that they might lose what held them together if they did not bind themselves in a physical way. Perhaps it was enough that they embraced and caressed. Why was it then, she asked herself, that as he slipped the ring on her finger it seemed heavy, its weight exaggerated to enormous proportions by an inexplicable foreboding? It was almost as if he had handcuffed her to himself. She flexed her fingers and said, 'I think I'll keep it safely in its box for a while.'

At that he looked alarmed. 'Don't you like it? I can change it. Doesn't it fit?'

'It's just a little on the big side. I might lose it if I wear it.'

He wanted to have it altered but she said no, there was nothing in it, and no doubt her finger would grow. It was so ludicrous a statement that he stared at her to see if she were joking, and she managed to laugh as if indeed the whole thing were a joke.

'I paid a lot for it,' he said. 'Don't treat it as if it were a bauble.'

'It wasn't my idea to buy it,' she retorted angrily. 'We don't need symbols of that sort. You never said you were going to buy it.'

'It was to be a surprise.' He almost added the fatal question

'Don't you want to marry me?' but he was afraid of forcing her to give an answer he didn't want to hear. He sighed heavily and with such obvious unhappiness that she put her arms around him and kissed him again, this time with real tenderness. He stroked the back of her hair as if she were a schoolboy. 'I feel my life is slipping away,' he confessed in a tone that made her tearful. She could not comfort him.

She examined the ring again and allowed herself to admire the flame of the ruby. 'It is beautiful,' she assured him.

'I looked for an amethyst. But that's a good specimen.'

'A specimen. You sound like a collector.' She shook her head. 'You say the most peculiar things.'

'I know,' he said wistfully. 'I know there are things you feel deeply about that I seem to miss out on. But I can learn. I expect you can learn from me too.'

'That's just what I don't want,' she exclaimed. 'I don't want to teach you or be taught by you. I want us to explore the world together, but – ' He had already explored much of it by the time she was born. That was her unspoken thought. She could never catch up. He could never retrace his steps to match hers. They stood in the centre of her room swaying slightly in each other's embrace, thinking sadly of the difference the years between them made, until Hugh moved back slightly so that he could look at her while he spoke.

'Most of the past twenty years I have been marking time. Maybe I have been waiting for someone like you. But all those years that might seem so long to you are nothing to me now. It is as if for twenty years I have ticked over – doing my job, treating my patients, making money. I often think it is a strange way to make money, yet I don't reduce my fees. I keep thinking there is something else in life for me. Maybe it's politics, perhaps something else. All I know is I need you. I can't imagine my future without you. The ring is a bribe, it's true. And it is a symbol. But I love you and I want us to be married and have children. I may be taking a terrible risk but I need to know how you feel.'

It was the longest speech he had ever made. His sincerity and earnestness won her completely. 'You make me feel a pig,' she said. 'The last thing in the world I want to do is to hurt you.'

'Then marry me, marry me. Soon,' he insisted.

'All right,' she agreed. 'But we'll just let it happen. Some day we'll say, "Let's get married tomorrow," because we feel like it.'

'I think you have to make arrangements,' Hugh said. 'The parish priest has to be informed.'

'Oh, Hugh,' she cried in exasperation.

He just managed to stop himself from saying there were procedures to be followed in everything. Instead, he kissed her on the mouth and held her and made promises about happiness together and unburdened himself of his earlier fears. In so doing some of his burden passed to Eve.

It is too easy to give comfort, she thought, and in an irrational moment she had the urge to hurt him, if only to rid herself of the sense of oppression. But how could anyone wish to hurt Hugh? And why did his ambition and his dreams seem so paltry? If he became a councillor, if he got into government, would it alter by a jot the misery of the women who came to her clinic? Political priorities would always be dictated by political expedience. His ambitions were shoddy in comparison with the needs of the people she wished to help and yet he treated her work as if it were some kind of hobby.

7

'Welcome, welcome, welcome.'

The greetings were accompanied by outstretched arms ready for embraces and chaste kisses on the cheeks. Eve responded warmly to Ruth and Bridget, standing in the hall. Hugh had driven her down for the engagement party. There were flowers everywhere, festooning the banisters and lighting dark corners with their brilliance. Eleanor's voice came booming from the drawing room.

'She's in great form,' Hugh said, nodding in her direction.

'That was a wonderful idea of yours, dear,' Ruth beamed, 'asking Adrian to come. We've persuaded him to stay for the weekend.'

'What fun to have the old house full again. Just like the old days,' Bridget said.

'You haven't met Adrian,' Hugh remarked to Eve. 'You'll like him.'

At first glance she knew she would not like him. The greying unkempt hair and the cynical twisted mouth were perfect accompaniment to the inquisitive look he gave her and the sardonic glance he bestowed on Hugh. 'I'm told I must congratulate you,' he said, rising and bowing to her.

'Not her, you fool,' Hugh protested laughingly. 'Me.'

'I beg your pardon, I have never been properly socialised. What does one say to the bride-to-be?'

'One doesn't have to say anything, if one doesn't want to,' Eve replied tartly.

Hugh's arm pressed warningly against hers. Adrian bowed

again, gravely this time, and sat down beside Eleanor, who was sipping brandy.

'You know, Adrian,' she said gaily, 'the bride ought really to be commiserated with.'

'That seems a little offensive.'

'No more so than being congratulated.'

'Well, I'm not much good at this sort of thing. I'm better at funerals.'

'You have the face for them, Adrian. All you need is the black hat.'

To Eve's astonishment, Eleanor traced tenderly with her finger the deep grooves on each side of Adrian's mouth. 'You had such smooth skin once. Is that loneliness or grief, or is it just time?'

'I remember your peaches and cream too,' he replied, and touched her face with the back of his hand. 'Is that time or bitterness?'

She placed her fingers gently on his hand and said, 'No. This is rage. It is sometimes confused with bitterness. I didn't know it showed so much.'

'Everything shows to the astute observer.'

'Is this a private conversation or are you going to keep Adrian to yourself all night?' Ruth asked, deliberately squeezing herself between them on the settee. 'It's a lot of nonsense, as you both know perfectly well. What do you people have to worry about? Look at my lines.' Indeed, her face was a network of tiny crinkles under the table light.

Eve joined Hugh at the french window. 'Look at the garden,' he said. 'Aren't they wonderful, the way they keep it in order?'

'It's beautiful,' she agreed.

'Let me see the ring.' Honora came to stand beside them. 'Oh, Hugh, you have such good taste. Look at Hugh's ring, everyone,' she called to the others. They came dutifully over. Eleanor, wilfully misunderstanding, peered at Hugh's hairy hand. Eve had seldom felt more foolish, standing there letting them stare at her hand. She could not look down but wondered if her nails were clean.

'What pearly nails she has,' Florence said, 'just like a baby's

76

But then she's not much more than a child, is she? At least not to us. We're such old hags. Though indeed we don't feel old.'

'You're always talking about age,' Florence said crossly. 'These unpleasant things should not be mentioned.'

The fire was piled high with logs and the heat was overpowering. Eve felt faint beads of perspiration breaking out on her forehead and upper lip. She did not want to attract attention by wiping them off. One of the sisters would surely say, 'Oh, are you too hot, should we open a window?' – their solicitude more unbearable than the heat. She might make an excuse to go to the garden. But at that moment the dinner gong sounded and her last hope of a reprieve was gone.

They assembled in the dining room, waiting to be assigned their places. 'You are guest of honour tonight,' Bridget announced, 'so you must sit by my right hand.'

One look at the cutlery told Eve that they were in for a marathon. There would be no allowances made for poor appetites. Refusal of a course or a partially eaten portion would be taken as rejection of hospitality. Her stomach shrank at the prospect.

'Please,' she said quietly to Bridget as the others sorted themselves out in their places. 'Not too much for me tonight, if you don't mind.'

A charitable, tactful acceptance was too much to hope for. 'Nonsense, nonsense,' Bridget declared in a loud voice at once, emphasising Eve's failing, and worst of all proclaiming her feeble attempt at hiding it. 'Any girl who is going to marry Hugh must have plenty of stamina. And you can't do without good food, now, can you?'

'Are you not feeling well?' Ruth asked, loudly compassionate. Eve longed to say, I hate smoked salmon. A kipper will do me for a whole meal.

Hugh intervened tactfully. 'Don't mind Bridget. She eats like a bird herself just to punish the rest of us.'

'Indeed I do not.' Bridget pretended to pout. 'We pride ourselves on our good table. These modern women diet too much. Mother and father never dieted and what harm did it do them?'

Hugh shook his head despairingly and Eleanor leaned across the table and explained, 'Their parents died in their fifties.'

'Early fifties. They were young,' Honora said. 'Young and gay. Not like us at all. Father died first; he was fifty-one. Mother went a few years later; she was fifty-four. Oh, how we missed them. Nothing has ever been the same since.' She wiped her eyes with the back of her fists and looked for a moment like a little girl, bewildered by the tragedy.

Eleanor reached over, patted her hand and said consolingly, 'It happens to all of us.'

Ruth frowned and said, 'Not like that. They were different. They were too good for this world.'

'Did you know,' Florence addressed Eve, 'that they were exactly the same age? Yes. Truly. On the same day in the same year. And they looked just like brother and sister. That's why we are all so alike. It's laughable, isn't it? Well, except for Hugh of course. Dear Hugh. We called him the changeling. He brought in the black hair.'

They sipped their soup.

'That was delicious smoked salmon,' Adrian said.

They chuckled and exchanged glances.

'It's very wicked,' Bridget said with some glee, 'but it is poached, you know. Oh, not by us of course. We don't fish. No, what's his name, young Doherty brought it and we smoked it ourselves.'

'Well, now we know it's not done in horse's piss,' Eleanor declared suddenly.

Bridget rose and pressed the bell. 'That will remind Rosie we're ready. She doesn't like to be rushed but she could easily fall asleep between the courses.'

'When you've finished your soup, Adrian, will you feel rosy all over?' Eleanor inquired mischievously.

Adrian burst out laughing.

Rosie came and went. At dessert Florence remarked on Eleanor's cream linen suit. 'It's nice to see you out of the slacks for a change.'

'I was afraid you might think I had grown wooden legs.'

'I don't like trousers on women,' Hugh said. 'If a woman has good legs she should show them off.'

'What about yours, Hugh?' Eleanor asked. 'I don't think it's fair depriving us of our little thrill. Is there a Creagh kilt you could wear?'

'You know what Thomas Dinely said of us all in his journal,' Adrian remarked.

'No. Tell us.'

Adrian stuck his chest out and assumed Churchillian tones. '"I observed at Ralahine a very ill scent to attend a great rain, and the west of Ireland generally is very subject to it."'

They all laughed, and Eve relaxed for the first time.

'Wait.' He raised his hand solemnly. 'There's more. It goes like this: "The men of Thomond are for the most part of large proportion of body and clear complexion. The women are not ill favoured, and as fair – fairer-handed, big, large, well bottomed, not laced, but suffered to grow at will, nothing set or curious of their feature and proportion of body, and with" – he paused for dramatic effect – "the largest legs, vulgarly, of any."'

'That's his party piece,' Eleanor said. 'I've heard it a hundred times before.'

The sisters were highly amused. 'What a rude man. It's a slander. Typically English,' they said.

'But,' Eleanor reminded them, 'those large legs were not of much help to them in penal days. They weren't able to kick the invaders out.'

'Well, the poor Catholics certainly suffered for their faith,' Ruth declared.

'The rich Catholics suffered more; if they didn't become Protestant, they lost everything,' Hugh reminded them.

'But it's all water under the bridge,' Honora said. 'And we do have Protestant relations. I remember grandmother saying that only for them the Creaghs would have lost everything. Most of it was lost. It's sad to think we are the last. If some of the family hadn't turned, everything would have been taken.'

'Never mind,' Bridget declared briskly. 'What's past is past. There's no use going over all of that again.'

79

'Let's toast to old Ireland.' Adrian stood up with his glass of red wine. 'United and free.'

Afterwards they pushed back the dining-room table. Ruth brought out a small button accordion and played some reels. Eve, Honora, Bridget and Florence danced, the sisters very precisely intoning to themselves the count, one two three four five six seven, pause, and a one two three, and a one two three. Then they faced each other in pairs and danced a four-hand reel. Honora sang 'Be-e-lieve me if all those endearing young charms', and Hugh sang 'The minstrel boy to the war is gone'. Adrian sang '*Anois teacht an Earraigh*', and they all joined in with gusto. Then everyone retired to the drawing room. Adrian sat uneasily on a slender Queen Anne chair. 'Oh, get off,' Eleanor said, laughing at him. 'You look like an elephant on a potty.'

'Really, Eleanor, you are awful,' Ruth said, handing him a large whiskey.

'Is there a pub anywhere handy?' Adrian asked innocently.

'You're not going rushing off and leaving us to our own company,' Ruth told him. 'I don't know what gets into you men. Cracked. That's what you all are. Cracked.'

'Women are drinking now, you know,' Florence said, downing an equally large whiskey. 'I believe it's disgraceful the way they crowd out the pubs. We always drink at home. Let the men go to their bars if they want to.'

The conversation shifted to politics and a three-cornered debate followed between Eleanor, Hugh and Adrian. Bridget occasionally interjected, forcing the others to lose for a moment the thread of the discussion. At such times, Eve noted, the three were poised as if in mid-air, suspended and isolated by the irrelevance of Bridget's remarks. But she continued and was supported with nods and other signs of approval by her three sisters. Eve could see that there was some kind of connection between her comments and the conversation, even if they acted merely as counterpoint to Eleanor's fiery expositions and Hugh's measured pedantry. Adrian displayed his talent for quoting, with relish, sizable chunks of poetry and social commentary. When politics turned to history and the three leaped back in time to Daniel O'Connell (having traversed the policies of coalition governments, the civil war, the establishment of the Free State, the 1916 Rising, the formation of the Ulster Volunteers), Bridget mentioned that the Defenders in Connaught had been press-ganged into the British Navy in 1795 and there was no one in the province to fight in the '98 rebellion. The three guests stared at her in silence, unable to appreciate the context of her information. Honora added further confusion by saying, 'Of course O'Connell saw the horrible effects of revolution in Paris himself.' When Ruth, as if to compound the puzzle said, 'When England sneezes Ireland catches pneumonia,' Adrian gave a loud guffaw. The sisters were offended and withdrew in a dignified parade. Eve thought it very insensitive of Adrian and she expected Hugh to tell him so. Hugh, however, sat for a moment stiffly in his chair before following the sisters, probably to console them.

So for a brief moment the complexities and intricacies of human motives and interests were seen to be beyond rational explanation and reasoned debate. Eve wondered, yet again, if the sisters were not much cleverer and better informed than they pretended. Their rag-bag of ideas might, after all, be the result of delicate and subtle discrimination, betraying a determination not to be swayed by fashionable opinion, the proof of their ungovernableness. Their little prejudices and foibles might be a wall erected to protect independence of thought. Yet how could they feed such thought? They appeared never to read. They declared themselves totally uneducated. Radio and television would hardly provide them with much intellectual stimulation. It was all a puzzle.

Adrian and Eleanor engaged in gossip about a mutual acquaintance, a member of the trade union who made fine speeches about justice and decent living wages. There were rumours about his marriage, that he treated his wife like a servant and refused to allow her to handle any money because of her incompetence. 'I think the poor woman had a bad case of post-natal depression after her last child,' Eleanor said. 'I know it's a long time ago, but I don't think she got the proper treatment then. In fact I'm certain she didn't. She's ostracised by her family now because she can't control her depression. Of course people like that are hard to live with. Perhaps it's too late to help her now. But that man! How he has the gall to go on about decent standards of living for the working classes when he treats his wife like a slave, I just don't know.'

'Well, politicians are a queer class of a bird,' Adrian said as Hugh came through the door.

'I hope that wasn't personal,' Hugh said affably and Adrian said yes, it was.

'I have a friend who is grooming herself for the next foray, the next election,' Eleanor interjected. 'She is going up as an Independent. I expect you to vote for her, Eve, and all your women friends.'

'They won't of course,' Adrian said with a slight sneer. 'Women always vote for men.'

'Your friend is wasting her time,' Hugh pronounced dogmatically. 'She'll lose her deposit. There's no place for Independents in modern politics. She will simply siphon off votes that our party could do with. She should have joined us.'

'She tried. I happen to know she looked for admission and was turned down.'

'She probably wanted the nomination without doing the donkey work first. It's not as simple as that.'

'Unless you have a brother or father or uncle in the party before you,' Adrian joined in cynically.

'Of course she went through the usual channels. Doesn't it sound like a drainage system? But that's what it's like. Underground sewers, full of intrigue and back-stabbing. If women did it, they'd be laughed at and called bitches. The whole structure is rotten. It's destructive of true democracy.'

'When you have found something better, let me know,' Adrian said. 'In my opinion women shouldn't get involved in politics.'

'Luckily your opinion doesn't count. If you exclude women you exclude half the population. Is that what you want?'

'You can't count women,' Adrian said. 'Women aren't really people.'

82

He meant it. Eve was certain. Eleanor burst out laughing. 'You know, I've always loved you,' she told him. 'You're such a pig and you don't try to hide it.'

'True,' he replied modestly. 'I don't believe in hiding my light under a bushel.'

There were great bunches of lilac in the hall and upstairs, outside the bathroom. Their fragrance pervaded the house. The long shadows of the evening stretched across the garden. Below them the sea lapped tenderly at the beach. The bathroom faced towards the mountain and, looking out through the window while she freshened up, Eve was glad of the sombre pine-covered slopes. She fancied she could smell the tangy scent. It provided relief from the excessive sweetness of the house. The sea even now, in early May, was cold. The breeze along its edges bore whiffs of Atlantic icebergs drifting too far south for comfort.

The landing window was a glass door which led onto a verandah with steps down the side of the house. Cautiously she tried the handle. As it swung open she jumped guiltily at Hugh's voice calling her from the foot of the stairs. She waited for him, feeling caught in the act.

'Ah,' he said, smiling, 'you're finding your way around.'

'It looks inviting out there.'

'I suppose. A bit gloomy though. My grandfather planted the mountain, to everyone's horror, I'm told. He was never a farmer and would certainly not have believed in spending his life chasing after sheep. He was a great landscape gardener, you know, in an amateurish way. The timber must be worth quite a bit now.'

'Who owns it all?' she asked, curious.

'Donogh does. But the sisters manage it. They sell the timber. And they are shrewd investors, though you might not think so to hear them talk.'

'I know they only pretend to be silly.'

'Silly? I wouldn't have thought they seemed silly. What a funny creature you are.'

How strange, she thought. Here was the impenetrable barrier again. The bond of kinship was like steel wire. Yet,

83

wasn't it natural, even admirable? So many families appeared to cherish undying hatred for one another. It ought to have been comforting to witness such devotion and loyalty. But it was not. 'Would we have time for a stroll before they begin the cards?'

'You poor lamb,' he said, taking her arm as they went down the steps. 'I think it is all too much for you. You are only a little mouse really. I think that's why I love you.'

'A lamb mouse. I'm quite a hybrid.' But she was pleased. The affection and compassion were genuine. It was hard to resist.

They followed the path to a stile which led into the wood. Close to, it was dark and airless. No birds twittered in the gloomy depths. A shingle path twisted through the trees. It led, Hugh explained, to a grotto where his mother had prayed every afternoon of her married life. Between three and four, she meditated. 'We never disturbed her,' he said.

Eve detected painful memories and held his hand in sympathy.

'She was going to be a nun, you know. Was actually on the train when my father dashed into the station and told her he would kill himself if she didn't marry him.'

'That was dramatic. And romantic.'

'I suppose so. But she was half a nun until the day she died. Quite unsuited for marriage and children, although she did her best to hide it.'

They reached the grotto. A niche had been cut out of the rock and in it stood a large plaster statue of the Virgin Mary. The blue paint on her cloak had been almost completely washed off. Patches of colour and a little glitter of gilt remained, but neither weather nor time had removed the flaccid expression which displayed not repose, nor peaceful contemplation, but merely a lack of energy. That such a representation could possibly remind its viewers of the tragic Jewish girl who had borne the Christian Messiah and watched him suffer for his challenge to the age seemed to Eve outrageous.

'They never portray her properly,' she said.

84

'She wouldn't be here if they did. Anyway, this is only Bernadette Soubirous's vision misinterpreted. An icon to assist contemplation.'

'It's an insult.'

From a clearing a few yards to the left they looked down on the estuary where it flowed into the sea. A single fishing boat chugged slowly homewards.

'He's a lobster man,' Hugh told her. 'And a poteen maker. It's a good mix of trades. The fishermen around here are jealous of their lobster rights. They guard them well. Any stranger moving in will find trouble.'

'I suppose you can hardly blame the locals for protecting themselves.'

'Perhaps not. But in a way we are all strangers. Blow-ins. It just depends how far back you want to go.'

'Maybe to the Firbolgs.' She laughed.

'Heritage is fine,' Hugh said. 'But it's what you do with it that matters. You are what you do. In some ways it doesn't matter who was here first. Ultimately it is the strong who have rights.'

'I believe that too,' Eve agreed. 'Women must get organised and physically fit as well. Because, as you say, might is right.'

'Are you talking about this women's rights thing? We should be talking about human rights. We all want the same thing. Peace and justice.'

'But you just said – ' She stopped, bewildered.

'Of course,' Hugh said, 'there are no rights without responsibilities. Feminists and women's libbers should remember that.'

'Why didn't you mention responsibilities when you referred to him?' She pointed to the vanishing lobster boat.

'It just didn't come up,' he replied, puzzled by her question.

'That's just it,' she said with an unnecessary tinge of exasperation in her voice. 'It only comes up when it suits you.' She turned abruptly away from him and half ran back towards the house.

'What did I say wrong now?' he called after her.

8

In the drawing room a discussion started about cards.

'We have an odd number,' Florence said. 'We can't play partners.'

'We can't play at all because we haven't got a decent pack,' Ruth said, a little fiercely, Eve felt. It seemed to be an old argument. Florence reminded her that they weren't playing poker so it hardly mattered. It was only A Hundred and Ten.

Only, only. Ruth showed her disgust openly. A Hundred and Ten was far superior to poker, which was only a gambler's game. It took skill. Great Aunt Flo had always said a person wasn't educated until she could play cards. Oh, what fun they were, those card parties of long ago. Wait, Ruth commanded and rushed to the bureau to produce a brand new pack, which she flourished triumphantly at Florence, who said a little guiltily, 'Oh, so that's where they were.' Eve wondered if she had hidden them from some perverse motive. But she had no time to continue with that line of thought for Ruth had produced something else from the bureau: a large album packed with very old photographs, each in its individual little window.

Eve avoided Eleanor's quizzical expression as she was ordered to sit down and look at the family. She needed little persuasion, and certainly no command, to examine the fascinating contents of the book. She turned the first pages eagerly, searching the faces of those long-vanished generations for touches of resemblance to Hugh. Ruth chattered beside her, pointing out the richer or more distinguished members of the family, or the young and beautiful who would always remain so, because they had died tragically before the camera could witness their decline.

The faces, Eve noticed, were invariably severe. She supposed it had been the newness of the technique that had made the sitters so self-conscious. But even in the more informal family groups, obviously taken by a loving amateur, the figures sprawling on lawn or beach showed no hint of merriment. The picnic photographs through the years were carefully composed, the children progressing from babyhood through adolescence to adulthood, until they stared at the wielder of the latest camera with the grim resignation of old age. Here and there a snapshot of a cook grinning amiably or a dairymaid caught defensively with a milk pail added a touch of vitality. Their employers, high-buttoned into respectability, were allowed no such freedom.

'It's very sad,' Eve remarked.

'You're quite right,' Honora agreed. 'We shall never see the like of those days again.'

'Perhaps it is just as well,' Bridget said surprisingly and took the cards from Ruth to deal.

It was hard to concentrate on the game, hard because it was an unfamiliar one, the rules amazingly complex, the pitfalls many. A mistake in judgement incurred offended silence from the partner and open contempt from the other players. This game apparently allowed no time for niceties and made no concessions to the rawness of the new player. Concentration was made even harder by the fact that the sisters, who seemed to have a marvellous ability simultaneously to talk and think and throw out the cards, reminisced about the past and their idyllic childhood. They had roamed the hills and rocky beaches without restraint, sometimes riding their little Welsh ponies, more often on foot. Every ancient monument and megalithic tomb was known to them.

One summer an archeologist had come to dig tentatively at the mound a few miles from their house. Each of them fell in love with him so none could have him. But it was better that way. They could never bear to think of growing up and leaving

87

home, leaving their place. They fancied themselves haunted by the ghosts of a thousand years. Following the track up the mountain, they heard soft footfalls behind them, and at night the clashing of weapons and the cries of the wounded in one of the interminable raids of the past reached their ears. In winter the remains of the castle against which their house had been built seemed fearsome, especially on evenings when the wind howled through the narrow windows. Then the maid would come shrieking for them, yelling at them to come in this minute or they would surely be killed, buried alive under tons of handhewn stone.

What had changed them from the adventurous lively children they undoubtedly were into the eccentric, slightly malicious women they had become? Eve saw for the first time the inner core of their lost youth shining through and she felt sympathy and even a little understanding. Then Donogh was born and they were sent away to school. Hugh was born a year later. But there were always holidays. Not quite the same, they said, but better than nothing. We were wicked girls at school, they admitted. Everyone hated us. They called us the Wild Irish. Oh yes, they went to school in England.

For a few seconds as they sat around the table they were suffused with melancholy and terrible, unmentionable grief as if that nightmare of loneliness and exile had come back to haunt them. Of course they had had each other, but they only met at recreation and at weekends, when they passed messages to each other in the crocodile walks in the parks. If they were caught, it was detention or no sweets on Sunday.

'We were content with little then,' said Florence. 'It was easy to amuse us.'

'Times have changed,' Ruth lamented. 'Now much wants more.'

'Remember the limericks we used to make up?' Bridget reminded them. 'I can remember one of mine:

'A widow of fame in Fanore
Went fishing one night off the shore
As she pulled in a shark

88

She said, Oh what a lark,
And she never went fishing no more.'

'Last line's a bit weak,' Adrian commented. They all tried.
Honora brought out pieces of paper and pencils and they
composed.

Eleanor wrote:

'There was a young fellow named Denis
A champion at ping-pong and tennis.
When a maiden from Clare
Said they'd make a good pair,
He said, sorry, my balls are in Ennis.'

Hugh wrote:

'There was a young man from Madrid
Who went to an auction to bid.
The first thing they sold
Was an ancient commode,
But oh, when they opened the lid.'

'You prefer anal humour,' Eleanor complained when they
chuckled at Hugh's and ignored hers.

'There's too much sex talk nowadays,' Florence remarked.
'We never had any of that sort of thing when we were young.'

'You mean,' Eleanor asked in mock amazement, 'there was
no copulation?'

'There wasn't so much talk about it. At least not in polite
circles. We weren't prudish, you know. We enjoyed a joke, just
like everyone else. In fact we were considered quite daring. But
there's all this coarseness and crudeness about everything.
Nothing is left unsaid any more.'

'No room for fantasies, I suppose.' Eleanor seemed to be
agreeing.

'It's all these women's libbers.' Florence's face turned red
and her eyes glittered with rage. 'They should be at home in
their little boxes where they belong. They don't know their
place. With all this education no one wants to do the menial
work. Who will do the menial work in the future?'

'How about you?' Eleanor asked. 'You'd be very good at it.'

'Women should be at home, minding their babies and looking after their husbands,' Ruth said. 'That's why they got married. And that's why we didn't get married. We knew what it would be like so we decided to stay single. We had plenty of offers.'

Eve could believe it.

'We're in the middle of a revolution,' Eleanor pointed out, 'and you don't even know it.'

'You'd think this was a new argument,' Adrian interrupted impatiently. 'Are we going to let it spoil our evening? Shut up, Eleanor, and concentrate on cards. Ruth is quite right. You make your choices. Women are always whining. I'm sick of them coming into my surgery with their nerves. Even in my little practice I have to dish out valium.'

'That's odd,' Eleanor said. 'I never have to do that. I wonder why. My patients all have good reasons to be depressed. A lot of them are physical. Do you send yours to the head shrink when they have cancer of the uterus or malignant tumours the size of footballs attached to their ovaries?'

'No one would do such a thing,' Honora said. 'Our doctors are the best in the world.'

'Let's not get into medical diagnoses,' said Hugh. 'We all make mistakes.'

'How come most of the mistakes are made with the women patients?' Eleanor asked.

'The law of averages,' was Hugh's answer. 'Most patients are women.'

'All I know is, if a woman comes to me with a pain, she has a bloody pain, and it's not, as Adrian puts it, "nerves". It might be betrayal, of course, that gives a pain. Perhaps Adrian is just too insensitive. Who's dealing?'

'Christ,' Adrian exploded. 'Why should I have to mollycoddle them? Most of them need a good kick in their beam ends. If I were their husbands, I'd give it to them.'

There was an appalled silence. Bridget rushed in reassuringly with, 'You don't really mean that.'

'He does mean it.' Eleanor had leaped to her feet. 'He's like a million other men who think that's the answer to everything. I have their wives with the proof coming in every week to my surgery. Women with broken jaws, split skulls, broken collarbones, fractured pelvises, where the Adrians of this world have kicked them on their beam ends, usually down the stairs. Only last week I attended a woman whose baby was stillborn while its mother lay at the foot of the stairs where its father had kicked her. You're nothing special, Adrian. Don't give yourself airs. You're just another paid-up member of the hairy-gorilla club. Do you think women should drink their pints out of two half-pint glasses because their gullets are too small to accommodate one pint but large enough to take two half-pints? And perhaps you believe that education is bad for a woman because it shrivels up her uterus, that learning creates some miraculous chemical imbalance between brain and womb?'

'Well,' Adrian said. 'You're in full flight. You're just like all the other women. You've probably got a little self-help club there in your surgery where you can whine away about the men in your lives. What do you call it?' He affected a high-pitched querulous voice. 'Consciousness raising. My dears, we must dedicate ourselves to the sisterhood and to consciousness raising.'

They glared at one another with venom. Everyone else in the room was ignored. Eve watched them. The great sex war which she had naively imagined was the figment of perverted imaginations was in full progress before her. Adrian should have been called Adam and Eleanor Eve and they could have bitten the apple together.

'Do you know what your trouble is?' Adrian said. 'You need a baby.' He spat the words out triumphantly. The final knife in the heart. Eleanor didn't even flinch.

'You'll give it to me, I suppose,' she snarled back. 'Retire to stud at last.'

Ruth clasped her hands in horror and exclaimed, 'You're getting very coarse. How can you say such things?'

Florence rose. 'I'm leaving. The poor Pope. What he has to put up with.'

Their intervention did nothing to stop the duel. If anything, it acted as a goad, for the pair launched into a tirade, dredging out of the past every prejudice and human foible they could recall, quoting and misquoting, from medical texts and sociological pamphlets. Each of them used words as if they were spears, goring and disembowelling with a frenzy approaching madness. They are all insane, Eve thought. Hugh is insane too because he sits there with his eyes cast down as if a discussion on the weather was taking place.

'As for a baby,' Eleanor was by this time yelling, 'if you're capable of it, you do it. I've had a baby. Have you?'

'That's not my function,' Adrian announced pompously.

'You don't have a function. You're just a freak. A lousy freak. With your lousy poetry and your lost language. You're typical of the sterile impotent male this country is bedevilled with. You couldn't even do it into an old sock.'

At that, Hugh pushed the card table back with such force it turned over and cards and glasses and ashtray went tumbling down. Eve had never seen him look so angry. His voice trembled with fury. 'I must say, you have excelled yourselves tonight. Both of you. You're a disgrace. My fiancée and my sisters have been forced to listen to your disgusting diatribes and witness your display of bad manners. I hope you will now apologise to them.'

They're nothing but a pack of cards, Eve thought in amazement, as she watched the passion and heat disintegrate, melt under the cold shower of Hugh's disapproval and his accusation of bad manners. Even Eleanor was restrained by the reminder of their duties as guests. Her life was spent among people for whom polite concern was a luxury, yet she could be muzzled here in this drawing room, not by a logical refuting of her argument, nor even by an opposing strength of feeling for which she might have had respect, but by a social custom which seemed laughably anachronistic in a country where every day terror and hate reigned. As bad as the argument had been, it had infused life into the evening. Distressed as she had been by the blatant emotions of both Adrian and Eleanor, Eve had to admit that at least they were honest emotions. The

92

sisters, with their sad, nostalgic memories, were dead wood. Adrian and Eleanor, with their verbal ferocities, expressed vitality, a will to live and explore. With them, there was still hope for a future. With the sisters, there was nothing. 'Please don't apologise for me,' she said. 'I didn't mind the argument.'

'There you are,' said Bridget. 'See how sweet the child is. She forgives you and so do we.'

With such magnanimity there could be no quarrel. Eleanor and Adrian apologised and peace was almost restored. Almost, because Adrian could not resist the last shot to Eleanor.

'If you ever feel you want a baby again, let me know. My service is free.'

Eleanor replied, 'How about now?'

'Enough is enough,' Florence said. 'I think it is time we retired.'

The women moved to help each other tidy up, pushing chairs into orderly positions, plumping out cushions to remove the gross body impressions, securing the wooden shutters on the windows, looping back the curtains. The two men stood at the door, silently watching and waiting. When the last ashtray was emptied and the drinking glasses gathered onto the tray, they wished each other goodnight and went to their rooms.

Eve read for a long time. The old house was full of creaks and groans and seemed to take hours to settle for sleep. She fancied she heard mice scuttle across the ceiling. Her room faced the garden but beyond it the sea boomed and crunched against the stones on the beach. Her window was open at the top and a large moth flew in, attracted by her bedside light. It spent half an hour trying to kill itself off the burning bulb, dashing in rage or confusion to the ceiling every few minutes before diving on its suicide mission again. Eventually she lost patience and pursued it until she caught it and threw it out of the window, firmly securing the latch against a second invasion. It was two o'clock. Her room was cold with the death-like chill of long non-occupancy. The sisters had begged her to light the electric fire if she felt the need for it, and a little guiltily she plugged it in. For a while she crouched in front of its cheerful glow, hugging her knees and scorching her toes.

The creaks and the scuttling had stopped and the house lay icily still. As she climbed back into bed, Eve thought she heard a soft murmuring from Eleanor's room next door. She listened intently and was certain. Eleanor had a visitor. Probably Adrian. What a sacrilege. In Donogh's room too. But the thought of their lovemaking, the warmth of their bodies embracing, made her feel lonely and sick with longing. If Hugh could shake off whatever chains bound him to this house and come to her now, she knew she would love him for ever. She lay waiting, willing him to come. It was five o'clock before she fell asleep, her arms wrapped around herself in pathetic imitation of a lover's embrace.

At breakfast Hugh assumed a mask of stony virtue and she knew she had been right about Eleanor's visitor. She and Adrian attacked their creamy porridge and grilled bacon with gusto, chatting between the mouthfuls with the casualness of complete empathy. Where was the fire and the hatred now? Dampened down temporarily by incongruous leapings on Donogh's bridal bed? Hugh asked Eve solicitously if she had slept well and when she lied he looked content. She had an annoying thought that perhaps he saw himself as the protector of her youthful virtue. When he said coldly to the other two, 'Would either of you like a bath?' she giggled nervously.

'You sound a little hysterical,' he said.

'Are men ever hysterical?' Eleanor asked vaguely, her mouth full. 'Is it only those of us who have wombs who can truly be said to be hysterical? What are men when they froth at the mouth?'

'Spare me one of your monologues this morning,' Hugh said.

'I think,' Adrian joined in, 'men never lose control of their reason. That's the difference. Unless under enormous stress, of course. I'm quite sure it is hormonal. The Greeks were probably right.'

'At what point last night,' Eleanor asked mildly, 'would you see yourself as being most reasoning and in control?'

'That's different,' Adrian answered, reaching for the toast.

94

'Hysterical giggles without any cause are hardly comparable to the drama of grand passion.'

Eleanor choked slightly but controlled herself. She looked him full in the face and asked, 'Why do you dislike the child so? Are you jealous?'

'Is who jealous?' Ruth asked beamingly through the door. 'More porridge anyone? More toast? More anything? You won't mind if I practise. I'll use the attic. I always practise at this hour. You don't want to rummage there, do you, Hugh?'

She kept the accordion in the kitchen cupboard because she said it needed warmth. In cold weather it sounded hoarse. Accordions were highly sensitive instruments, needing very careful handling. A good carpenter, she reminded them, needed good tools and a good musician needed a good instrument. And vice versa. It was a partnership which could not survive where there was neglect. He depends on me, she said.

They heard her labouring up the stairs with the instrument. She stopped at the first landing and played a little scale before continuing. Her devotion to her accordion was touching. The tender, protective air she assumed when she spoke of it endowed her with qualities more likeable than the brittle mannerisms and dark innuendoes with which her normal conversation was spattered. In much the same way, her sisters' dedication to the shell pictures redeemed them and made them not simply eccentric or malicious women but artists, and therefore excusable.

Eve wondered if the extraordinary attachment between Hugh and the sisters was also shared by Donogh. Their passionate loyalty to him was obvious whenever they mentioned his name and was a part of their antipathy to Eleanor. But did Donogh feel the same way? If he did, why did he never return to the house, even for a holiday?

After Ruth left, Adrian suggested a walk by the sea and they hurried for coats and outdoor shoes. It was a magnificent day. At the far side of the bay the windows of houses glittered with reflected sunshine. A few fishing boats trawled slowly and a curragh made its homeward journey. The air was calm but the sea was agitated and heaved restlessly off the rocks. The small beach below the house was horseshoe shaped and they sheltered in the sunny arm of its curve, watching the spray and the cormorants and the boats at work.

Eleanor moved away from them, typically without a word of excuse or explanation. Adrian ambled after her, saying, 'Might as well see what she's up to.' Hugh nodded without answering. For once Eve did not feel it necessary to speak. She was pleased at her new self-control. It must be a sign of maturity not to have to rush in with babble every time there was a gap in the conversation. Not that there had been many gaps so far in the weekend. No companionable silences; only voracious dialogue or inexplicable innuendo. She wondered for the hundredth time what she was doing here.

Hugh took her arm and said, 'You're very quiet.'

'So are you.'

'I'm just thinking.'

'So am I.'

'It was a mistake to invite Adrian. Eleanor – well, what can be done about Eleanor? She'll never change.'

'Poor Eleanor.'

'I wouldn't waste any sympathy on her. That lady can take care of herself. She only has herself to blame for the mess she's in. I suppose she told you all about Donogh? Her version.'

'Well, I asked her. But she didn't say much. Just that she had had a child. I think it is very sad to lose a child. Especially for a mother.'

'Fathers have feelings too. It was her own fault. She didn't fight hard enough.'

'Did anyone help her?'

Hugh frowned. 'I don't know if she had any family to help her at the time. Her parents were dead. I think she has one brother abroad. She never mentions her family. Always seems something of an orphan. My sisters are very kind to her. There is no real need for them to ask her to stay. But like you, they feel sorry for her.'

'Poor Eleanor.'

'There you go again. Wasting pity.'

'That's a silly thing to say. You can't waste pity. I feel sorry for her being on her own. She has a lonely life. It's hard on divorced women.'

'True,' he said. 'Emancipation for women doesn't change the biological factor.'

They argued along the sunny but cold beach. Why did he have to reduce everything to the physiological? Didn't he believe in ideals? Didn't he have any vision? Ideals, he said, are the prelude to cynicism. He wasn't a poet; was she? He wasn't a philosopher; was she? 'I might be,' she said. 'I might be both.'

'I'm a man of science. Philosophy and science don't mix. I'm a politician too, at least by intent. Philosophers are the enemies of the state. They take upon themselves the pain of truth. Could you live with that?'

'You're arguing again. Is it worth it?'

'You're changing,' he said. 'I think Eleanor has an influence on you. Sometimes you seem very far away. Even when I gave you the ring you seemed to back away before you let me put it on your finger. You're not wearing it now. Is there a sinister significance in that?'

She lied. She said she was afraid the sand would get into the setting and spoil it. It was a beautiful ring. It was a pointless conversation. Why should she feel guilty at not wearing the ring? Why should he make her guilty? And why had she accepted the ring? She hadn't really wanted it. It didn't even belong on her finger, but on the hand of some exotic mythical woman, anointed with oils, perfumed, fed on honey and choice foods, a kept woman, splendid in lethargy and erotic in captivity. It's only a thing, she said to herself miserably as they sat on a rock staring glumly out at the sea. Why don't I wear it and use it as a knuckle duster? There would be some purpose to that. If only Hugh had come to her last night when she had waited for him, willed him to come, imagining that her desire was so strong it would draw him to her bed. Instead, Adrian had gone to Eleanor.

What would Hugh have done if she had arrived in his bedroom, if she had made a blatant suggestion to him, instead of waiting for him to take the initiative? But what words could

97

she have used? She could imagine him getting embarrassed and leading her back to her own room. Thank God she hadn't done it. It might have been such a fiasco that she would not have been able to face him again. It was good to be able to look at him and ask the apparently innocent question, 'Is something wrong? You were in bad form this morning.'

His mouth closed in that mulish way she had lately noticed. She was sorry she had asked. It was treacherous. An act of deceit.

'Those two.' Hugh got up from the rock and began to stride after Eleanor and Adrian. 'They behave like children at times. Wicked, malicious children. They don't know when to stop. I'm surprised at Adrian. He was always an odd fish but I never knew he was like this.'

She had to run to catch up with him. 'Do you think they are in love with each other?'

'In love with themselves, I should think. Or perhaps it's just lust, if you'll forgive me mentioning it.'

'I'm not a baby, Hugh,' she said desperately. 'I do know about all that. I've had several boyfriends before you.'

'I know you, Eve. Your relationships would always be – pure.'

She stopped so suddenly that he had gone several yards ahead of her before he noticed she wasn't with him.

'Come on,' he called. 'We'll catch up with them if we hurry.'

When he had used the word 'pure' her heart had pounded so fiercely that she had been forced to stop. 'Lust,' he had said. And then 'pure'.

He stretched a hand back for her to take as he kept walking. She deliberately ignored it and stepped to his other side. He put an arm around her waist and squeezed her affectionately. 'I've been a little out of sorts, lately,' he admitted. 'It has been a strange experience coming across the letters from that woman, Honora's namesake. It's hard to explain, but it's almost as if I never really knew who I was before. It's as if I am only now discovering, first through you, and then through these papers. I'm not the most self-analytical of men. I plan ahead but I don't examine ideas much. I suppose I have been too busy. But

98

I've always tried to be honourable. It's an old-fashioned word, but it's important to me. And I've always felt I belonged to an honourable family. Donogh didn't treat Eleanor too well, and that was a blot, but then Eleanor – well, you know what she's like.'

'Have you found a skeleton in the cupboard? A highwayman or two?'

'Of course not. Nothing like that,' he answered brusquely.

'I'd like to understand,' she said. 'But does it really matter what happened in the past, or who this Honora person was? She's dead. They're all dead. It's now that's important, what we do with our lives. And there is so much to do. So many people need help. But where to begin?'

'We can't cut ourselves away from the past. We don't just leap into life from nowhere; we are the extension of something else. Life is a continuous chain. I have always been very proud of my family. When times were hard they shared what they had. They were good-living, honourable people. We had a soup kitchen in Tower Hill for the poor people who lived around here. There was quite a big population then, you know. You can tell by all the little gables and ruined houses. But they died or emigrated.'

'It's very sad,' Eve said. 'But it's over. Awful things happen today as well. And we can do something about today. We can't change the past.'

'We can learn from it,' Hugh said obstinately. 'We must learn from it. We must have something to build on.'

'Well, I just think,' said Eve, 'that every child born creates a new world. We have to learn everything for ourselves. Everything begins again, constantly.'

'I suppose it is hard for you to understand just how much the people around here suffered,' Hugh said.

'I wish you wouldn't be so patronising. You never listen to anything I say. In the past few months I have met scores of women who are suffering in the most terrible way – being beaten, being humiliated, not given money. I've tried to tell you.'

'Look, Eve,' he said, 'don't bring up that business of

99

battered wives again. We have a social welfare system, we have social workers, we have our own government, we elect our own representatives in government. These women have a vote. You have a vote. Why don't you use it?'

'The women vote the way their husbands vote.'

'Well then,' he said. 'You see?'

'They think they're stupid. Don't *you* see? They really believe they know nothing. They think men know more. They think men are cleverer. They think men are stronger. They feel helpless.'

'Things are bad for everyone just now, my love,' he said compassionately. 'I admire you for being so concerned. But must you be so obsessive about it? Wait. Wait. Where are you off to now?'

She had run on ahead of him. Her toes left odd little marks on the sand. He followed their prints in a half-trot, puffing as he ran.

What could he tell her that she wanted to hear? Why did she insist on mentioning those women all the time? He couldn't bear to think of their sordid lives. Violence had always distressed him. Donogh was the one for sports and violent games. Hugh had been the sort of child who wept over a wounded bird on the beach. He had hysterics when he saw the cook plunge a live lobster into a boiling pot. He was sick when he saw fish heads lying in newspaper on the back kitchen sink. Donogh had once locked him in the cold room at the back of the house where the pheasants hung to ripen, and he had been so ill that for days afterwards he had missed school. He had been sent to stay with his uncle, the doctor in Limerick, to recuperate. It was then that he had decided to make medicine his life. He was brought around the wards by the nurses. Everything so clean and orderly, illness in its proper place, washed out and disinfected. Until then he had always grieved more for sick animals than for sick people. People could take control of their own lives. Animals could not. That made the crucial difference.

He stooped to unfasten his sandals. The tide was coming in, the sea flinging itself forward in great surges, heaving with frightening energy its billions of tons of water onto the shores.

It advanced and retreated, gathering itself with tremendous force to crash off promontories and rocks. A boiling wave rushed to cover his feet, then receded and faded. Was that his life now? Would this last anguished effort fade with his ebbing tide?

He slowed his pace to follow Eve more sedately. She had stopped running. More accurately, she had stopped moving forward. She was jogging in a standing position. Ahead of her Eleanor linked arms with Adrian, who had his head down and seemed to be shuffling the sand with his feet. Then Eve turned and ran towards Hugh. He waited, smiling. When she reached him, arms outstretched to embrace him, saying, 'I don't want to quarrel,' he pulled her to him, his eyes glistening with tears of relief. Then, arms wrapped around each other, they walked slowly back to the house where Bridget, Florence, Honora and Ruth waited.

Adrian had caught up with Eleanor just as they were out of sight of the other two. 'You're a bitch,' he said. 'The way you stalk off with not a word to anyone. Did your mother never teach you any manners?'

'You're a bastard,' she rejoined coolly. 'Our mothers must have been nurtured in the same tradition. Our manners about match.'

'My mother was a fantastic woman.'

'So was mine. And so was my father.'

'A fantastic woman? Well, that explains everything.'

'I didn't know either of them very well, of course. He died when I was eight. She died when I was eleven.'

'Oh Christ, Eleanor. I forgot. I forgot you were a deprived child.'

'Shut up, go away, and leave me alone to think.'

'I want, I want to be alone,' he sang in a high falsetto. 'We weren't too bad last night. Considering our lack of practice.' He pulled back his shoulders and beat a tom-tom on his chest.

'Speak for yourself,' she said. 'I've had plenty of practice.'

'Admit it,' he jeered. 'You haven't had a man since Donogh. Admit it.'

She sat down suddenly and he stood on a rock towering against the sky, letting the spray from the waves splash his trousers. 'Finn McCool,' she said mockingly.

'I wish I was,' he answered wistfully. 'I wish I was a warrior bold, hunting in the woods of Clare, or a St Brendan scouring the oceans in my leather boat sewn up with twisted hides waxed with beef fat. If I had been Hugh, born here on this rough challenging coast, I would have been different. What can you do with your life when you are born in a narrow side street of a narrow town, with Redemptorist bells forever ringing in your ears? Prayer and suffering and resignation. It's not much of a diet for a small boy.'

'Is that what it was like?' Eleanor asked in amazement. 'I don't know why, but I pictured you in a different setting. A suburban villa somewhere vaguely in the precincts, rural relations and a Kate O'Brienish mixture of intelligence and even sophistication nicely leavened with country cunning. And certainly a strong dash of culture.'

'Oh, there was that too, but I was a deprived child also.' He laughed. 'Well, it was either that or the climate.'

'You're not a failure,' she said. 'If that's what you're hinting. I think you've made something marvellous out of your life. But I agree, the Celtic sagas are attractive. I have my fantasies too. I think I should have been a great virago of a woman with my big white arms waving at the battalions to stop: we can't fight today because I'm getting my period, but in four days' time I'll be at my peak and we'll beat all comers.'

'We were born too late,' he said. 'Or maybe too soon.'

'It's not the time that's wrong. It is ourselves. We go against the conventions but we don't go far enough. We make too many compromises. I suppose we made the wrong choice. We chose survival.'

'I could just imagine you in your passion-killing woolly knickers.'

'If you hate women so much,' she said unexpectedly, 'why are you bothering with me?'

'Who said I hated women?'

'It's obvious. Don't you think I am a woman?'

102

He studied her calculatingly. 'Biologically, yes. Temperamentally, no. You ought to have been a man.'

'It might surprise you to know that I have other dreams. Not of being a man but of being like Eve there. A frail flower perfuming the air. An ornament for the delectation of others.'

'It sounds like the beginning of a poem. Do you mind if I take notes?'

'Sneer away. Why shouldn't I dream? On the other hand, why should others not smell sweetly for me? You, for instance. Be a muse to my art? A cockscomb male preening in satin and perfumes is no more ridiculous than a woman furred and feathered and scented as an expression of her so-called femininity.'

'Phew,' he whistled. 'I've got to use that. Where's me biro?'

'You're no better than Hugh,' she said. 'He's nothing but a big medical textbook and you're nothing but a big poetic myth.'

'That's the nicest thing anyone ever said to me.'

'It isn't meant to be a compliment.'

'All the better for that. Thank you, my dear.' He bared his teeth wolfishly.

'Oh, Granny,' she joined in the game. 'What a great big thing you've got.'

Laughing, they rolled together on the prickly sea grass.

'Why don't you crush me in your big strong arms,' he said, 'and shower passionate kisses on me. I promise not to swoon. And if you want to carry me off in your strong arms to your white charger don't bother wrapping your cloak around me. I don't get the vapours.'

She lay on top of him, looking into his cold cat's eyes.

'You're divine,' she breathed huskily. 'You're so perfectly formed. What a shape, what a body. With your looks and my brains we could go a long way together. Howabout it, baby?'

'Oh,' he said faintly. 'I'm overwhelmed. This is so sudden. I never knew you felt this way. But it's not right. We mustn't. No. No. We mustn't. Dear God, give me strength. God, you're a ton weight. Would you get off my bloody chest. There's a time and a place for everything.'

'See,' she said as they rolled on to their backs. 'You couldn't stick it even for a minute.'

'The script was wrong. That's all. Your choice of phrase is strange. And you are a hell of a weight. Is it muscle or fat?'

She didn't answer.

'You're too old for stony silences. Martyrdom is for the young and beautiful. But I meant what I said last night. I could give you a baby. I'd like to. I feel I owe it to society before I die. But don't expect anything else. I am a bastard. What do you think?'

'It's not much of a deal,' she said. 'And it's risky. At my age I could have a Down's syndrome child.'

'I hadn't thought of that.'

'You wouldn't. You think you're doing me a great favour. You keep forgetting I have a child. Somewhere. Some day I may find her.'

'You stopped looking a long time ago. And she's not your child any more. I'm not so bad. I think we could work something out. I just don't want to make promises I can't keep.'

Eleanor did not answer. How could she argue across the unbridgeable gap? She was forty-five years old, a woman of strong will and intellect caught in a civilisation so patriarchal in structure that there could never be any proper dialogue between her and any man because she could never forget the disadvantages or forgive the injustices. There were some compromises she could not make. Adrian, Hugh and Donogh in their different ways and with their differing personalities were all flawed and coarsened as she was herself. Her foolish efforts to restore some sense of balance in her life had ended in her own destruction. She had become a half-man, a figure of fun to many, with her rough ways and her rough tongue. Rebelling against the hypocritical modesty which had sterilised the lives of so many women, she had made the fatal mistake of imitating the tough vulgarity of the stereotyped male. Both were travesties of what might have been. Men and women cannot live together, she decided. We have destroyed innocence and our lives with it. For a brief moment

104

she pitied the harsh desert nomads groping for explanation in the story of the Fall. The woman tempted me and I did eat. Who could live like that? What woman could endure such a lie? Swallowing the lie meant you became the lie, a treacherous sow devouring your young. Yet what defence was there against it? Only brute force, the denial of the life-giving womb, the death of the world. Perhaps it would come to that. Women in battle. Men spilling their seed and scooping it up, trying to create it for themselves. Test-tube babies, laboratory tricks.

'I'm not sure,' she said, 'that you would be a suitable father for my child. You're intelligent, but only slightly above average. Your neuroses might be inherited. How do I know you won't pass them on to my daughter? I'm not sure I can take the risk. I may have to look elsewhere.'

'You're only bluffing. You know you won't find it easy. Who will you ask? One of your patients? You'll be had up for rape.'

'What a truly male chauvinist pig you are,' she exploded. 'You and Donogh are very alike. Do you think I'd risk that again?'

Oh well, off she goes, he said to himself. Paddling along like a duck in a wet field. It was worth a try. A few weeks with her might have been diverting. But he could alter the wall hangings, do a bit of spring cleaning. His genuine Turkish saddle rug could hang opposite the door where it would be most effective. He might move the big marble-topped wash-stand into the centre of the reception hall with the brass church urn on it and the dried grasses in the urn. Or was that a cliché? Everything was a cliché. The printing machine, radio and television created minefields of clichés. The glossy magazines had done the same for visual art. Visual Art. That was another cliché. Man was a cliché. Woman was a cliché. Could they be erased with Tipp-Ex? Or would it take the bomb?

Everything had become too easy. Slovenly habits so quickly turned to addiction. There were times when the effort at composition was too great and his poetry suffered. He either wrote none or the sweat showed. Composition ought to be a spontaneous delivery. Birth without pain.

Thought was a mechanical deliverer. Everything should be conceived of the gods, the anonymous ever-present, mythical gods in all their shapes, love, fire, air, water, war. Or goddesses? He shrugged the sentiment aside and continued to amuse himself. Gods of earth. Goddesses? Fertility? Love? He was back full circle. He waddled duck-like in deliberate mimicry after Eleanor.

9

In June, Adrian was in Limerick buying equipment for his home-made wines and found himself caught in a queue of cars in one of the narrow side streets. He could move neither forwards nor backwards. The source of the delay was soon apparent – a procession of people moving down the main street. Among them a group carrying banners sang hymns. On one of the banners was an image of Christ's mother painted in the style of a Russian icon. Another bore the words NOVENA IN HONOUR OF OUR LADY OF PERPETUAL SUCCOUR. Of course. It was the time of year for the nine days' prayer. He knew that in Limerick it reached particular fervour. An order of priests who had the imagination to employ a PR man ran the event with the aplomb of a highly efficient multi-national company. Each day of the Novena thousands flocked to the church to pray and sing hymns and listen to sermons. Out of curiosity and perhaps a touch of nostalgia he decided to participate. He followed the surge of traffic behind the procession, parked the car dutifully where he was directed and, self-consciously sheep-like, pushed with the crowd into the church.

It was a building of Gothic design with huge marble pillars and a high domed sanctuary. Splendidly triumphant, it reeked of majesty and authority. How was it, Adrian reflected as he was ushered into a seat by an official, that Hugh never considered the great churches and cathedrals as expressing whatever it was he felt should be expressed? Far removed from the little beehive huts of the ancient Irish monks and the pleasant functional monasteries of the early Christians, this

107

was surely a magnificent monument, a flamboyant celebration of the humble life of Christ, as proud and challenging as the pagan tomb of Bru Na Bóinne. Built at a time of poverty and near starvation, such a building could be seen either as a justification for the people's suffering or a further symbol of exploitation. Adrian didn't care which it was. He sat back in his seat and wallowed in memories.

As a boy he had scarcely been aware of this church's architecture. He knew only that it was a place of quietness and peace where the faint smell of polish mingled with the scents of burning candles and incense. At night the glow from the sanctuary lamps outshone the flickering candles before the side altars, with their special dedications to special saints. When he accompanied his mother on her evening visits for prayer and meditation they shared a magic world of dreams and shadows. It seemed now, as he looked back in memory, that the warm glow of sanctuary lamps and candles pervaded his childhood. The religious certainty of that time was a happy taste of paradise. It was good to be able to reach out and touch it with his thought.

Each evening he and his mother waited for the lay brother to extinguish, one by one, the altar lights and the candles until the soft dimness was overcome by the velvety smoothness of the dark. The single light in front of the tabernacle would never be extinguished. That was the light of the world. If that went out, evil captured men's hearts. As he left, he always turned to look again at the lamp while the lay brother stood patiently, rattling his keys to encourage their departure. Up at five o'clock each morning to practise the virtues of chastity and obedience, without any of the recognition given his priestly superiors, he must have thought their last reluctant walk was yet another cross for him to bear. Adrian used to watch him fearfully as he scurried out but there was never any response. His mother would murmur, 'Goodnight, brother,' and the pale long face would dip in acknowledgement. At home by their own fireside, his mother sighed for the lonely, cold life of all lay brothers, as they made their way through stone corridors to their bleak cells. His father would laugh and shock her by saying they were all probably rushing to tipple at the altar wine.

As he sat packed with a thousand others in neat organised rows, the suppressed excitement of the audience was almost palpable. In the gallery above, the organ tuned up. The altar was vivid with flowers and, even in the bright sunlight shafting through the windows, hundreds of candles added their pale light to its magnificence. The light of Christendom battled with the light of the natural world. The organ pealed out a triumphant Ave and the congregation rose to greet the priest, who made his way quietly to the pulpit, wearing his long black soutane. The performance began.

Adrian was not interested in the words the priest used, or in the message they conveyed, but only in their great rolling sound. They echoed through the church, bouncing off the pillars, swooping in great curves to penetrate the hearts of the hearers. They filled every crevice in the arched ceiling, each corner of the side altars, so that the whole building became nothing more than a gigantic receptacle for the words of this one man. Adrian was overawed by the power invested in the preacher and every now and again he glanced furtively at his neighbours for evidence of inattention or even incredulity. There was none. Their attention was unbroken. They were admonished and exhorted and they took it with the utmost equanimity. The Mother of God was described in the glowing terms of rhetoric but the preacher never exceeded himself, never ventured too far into his flights of fancy.

His sudden swoops down to earth came with reminders of the practical favours granted by God's mother to her earthbound children. Examples were read out of exams passed, illnesses survived, even the grace of a happy death. The congregation was urged to pray for the safe return of some fishermen who had been missing off the coast for several days. Adrian, feeling that such pleading must be heard, silently added his own prayers to theirs. Willingly, he was swallowed up in the fellowship of common prayer, became part of the one great spirit, and abandoned without qualm his individual need. He was not even surprised when, just before the close of the service, a man ran up the centre aisle holding high a piece of

109

paper and with great solemnity handed it to the priest. A hush of anticipation fell over the church. A woman sitting beside Adrian cried, 'Oh, Jesus, help us, Mary, blessed mother, succour us.' The man in the pulpit read out in quietly controlled tones, 'Our prayers are answered. The fishermen are safe in harbour. Let us give thanks.' The congregation rose and sang the Alleluia.

Adrian's hands trembled. If he had cried no one would have noticed or cared. Around him noses sniffed. Handkerchiefs were everywhere. He was moved to love and being so moved wished to weep out loud. Memories of his mother taking him by the hand up to the altar, lighting the candles, encouraging him to insert the pennies in the slot, telling him about the love of Jesus in the tabernacle, overwhelmed him.

He had recovered somewhat by the time he called at Eleanor's house.

Her greeting was casual, friendly. He should have remembered her style, the way she didn't allow quarrels to drag on, displays of emotion to be sealed into permanence. It's all part of life, she used to say when they were young. Ups and downs. Here we are swinging into neutral.

He told her of his visit to the church, wondering if she would laugh but anxious to confide in her. She smiled once, sympathetically, but she didn't laugh. She didn't even make a joke. 'Strange,' she said. And that was all.

After dinner she showed him her garden. Long and narrow, it was wedged between neighbouring brick houses.

'Your house looks as if it was an afterthought,' Adrian said. 'Somehow I never think of you as pottering around in a garden. Is it a sign of something, or shouldn't I ask?'

'I'm sure you never think of me at all,' she answered drily, ignoring his question. 'Did you even think of me since our last get-together?'

'"Get-together",' he mocked. 'Did you think of me?'

'Yes,' she said, and bent to pick a weed.

It would have been more comfortable if she had made a joke of the affair. It was what he expected, perhaps even hoped for. It was the only sane way to treat the whole business. Eleanor

110

could always be relied on to make the ironic comment which put everything into perspective and allowed one to build up reasonable walls of defence. And here she was, tough, confident Eleanor, betraying his trust by looking almost pathetic. Perhaps, he thought in panic, he could find an excuse about the holiday. Urgent business or death in the family. What family?

Eleanor said, 'I thought about you and I thought what a bloody nerve you had with your big offer: come and live with me. "Come and live with me",' she mimicked him harshly. 'If I had said yes, you would have dropped dead from fright.'

His sheepish look made her laugh.

'You're so transparent, Adrian, you should wear a mask. But don't worry. It's true I'm going through a bad patch but I'll come out of it. I know all the advice to give myself. If it works for others it should work for me. I'll even believe myself because I'll have to. Who else is there to turn to? Certainly not you.'

The last was said with bitterness and it made him feel angry and defensive. But what could he say? Denial would turn to justification, and God alone knew where that might lead him. Straight into the garden of Eden with a serpent lurking behind every bush? His best hope was to continue to bluff it out, knowing that she would know he was bluffing, but relying on some measure of tact in her which would rescue him. She surely would not let him trap himself in a situation from which neither of them could escape.

'If I can give you any help,' he said formally, 'you know you only have to ask.'

Her peculiar whinnying chortle was the insulting reply.

'You're a difficult woman,' he said.

His hair needed trimming. A lank straggle looped over one ear. His big soft face was melancholy and his mouth twisted into the two furrows on each side. She wanted to put her arms around him, to press her body close to his. She was alarmed at the strength of her desire and the premonition of the pain it might bring. But she reached for his hand impulsively and held

111

it in hers. 'You have soft hands. I wish I could be soft. Perhaps you need that. Someone melting and feminine. But I've learned to be tough and I can't unlearn it now.'

'You paint a grim picture. Very melodramatic.'

'That's the kind of thing Hugh would say. I expected better of you.'

She was not playing the game properly. She was saying and doing all the wrong things. In spite of herself he was moved to feelings he could not accurately interpret. He had a sensation of pity, a sad and savage pity. He released his hand and drew her arms around his waist, embracing her while he said into her thick, grey-streaked hair, 'You poor old slob.'

He allowed the tremulous stirrings of his flesh to take possession, and was about to draw her into the house when she moved away from him, took his hand and held it against her cheek. 'Thank you for that,' she said, smiling.

She was letting him go. Instead of being grateful, he could have cursed her tact and, even more, her affection. The moment was lost. His shoulders seemed to slump, his body suddenly to sag. Eleanor fixed him with her comical, quizzical expression. For a moment he wondered if he should take the initiative. But the risk of her laughter was too strong.

She stooped again, this time to pick up a bunch of withered flowers. With an exclamation of disgust she let them fall, the slime from the stalks trailing on her fingers. 'I dropped them out of the window this morning,' she explained. 'They were in the vase for a week. Horrible smell, isn't it? Especially off the stalks of Sweet William. Dead matter is repellent. It's too gross a reminder, I suppose. Do you think, Adrian, that our senses often deceive us? We love and hate all the wrong things. Should we be in love with death?'

He shrugged. 'Perhaps we have forgotten too much. We don't interpret the signs any more.'

'I wonder if it isn't just a lack of courage we suffer from. We don't take chances in case we make fools of ourselves. Only gamblers really live. The rest of us just drag on from day to dreary day.'

'A kind of divine folly. Yes. But you always seem to take

chances. You certainly don't mind what people think of you. I thought you made rather a virtue of that.'

'It depends on the other people. I care what my friends think of me. I think I do mind what you think of me.'

'I'm glad,' he said.

Hugh was held up by traffic on the same evening, but for a different reason. A protest march had blocked one of the side streets. A band of about fifty women bearing placards marched solidly in rows. A dozen or so men walked with them. CIVIL RIGHTS FOR ALL, FREE LEGAL AID, FREEDOM TO WALK THE STREETS, FREEDOM FROM RAPE, proclaimed their messages more effectively than a loud hailer. It was the crowning touch to a day full of frustration. Then a familiar flowered rain hat on one of the marchers caught his attention. Eve was there with her own private banner: BATTERED WIVES ARE YOUR MOTHERS AND DAUGHTERS. He supposed there hadn't been room for the word sisters, or perhaps 'sisters' had other connotations, he thought sarcastically.

Around him the snarled traffic rebelled. Angry faces at open windows shouted abuse. He was humiliated and furious. He had never believed she would go so far as to make a public spectacle of herself. A car pulled up beside him and its angry occupant shouted, 'They've had a rush of blood to the head. Too much freedom they have. Go home and cook your husbands' suppers, you little –' He trailed the epithet off under his breath. 'A good whacking is what they all need,' he confided loudly to Hugh. 'Keep them in their place.' Hugh ignored him but the man continued, 'They should be down on their knees this minute, praying to the Blessed Mother of God in the church. I'll tell the priest on yiz,' he roared to the group just ahead of him. 'Not that they care. Church or state they don't care for. Hoors all.' He wrenched up his window and reversed back, crashing into the car behind. Hugh spotted an opening to his left and cut across, ignoring the irate horns.

It was depressing to be involved in such a display of vulgarity. Why could Eve and her friends not use the legitimate structures for redressing grievances? Why could they not be more restrained? He had no sympathy for street politics. Headlines leaped at you everywhere you turned. Equal. Free. As if there ever could be true freedom or true equality for all. Unequal and unfree we were born. Chained to tyrant earth from the moment embryo tissue formed in a mother's womb.

In one of her letters to her husband's brother, Pierce, Honora Creagh wrote:

> *I am tied to this box. My legs being poisoned by wounds, the physician O'Dea did cut them off. My sister's husband, Turlogh, hath made this little carriage for me by which I move myself along the ground. It is but a wooden box and hath four wheels and I do trundle merrily enough using my hands. I am resolved never to speak the Irish and am resolved, though Turlogh is against it, to turn Protestant if my lands will be returned. You have not said your mind on this. Our cousin James has been seized of his mill near Ralahine and all his merchandise. If you are not dispossessed I beg you to send me word. You have my ruby. All else is gone. I am housed here in charity; though given in good heart it grieves me much. I had hoped to die before this month. Death comes not easily and my heart is black with hate. I may not die in peace. I nightly pray revenge on those who brought us all to this, not merely English, but others who were traitors. The whole of Clare is burned. Our friends have all been murdered, even the little children. I pray I will receive an answer soon.*

Why was there no mention of any response to poor Honora Creagh? Hugh questioned his sisters about the papers but they were not interested. 'That's all in the past,' they said. 'Why should you bother with it now? You never cared before.' Bridget said she had once helped their father sort things out but no one had concerned themselves about this Honora Creagh. 'She wasn't even a relation. She was the widow. And there was a story that she had killed a man or had him tortured.'

The image of her truncated body riddled with hate clung to Hugh's imagination. One night he dreamed of her pushing herself along the dark floor of Turlogh's house, obsessed with the need to recover her lands. In the dream she turned into Eleanor and he woke sweating with fear. He was losing Eve and he could not understand why. She was changing from the carefree girl who had admired him and listened to him with respect. Even when they did not argue, he sensed her disagreement and braced himself for some challenge to his opinions. Honora Creagh became more real to him and more comprehensible. At weekends his sisters exchanged glances when he went to the lumber room. He knew they disapproved but he did not care. He untied bundles of documents, perused land maps and title deeds, looked through hundreds of letters from emigrant relations and friends hoping to find an account of a response or an explanation for the lack of one. There were only two items of any relevance. One was a copy of a petition to the Court of Claims established in Dublin in 1700. It was on behalf of Patrick Creagh of Kilfearagh, Gent., and said that in 1673 Lord Clare demised to him the town lands of Kilfearagh and part of Farrinbeg for the lives of himself and of his wife, Margaret, née McDonnel, and of Patrick FitzAndrew Creagh at the yearly rent of £24 and a fat beef, or forty shillings in lieu thereof. The usual covenants for building a house and planting an orchard were contained in the lease. The other item was a page of beautiful copperplate writing with elaborate capitals headed *Translated from the Irish by Finola Creagh.* It said:

This day I have resigned myself and welcomed Christ Our Saviour to my heart. The friar from Quin hath visited me though in much danger to himself and has stayed with us in hiding for five days. My lands have been put up for sale and I believe are bought, although the castle house was ruined and even the two beech trees cut down for firing. By Act of England's king we are declared attainted although we could never be in treason since all was ours of right. This king and those English who supported him are traitors and we have had no justice but now expect none. My justice, I believe, will be with Christ hereafter and with His holy mother and the blessed saints. I have repented of my hatred and also of some deeds which I committed to protect my own. But, nonetheless, I do not forgive, nor ever will, though Christ may judge me, those who brought us all to this. We wished only to live. Now we are all thrown out like dogs upon the roads to ramble where we may and beg for bread. Turlogh is ill. My sister weeps all day. Her daughters have been taken as servants in Mr Hickman's house, who is an Englishman. I hope I soon may see my dead sons and my husband and my little girls who died of fever long ago. They loved your tall black house in Limerick. You may remember. I do not hope for word from you though it would give some comfort to know how you have fared. Pray for my soul.

Hugh sat for a long time among the dusty papers after he had read that letter. He let his mind wander back through the centuries to the dark penal times from which she wrote. As the room filled with the shadows of the late evening he felt himself almost possessed by her insistent voice. Unremittingly remorseless, it reached out to him, repeating, as if it could never weary even when death had silenced its owner, the endless litany of disaster and betrayal. Most poignant of all was what she had left unsaid but it did not take much imagination, or much knowledge of the history of the period, to know what suffering lay behind that silence. The letters made him wretched. Their existence implied some terrible callousness or indifference on the part of their recipient. But perhaps it was only cowardice. Somehow that was more forgivable.

Eleanor had been more affected by Adrian's account of his visit to the church than she had pretended. His description of the sermon and the prayers reminded her of her girlhood faith. After he had gone she sat in the patio outside her kitchen and watched the moon climbing over the cathedral spire. It was a pale wisp of a moon haunting the summer night. Her garden was fragrant, releasing its scents as the day faded. Before Adrian left she had said, 'You're lucky to have held on to religious faith.'

116

'No. It's nothing to do with luck. I made a rational decision. It's a question of will with me, not faith.'

'Typically casuistic and male,' she said. 'Women are much too honest.'

'How about stupid?' He laughed. 'You should try going to mass again. Maybe you miss all that ritual.'

She did miss it. There were a lot of things missing from her life, she thought. Seasons of prayer had been as much a part of her youth as the seasons of leaf fall and rising sap. Celebrations at Easter, mourning during Lent, repentance and rejoicing, were the pillars on which her young adulthood had been built. Like some great angry Samson she had deliberately shaken those pillars and brought the whole edifice crashing about her head. Was it a mistake to have thrown away such certainty, such belief in the eternal human soul? Suffering and death were the crucibles in which the everlasting spirit was forged.

It was so long since she had cared enough even to argue about religion that her response to Adrian's experience came as a shock. Such feelings should have been buried and forgotten. Their revival brought back old resentments at the prejudice and obtuseness of the religion in which she had been so lovingly baptised. It was hard to believe she had ever been so idealistic, yearning for perfection, longing for truth. Her life had once been regulated and encompassed by faith in this one Church and yet she had been forced by her very need for truth to abandon it.

As she sat watching the moon strengthen slightly, Eleanor thought of the morning offering it had been her custom to say on waking. She tried to recall the words. Was it O Jesus or O God? Was that how it began? Or dear Jesus? Or my Jesus? Then there were all those capital letters expressing respect. Sanctifying Grace. Actual Grace. How had the prayer gone? She tried again and murmured aloud, O Jesus, through the most pure heart of Mary I offer you all the prayers, works and sufferings, thoughts, words and actions of this day for all the intentions of thy Divine Heart. Had she all the capital letters in, she wondered fretfully. At night, she knelt beside the bed and said her three Hail Marys for the virtue of holy purity, an act of contrition for sins committed. How had that gone? O my God, I am heartily sorry for having offended you and I detest my sins because – because – she had forgotten the rest. But she remembered the end. And I firmly resolve by thy holy grace never more to offend you. Amen. She wished she had kept some prayerbooks so that she could look it up. Did she burn them or throw them away? She couldn't remember.

But she remembered that each day began with a dedication to God and ended with a renewal of commitment. And when she at last refused to make the commitment because no woman with a shred of self-respect could be a member of a church which so obviously despised and feared her, her denial was revenge for betrayal.

She stood up, shaking her hair and laughing at the moon as she recalled the tearing up of that particular contract. On a stormy day, standing on a rock dangerously overhanging the wild seas of Clare, she had yelled into the wind and spray, 'There is no God.' She waited to be struck by a thunderbolt or to be washed into the sea and hadn't the nerve to repeat the experiment. The gesture had been made, the last ritual performed. Afterwards other rejections were easy. In a strange way, the statement brought her peace. There was no more need to struggle with waning belief, no more need to bury the anxious questions, no need to compromise.

All that was in the past. Why should she now feel regret? And why was it that she had lately been unable to comfort her patients who had at last to come to terms with death? She almost found herself snapping, 'Stop worrying. We all have to die. Be prepared. Face it.' How could people who had never faced life be prepared for death? Hugh's family would surely die in terror for just that reason. Unless, she thought jealously, their funny superstitions hid untarnished religious faith. She had often laughed at them, but she might have been wrong. When Ruth hung the picture of the Sacred Heart out of her bedroom window to discourage marauders, or to bring rain or to drive it away, perhaps she was negotiating in the purest way with a supreme power. When Eleanor's aunt had insisted she

118

bless herself with holy water each time she left the house, was that reaching out to the unknown merely a practical recognition of human frailty and mortality? Perhaps that faith, touching and trusting, was more admirable than her own denial. Arrogance and pride were sins of Satan.

One of the things she most admired about Adrian was the way in which his self-centredness lived comfortably with his religious faith. His belief was adapted to his needs. No agonising scruples came between him and salvation. He had approached medicine in the same practical way – not as a vocation, but as a profession with prestige and the promise of financial reward.

'I'm not cruel,' he protested, when she mentioned it to him. 'I'm not even unkind. I wonder, could the same be said of you?'

'Probably not,' she answered. 'But my patients know that I care about them. I don't fob them off with a few tablets. I do listen to them.'

'So do I,' he exclaimed. 'If they don't go on too long. And if they don't make their own diagnoses. They can't expect me to listen to every fiddle-faddle from the pain in their big toes to the way their husbands neglect them. Men get to the point much quicker than women, or haven't you noticed?'

'Men are cowards. They don't want to be told so they don't ask.' Adrian cast his hands up in despair and Eleanor smiled and said, 'Call it quits.'

It was disconcerting to find herself thinking so much about him. His presence intruded when she least expected it. It was sometimes no more than a vague, shadowy awareness, a gentle recollection of his face. She became fidgety and dropped things, at times even forgetting what should have been the most ordinary and routine of tasks. Once or twice she fancied she saw him in town and her heart beat faster and she craned her neck to catch a glimpse of him, only to discover that it was a complete stranger.

As the summer progressed she daydreamed about the holiday they had planned, at the same time trying to forget their one indulgence in sexual passion in Hugh's house.

119

'It's only sex,' Adrian had remarked, and yet it both drew them together and was a barrier between them.

Her surgery seemed to have more than its usual quota of women complaining of depression. Stories of despair, frustration, lack of love abounded. Her patients lived with people who did not love them and who would not be loved. Ungrateful children, selfish husbands had ruined and laid waste their lives. They were trapped in an endless round of drudgery. Inevitably they blamed themselves. They rose from the chair, gathering their bits and pieces, bags, scarves, shopping baskets, parcels. Their burdens were everywhere and they heaped them on themselves with suicidal intent. For Eleanor, their despair and resignation, their timidity, their unwillingness to risk all in a burst for freedom were frightening. She no longer seemed to have the will to advise or explain. Occasionally she ventured opinions, made suggestions about the women's lack of power and their inability to make decisions for themselves. But what was the point in one woman doctor attempting to revolutionise the apathetic masses? She wished an armed revolution might take place one weekend when all those disillusioned, oppressed women, having at last learned the lesson of history, might take to the streets.

There were, in fact, occasional street marches and she knew that Eve participated in some. There were protests about law and order, demonstrations for peace in the North, marches for a kidney machine in the local hospital, marches against the housing of itinerants, for the prisoners in Long Kesh, even one march against rape. But there was no great public expression of the anguish she listened to each day. Often she felt like a confessor and she wished they could all go back to the days when the priests sat in their wooden boxes for hours on end saturated with the woes of others. Her women patients had lost confidence in the wisdom of a celibate male clergy. Apart from a few organised voluntary workers, no one else was prepared to take responsibility for fragile and ailing spirits.

Adrian called one evening, with the itinerary for their holiday worked out. She was gratified by his enthusiasm.

'I'd love to close up for a month,' she said, 'and travel through Europe.'

'Why not?' he replied recklessly. It was a warm sunny day and the blue skies gave him courage.

'What about our patients?'

'Good locums are easy to find.'

It seemed a marvellously irresponsible thing to do. The chance of a lifetime. No strings attached. Everything behind her. 'Well. Perhaps it's a foolish idea. People depend on me. I don't think you have ever taken your practice seriously. What are you laughing at?'

'I'm not laughing – well, not much. I'm just amazed at your conceit. Why do you assume I don't care about my practice? I don't have a sentimental attachment to people who would leave me in the morning if I made the smallest mistake.'

'I never make mistakes.'

'God help you then.'

'There is no God.'

'Are you going on this holiday or not? Make up your mind.' He turned restlessly away from her, the grooves on his face deepening.

'Sorry,' she said.

He turned around. 'You can be very childish at times.'

'So can you.'

'I suppose it's a good thing, now and again.'

'Do you think we could put up with each other for a month?'

'What have we got to lose? A month?' He hesitated a moment and she could read his mind. He was thinking, my God, that's four weeks. Twenty-eight days. 'We're both lonely,' he said, a little too glibly, 'even though we won't admit it.'

Perhaps he was being honest. It seemed only fair to respond in kind. 'That's the trap, isn't it?' she said.

'It's only a holiday.'

'No, Adrian, no. It's more than that, and you bloody well know it. I don't know if you're afraid, but I am. I'm afraid I'm going to leave myself open again. Pains I have recovered from.

You know what I mean. Getting attached. Being rejected. Or just as bad, rejecting.'

He was astonished to hear Eleanor stumbling over words.

'All that,' she almost stuttered. 'All that. Liking someone, maybe finding they're not worth it after all. Disappointment and grief. I had six years of hell because of a man and I was young and resilient but even so it left its mark. So now I'm afraid. It frightens the shit out of me. I'm afraid to like you. I can't take that. I try to be tough but the truth is I don't have the malice for it.'

'That's just what's wrong with both of us,' he answered quickly, as if the speed of his words might reassure her that she hadn't made a fool of herself. 'We could bury ourselves alive because of the fear of sunlight. I like you. I always have done. You know that. Or you should know it. You also know I'm a selfish bastard. Don't expect any great emotional commitment from me. I don't want it from you either. We get along together. Shouldn't that be enough for now?'

It should be. In some ways it was. Nonetheless, she was afraid. It was the kind of terror she had vowed never to experience again, not even at the moment of death, demoralising and humiliating. The years of dealing with others' fears had for a while released her from her own. For all her briskness and vitality, she had lived vicariously. She pushed the thought aside. If middle age held any rewards, surely one was the chance to be compromising and self-deceptive without guilt.

He stood in front of her waiting for an answer, solemn and childlike. She remembered her Aunt Anna saying, 'Men are only children and have to be treated so, humoured and persuaded.' That was the reason Anna never married. 'I could not bear to treat a great gorilla as if he was a baby monkey. I should constantly laugh. You cannot spend your life constantly laughing. It's flying in the face of God. There's work to be done, soil to be tilled, seeds sown, fields planted.' Aunt Anna marched out to her half-acre and weeded the carrots and thinned the beets with ferocity. Aunt Anna also said that she would have loved children if she didn't have to go through that messy business with men to have them. Once, in a rare moment of coarseness, she had said, 'Men are all balls. Never forget that. When Freud got lost in the swamp of sexual psychology, he was thinking only of men.' A pity she had died before test-tube babies and post-Freud revisionism.

'You've a funny look on your face,' Adrian said.

'I was thinking of Aunt Anna.'

'You sometimes look as if you were locked in a steel cage. It would take a Houdini to get you out.'

'No, it wouldn't,' she said. 'It would only take a real, live, adult male, preferably human.'

He flushed and made for the door.

'Adrian,' she cried out after him. 'I didn't mean what you think I meant.'

'It's lucky,' he said, turning around, 'that I am not a violent man like Donogh. I'm bigger and stronger than you are.'

'You're threatening me?'

'You'd try the patience of a saint.'

'I wish I could tell you how good that makes me feel.'

'I know. You take pleasure in being difficult.'

'I don't. It's just that you sounded as if you cared a bit.'

'Sometimes I wonder if you really are as thick as you sound or if you're just plain stupid.'

'Stupid,' she said, grinning. 'Stupid will do.'

'Would you be stupid enough to come fishing with me this weekend?'

'That wouldn't be stupid. That would probably be the most intelligent thing I could do. Yes.'

Her back ached. Was it womb drop or more sinister fibroids? Or simply tension, or even some new inexplicable demonstration of the love bug? She wanted to shout out loud, hardly caring whether the words were true, 'I love you, Adrian. I love you madly, passionately, you great unlovable slob.'

Instead she made practical arrangements for the weekend. Adrian told her that the mackerel were running. They discussed baits and spinners and reels. Marvellous, marvellous to be on a slippery ledge, washed with spray, all that ocean stretching as far as America. Rows of figures along the cliffs.

123

The whipping of the rods as they swung backwards and forwards to cast out into the shoals of fish. The taste of salt and the smell of the sea. She licked her lips and inhaled deeply as if to bring the memory to life.

There was a kind of perversity in the way Hugh's sisters lived so close to the sea without being affected by it. They neither loved nor hated it. She could never remember having seen them standing at a window simply staring, as she did. They stood with their backs to the windows. Their tiered gardens were designed to climb away from the sea rather than descend to it. The shells and crooked timbers were hunted for surreptitiously, as if their acquisition was illegal. Eleanor had remarked once to Florence that the black-velvet-backed pictures on which the pretty shell designs were displayed had an appearance of bereavement. 'They don't belong there. Don't you feel that?' she asked. But Florence was insulted and had gone off in a huff.

Any attempt at cutting through their brittle consciousness was repelled by silence or scorn. If they had deeper feelings or a genuine awareness of the world into which they had been born, they did not show it. Locked in a circle of ever diminishing smallness, it seemed as if they must eventually be stifled by its encroachment and fade away without leaving an imprint. The gardens would quickly revert to wildness, and the sea, which each year eroded the coastline in great chunks, would some day claim the house which had become their tomb.

It filled her with rage when she considered their fruitlessness, just as it filled her with rage to observe the complacency of so many of her acquaintances and the ravaged lives of her patients. Donogh had told her that she was a fool to have chosen medicine as a career. She ought to have painted in oils and lashed the canvas with her furious vision. Blazing colours would celebrate life more effectively than words or deeds. Part of Adrian's attraction for her was *his* attempt at artistic expression.

As he was leaving that day he invited her to the next poetry reading he was due to give. To the local blue rinse, he said.

'What do you mean?' she asked stiffly.

'The local ladies' guiid, if you prefer,' he said, with the slightly patronising smile which infuriated her.

'If you have so much contempt for these ladies, why do you bother to give readings to them?'

'Who said I had contempt for them? I love them. I appreciate them. They're the only ones who will listen to me, apart from randy young apprentice poets who come to steal my best lines.'

'I hope they boo you and throw rotten eggs.'

'Why do you take everything so seriously?' He gave his resigned sigh and slumped his shoulders about six inches.

'Straighten up, for Christ's sake,' she said. 'Knowing you is like being companion to a yo-yo.'

He went off laughing and she was left with the familiar ache. From pleasure to pain and back again. She might never survive it. God, she wondered bitterly, are all men like this? Incapable of real feelings, incapable of real affection, so full of self-interest they can't even transfer the most trivial emotion to another person? What am I asking you for, God? You're not there.

10

Adrian delivered the same invitation to Hugh with a plea for his male support. 'Please come,' he said, putting great emphasis on the 'please'. 'I've talked to Eleanor about it, but I am tired of women audiences. My parish priest says he doesn't believe they ever listen to a word he says, and I'm inclined to think he's right. They're probably just thinking of their hair-do's or the Sunday dinner while he's giving his all from the pulpit. God knows what they're thinking when I'm baring my soul. Have you noticed the glazed look that comes over their eyes when we are being particularly intelligent?'

'No. I can't say I have,' Hugh replied. 'I'll bring Eve, if I may.'

'By all means. By all means. She's more than welcome. I didn't think she'd be interested. Spend the weekend with me. Or will you be staying with your sisters?'

'No. They don't like guests in September. They usually take off for drives and sometimes spend a weekend in Kilkee. They like to feel unfettered for the whole month.'

'Good for them,' Adrian said enviously. 'They've a great life.'

Eve said it sounded like fun, so long as the poetry reading did not last too long. 'I hope he reads well, your saturnine friend, and doesn't drone on in a monotone like most of them, or emphasise each syllable like the rest. But I'd love to see his castle.'

'It's only a tower, rather like the one at home. I can never understand why he bought it. It's of no historical or archaeological significance, and it didn't belong to his family,

126

so there can be no sentimental reason for living there. And it's cold.'

'Well, it will be nice to see how the idle rich disport themselves.'

'He's not idle, or rich. Far from it.'

'Very middle class, though, wouldn't you say?'

'Middle class?' Hugh said crossly. 'And what am I? What are you? Are you suggesting that we are not workers? Will you wave banners for the so-called "workers" who never did a day's work in their lives?'

'Don't get angry,' Eve said, but without too much concern. 'I suppose I move in different circles.'

'Indeed,' Hugh grunted.

'What does that mean?' She stared at him. 'Don't you approve of my friends?'

'I don't know them very well,' he hedged. 'But I think you should be careful who you get mixed up with.'

'Don't you think my friends are my concern? Do I ever suggest that you shouldn't see so much of Adrian? I'm not sure that he's good company for you.'

He was relieved to see her trying to hide a smile. 'For a moment I thought you meant it,' he said. 'Adrian wouldn't hurt a fly.'

'And my friends would?'

'I just don't see the point in what you are doing. I'm sure you all mean well ...'

'Oh, thank you,' she said without smiling.

'I don't want to quarrel.'

'Neither do I.'

'Well then. Come with me tonight to the council meeting. You know I'm being co-opted, unless someone throws a spanner in the works.'

'I'm really sorry, I can't come. As I told you, it's my night at the clinic. There are so few of us I can't get out of it. It's not fair on the others.'

'Aren't there social workers for that kind of work? Isn't that why we pay taxes? All you are doing is removing the responsibility from the government.'

'When you're elected, as I'm sure you will be, some day, to the Dail, maybe I'll be able to leave it to you.' She stood on her toes to kiss him, wrapping her arms around his neck.

He untwined them. 'You're different since you joined that group. Sharper.'

'I've got a bit more confidence, that's all. At least Eleanor will be pleased.'

'I hope you don't take any notice of her. She's no example for anyone.'

'Darling, darling Hugh,' she said, kissing him again, ignoring his coolness. 'Relax. I love you. No one's going to change me. I won't turn into a wicked witch, believe me! So long as you don't turn into a frog prince, of course.'

'I never read fairytales,' he said, 'so I don't know what you mean.'

'And I don't know what all this co-option is about. Has someone died?'

'I'm sure I told you.' Hugh sighed. 'It's because of John Morrison's death. There'll be some opposition from the mavericks in the council, but I think there's a deal being made. It's important to me. It's my foot in the door. There may be a general election next year and a high profile will do me no harm.'

'I never knew you were a man of such intrigue.' She kissed him again and hurried away from his house, leaving behind so faint a trace of mockery he had barely picked it up when she was gone. Three kisses in a row, he thought discontentedly, and what had they meant?

They had had supper earlier. Usually she helped him stack the dishes in the dishwasher. But tonight she had more important things to do. Now he began to scrape and rinse and pack the plates and tea things.

In his bedroom he undressed and stared at his image in the long wardrobe mirror. He turned sideways, observing his well-fleshed buttocks and legs and slightly protruding abdomen. He bent to tip his toes, knees straight. It was an effort, but he managed. One, two, three, four, five, he counted in gasps as he came up for air. He lay on his stomach and tried some push-

128

ups but collapsed after four. He rolled over and closed his eyes.

From his window Hugh could see the great stone towers of King John's Castle and below them the river cascading over the Falls. While he was dressing he looked out, noting the repair work on one of the towers, the new pillars on one of the two bridges. Honora Creagh must have passed over the original ford on the journey into Clare and new terrors, with more apprehension than he could ever experience. But perhaps she did not know the meaning of fear. Perhaps she was one of those tough, brawny women who threw bottles and stones at the invaders and died screeching in hatred and rage. He shuddered, and turned away to select an appropriate tie.

As he knotted the tie into place, he realised he was arming himself for the evening. Without making any conscious decision, he was preparing for the council meeting. He had put on a green speckled tweed jacket, darker green trousers and a pale lemon shirt, an outfit Eve called his St Patrick's Day parade. Aware of the symbolism, he faced his reflection squarely in the mirror, tucking in his stomach and straightening his shoulders before smoothing down his greying forelock. Reflectively then, he touched the top of his scalp with his fingers. No. He was not going bald. He breathed in deeply, stole a last glance at himself in his St Patrick's Day parade and set out on his journey. There might be no brass bands tonight, but he would ring the bells of disaster with flamboyance.

It was in fact the bells of success that rang for Hugh that night. He came out of the council chamber a successful politician. His co-option had been planned and executed with efficiency. It was his initiation into a power game and it thrilled him. How had it been for the Creaghs who had become aldermen in the nineteenth century, he asked himself days later. The number of highly coloured oil portraits they left to their descendants was proof of their respectability, although it must have been attained only after overcoming handicaps he would never experience. Given the odds against them, the Creaghs must have worked and schemed and used all the astuteness in their makeup to become the pillars of society exemplified in the portraits. They were not brilliant or daring.

They had simply survived. Some time in the mid-eighteenth century they had become wine dealers, purchasing the house not just because it was attached to the tower originally owned by Creaghs, but also for the sake of the wine cellars which connected by underground passageway with the sea. Hugh's grandfather had the passage blocked off after a near fatal accident to one of his children when a portion had caved in. No doubt, as for many others on that coastline, smuggling from the continent had been an important part of their business.

So, struggling to hold on to a religious belief which became part of their obstinate will to survive, reminding them of their ancient rights, the Creaghs made money and built houses and sent their children abroad to be educated. Honora's ruby and the papers and letters were the haunting relics of a completely different world, now destroyed. How had that earlier passion, that immense hatred and will, become so watered down as to produce himself, bland and conservative, and his sisters, eccentric and isolated, their lives draining away as if they had no meaning? However it had happened, it was time to change and make amends. He could not take up a sword to avenge the treachery of the past, or the cowardly neglect, but he could and he would make his mark so that the Creaghs might live again. Thank God he had met Eve, who was young and resilient and spirited, for all her shyness. It would be wonderful to father a son who would be a hostage to fortune. Donogh and Eleanor had messed up their chance. So far as he knew, from the brief communications with Donogh at Christmastime, there had been no second family. Even if there had been, the children would be first-generation English, lost like the millions of others to their ancestral land. If only Eleanor had been easier to live with, he mused, things would have been very different.

At that moment Eleanor was on her way to Maryfield on a late night house-call. A woman had phoned her to say that the police had been summoned to the house next door and they had asked her to fetch a doctor.

'Why does it always have to be me?' Eleanor complained. 'Can't you get anyone else?'

'It's Miranda Connors, miss,' the woman said. 'Don't you know her?'

'Oh, indeed I do,' Eleanor groaned. 'I'm coming.'

Miranda had blamed her last miscarriage on the kicks she had received from her husband during one of his drunken sprees. When Eleanor told him what he had done, he called her an interfering bitch. Miranda was his wife and it was nobody's business but his own what he did to her.

On this occasion Miranda lay at the foot of the stairs, her face already swelling, her arm lying crookedly behind her back. She refused to have an ambulance or be brought to hospital.

'He'll be back in the morning and he'll take the children on me,' she moaned. 'And he'll kill the eldest because he hates him.' She looked up at the four small figures cowering on the landing, eyes dark with fear.

Eleanor glared at the policeman. 'Have you arrested him this time?' she asked. 'Don't tell me you haven't enough evidence this time.'

'He's gone. Slipped out the back way as we came in the front. But we'll get him. Will you summons him this time, Mrs Connors?'

Miranda nodded fervently.

'Can you come down to the station and fill in the form.'

'She cannot,' Eleanor said. 'Even you should have enough intelligence to see that she won't be able to move for days.'

Miranda had a compound fracture of the left arm. When the jumper she had worn over her nightdress was cut off, a sharp splinter of bone showed through the lacerated tissue. Her shoulder was dislocated and she might have a fractured jaw.

She eventually agreed to go to hospital when Eleanor promised to take the children home with her. While their mother lay awake in hospital, they slept soundly in her spare bedroom. Next morning Eleanor made arrangements with the social worker for the area and left the children and their problems to her. But she could not forget them, and when she saw Miranda in hospital she found it hard to steel herself against her pleas that she be allowed home and have her children returned to her.

Miranda loved her children with a primitive ferocity, perhaps because she had to protect them so often from their father. She had left him four times. Each time he had found her and persuaded her to return, sometimes by threats, sometimes with promises that no man could keep, least of all a man like him. Sometimes he wooed her with gifts and with words, took the pledge, got a steady job. The conversion might last for three months, but never beyond that, and by then she was safely pregnant, and even more vulnerable.

After Miranda's eighth pregnancy and her fourth miscarriage, Eleanor had fitted her with an IUD. Miranda was unhappy: it was against the Church, and she was a good woman who kept up her religious practice in spite of everything, and she wanted her children to be brought up decent with a mother who knew right from wrong and wasn't afraid to choose the right thing even when it was hard. Some day, Eleanor knew, Miranda would have a hysterectomy and her husband would accuse her of not being a proper woman, of being no good to any man. To prove his virility, he would sleep with any willing woman and would boast about it to his mates and to his wife afterwards. Eleanor had heard the story so often and knew the pattern so well that she could foretell each chapter in their lives. She understood the anguish of broken relationships, of rejected love, the hopeless love of one human being for someone totally unworthy of that love, but she could not understand Miranda's refusal to leave her husband for the sake of her children.

Miranda had been christened under protest by the parish priest, because the name was not a Christian name. Miranda Mary was finally agreed on. She was a glamorous baby with yellow curls, as her pictures on the wall portrayed. She was a glamorous teenager and a glamorous bride in white, and at twenty-nine she was a gaunt woman with dyed-blond hair and muddy skin but still with a fierce, bright spirit willing the world to be a joyous loving place. At thirty-five, Eleanor knew, she would finally be beaten and demoralised, believing that she was no good at anything, especially not at lovemaking, because her husband was too drunk to manage it. She would by then be totally incapable of making an independent life. Only a few weeks earlier, Eleanor had told her that she would be an old woman at thirty-five.

'I give you five more years if you stay with that man. If he doesn't kill you in the meantime.'

'But where can I go?' Miranda asked hopelessly. 'What will I do? Who will mind the children if I do get work? All I know how to do is clean and I don't know if I'm able for that now.'

Where can I go! What can I do! Eleanor closed her mouth to prevent the answer from leaping out. To the Whorehouse. Or get thee to a Nunnery. The stock answer to the classic question. Cleaning, whoring, praying, bearing children.

'For Christ's sake, Miranda,' she burst out. 'Believe in yourself. You're brave and strong. You don't need me to tell you what to do. You don't need to lean on anyone.'

'Who will mind my children?' Miranda repeated. 'They're not to be put into foster care.'

'Can't you put them in a crèche?'

'What are they? Don't they cost money?'

'I'll find out,' Eleanor said wearily. 'I'll ask around.'

Perhaps Eve, with her little women's group, would know something, or be able to do something. If they couldn't do that, what use were they?

'And besides,' Miranda whispered, 'I need a man. Sometimes he's not so bad. Sometimes he can be very nice. He's the only one I've got.'

'Oh that?' Eleanor said. 'That's only sex. We all need that. It doesn't have to turn us into slaves.'

'I'm not like you. I'm not educated. You can do things I can't do.'

What did she mean, Eleanor wondered. Could she possibly believe that 'educated' women were in a better position to hunt for a man, to procure his services, his loving attention? What an appalling mess it all was.

It was obvious that Miranda still had faith in men. Who could blame her? Since they governed and made laws and

133

pronounced on morals and manners and preached and lectured and made all the rules, and fought and conquered and made history and decided whether a woman should conceive or give birth, which crops to grow, which houses to build, which animals to breed from, which bombs to invent, they must be wise. Miranda knew that. Some day the wisdom hidden in her husband's heart would surely show itself. All she needed was patience. Griselda-like, she would wait. Miranda knew that, for all the talk about liberation, she herself could never be free. Some day her husband would be what he ought to be. She was chained to that faith as she was to her religion. Eleanor, seeing only another drunken lout, a bully and a coward, could not imagine such dreams, and would have been very angry if she could.

Miranda's injuries brought Eleanor and Eve together again. One of the children had attended the assessment clinic and revealed that the father had regularly got into bed with her, and while not going so far as to have intercourse, had, as the doctor in the clinic described it, sexually molested her. When Eve visited her to talk it over, Eleanor could hardly conceal her irritation at Eve's distress.

'Crying doesn't help these things,' she said brusquely.

'These things. How can you be so callous?'

'Little Eve. Little Eve. How can you be so naive.' Eleanor chanted mockingly.

'Don't you ever cry, Eleanor? Don't you ever weep for the human condition?'

'The human condition! Jesus, Mary and Joseph. What in hell is that?'

'I never knew you prayed.'

'Holy Mary, Mother of God, pray for us sinners, now and at the hour of our death, amen. How's that?'

In spite of herself, Eve smiled.

'Better and better,' Eleanor said approvingly. 'Now. Back to life and the real issue: isn't that what you would call it? The real issue at this moment in time!'

'It's not funny.'

'It is funny. I sometimes think I'll kill myself laughing.'

'I hope I never get like you. No matter what I see or hear, I hope I don't end up like you.'

'You should be so lucky. Haven't you come across a family yet where life is lived in the raw like in one of those blockbuster novels you and your friends read? I've met families where the whole gamut of human emotions is run through in the space of a day.'

Eve ignored the comment on her reading habits. 'I just didn't think there could be much of that.'

'How much is much? Are we going to get into statistics? All I can tell you is that I have come across families where several of the little girls were, as you put it, sexually molested. The father usually starts with the eight-year-old and when she reaches puberty he starts with the next eight-year-old.'

'It's horrible.'

'I suppose it is. But at least it isn't rape. That happens too, or didn't you know?'

'I suppose I seem very foolish to you.'

'A bit too protected, I would think.'

Eve was angry and embarrassed and unable to defend herself. 'These children,' she said weakly, 'they must be permanently damaged.'

Eleanor made a blatant effort to be patient. 'Maybe. Maybe not,' she said. 'It can make them what we choose to call promiscuous. They sometimes end up on the streets. Or it can turn them off men for ever. And maybe that would be the best thing. For all of us. Life would be so much simpler if we could really hate the buggers the way they deserve.'

'I got the impression,' said Eve, with a touch of malice, 'that you liked Adrian.'

'There are always exceptions to every rule. But to get back to what we were talking about – I hope you didn't show your obvious revulsion to Miranda's little girl. And why didn't you get in touch with me?'

'I've just done that. Of course I didn't show my feelings. I thought you might understand.'

'I do understand. Only too well. But let me give you some

135

advice yet again. You can't take the burdens of the world on your back. You don't change things overnight. Most of us are just groping our way in a dark tunnel, hoping there's a little light somewhere, but knowing it's a long way off. I'm sure there's a good maudlin song to ease that particular pain. "Light a little candle as you go on your way."' She sang the words mockingly. 'Don't you know we are all savages at heart? Civilisation an epidermis deep.'

'Can anything be done for the little girl?'

'What would you suggest? A court case? What good would that do?'

'But incest is taboo everywhere, even in primitive societies.'

'So? I don't feel like unravelling anthropological puzzles just now. I'm going to have an early night.'

'I wouldn't dream of robbing you of an hour's sleep, especially over a silly little thing like incest,' Eve said haughtily.

'It's my belief,' Eleanor said, rising to escort Eve to the front door, 'that all women feel violated at some time or another. Does it matter who does it or how early it starts? For all I know, men may feel it too. It's a condition of our being. Like childbirth. The sooner we come to terms with it, the better. Like death.'

'That's the most terrible thing you have ever said,' Eve cried.

'You know it's the truth.'

'If I believed that, I would enter a convent or go mad.'

'Try both. It would be a happy combination,' Eleanor said as she opened the door.

Eve slammed it behind her.

'A condition of our being!' Eleanor grimaced in the bathroom mirror, spitting out toothpaste froth as she vigorously applied the brush. 'I sound like a bishop delivering his pastoral letter.'

She envied the tears in Eve's eyes, envied them with a dry sense of loss, in a permanent, aching longing for innocence.

11

The telephone was ringing as Eve inserted the key in her apartment door. When she picked it up, she heard Ann's voice, calm of tone, but husky, which was a sign that she was worried. Ann always made an effort to keep her voice level and light, even when under stress, but some contraction of muscles in her larynx gave the game away and that husky apprehensiveness was the result.

'I'm sorry to bother you, Eve. Is it an inconvenient time?'

'No. Of course not,' Eve replied, bracing herself for the blow, and wishing for a cup of tea. 'I'm just in the door,' she added, giving as much a clue to her hungry condition as good manners would allow.

'Well, when you've had something to eat, could you come over here straightaway. I've a problem. She's here with me and Clem's away for an hour or so and I'd sooner have it sorted out before he gets back.'

'What kind of a problem? Shouldn't you bring her to casualty if she's hurt? Does she need a place to stay?'

'I can't talk on the phone now. Just come. Please.' She put the phone down.

That was an infuriating habit of Ann's. You were left there high and dry, holding a can of worms and not knowing what to do with yourself or with them. I won't go, Eve thought. She can sort it out herself. I'll ring Hugh.

She dialled his number and, when she heard the first ringing tone, she put down the receiver. She made herself a sandwich and a cup of tea. She went into the bathroom and stared out at

137

the long garden, the walls and rooftops, the other long gardens, sheds, old coach houses, that were part of the Georgian terrace, part of Limerick's past, part of her life now. A cat basking on top of a garden shed caught the evening sun, exuding such an air of contentment that she longed to be lying there with him. The rooftops looked safe, harmonious, beautiful. Even the missing slates left properly proportioned gaps. She could stay here all evening, and simply gaze at rooftops and basking cat and sunshine and never face what made Ann's voice husky. She could telephone Hugh and talk to him. It was cruel to have let the phone ring, even once. Supposing he had heard? It might have startled him. She dialled again. She needed the comforting, reassuring sound of his voice. There was no reply. It was always the way. Just when you needed people they weren't there.

The evening traffic had thinned a little as she drove to Ann's house. It was tucked away in a cul de sac, off the main road, an end house in a small estate of identical modern houses. Each had small, brilliant-green lawns, artistic shrubberies, neat flowerbeds. The curtains hung in perfectly symmetrical lines. She was relieved to note a few rebellious dandelions on Ann's lawn. A child's wheelbarrow lay upside down on the gravel drive. Four bicycles leaned tipsily against the garage wall. It all seemed blissfully normal and safe.

A little girl of about nine answered the door. 'Please come in. Mama says I'm to tell you to go upstairs.'

From the kitchen a toddler made his way, chuckling, and the little girl scooped him up into her arms and planted delighted kisses on his face. 'Oh, you villain,' she cried lovingly, as he tugged at her hair and wriggled to escape her embrace. 'I told you not to go into the kitchen.'

Then she beckoned Eve imperiously. 'It's up there, in the guest room. The room next to the landing.' She placed emphasis on 'guest room' with a comical touch of hauteur. Eve followed her instructions obediently, smiling at the picture the two made, and knocked at the guest-room door before entering.

It was the prettiest room she had ever been in. The evening

138

sun poured through lucent windows onto a plain carpet of palest pink. It shone on walls painted an even more delicate shade of the same colour, though it was hard to imagine brush or roller touching so smooth and perfect a surface. Bed coverlet, curtains, lampshade picked up the colour in dainty flower sprays with touches of sea greens and blues. It was a room that seemed to breathe serenity and tranquillity. The built-in cupboards were of light ash or beech. One shelf held a few books and a vase with a single rose. By coincidence or design, the rose motif was repeated on the washbasin in the corner. Eve took all of this in at a glance, and then saw the girl sitting with her back to the light, face averted from the door through which Eve had entered. Ann sat on the bed near her.

Ann barely nodded to Eve, her attention completely focused on the girl. 'I came as quickly as I could,' Eve said.

'I knew I could rely on you,' Ann said without taking her gaze off the girl. 'Don't cry,' she said, although there were no signs of tears on the face so near her own. There was a great red weal and a puffiness around one eye. She wore a short red skirt, a multi-coloured shirt or blouse, and high-heeled white shoes. She looked about nineteen because of her slight figure and the almost childish legs.

'This is my friend Eve,' Ann said.

'Hello,' Eve said and smiled.

The girl did not reply, did not lift or turn her head.

'I'll get you a cup of tea,' Ann said, and led Eve by the arm out of the room into the hall. Eve was about to question her when Ann put her finger to her lips and ushered her into another bedroom, this one obviously shared with her husband. Their clothes mingled companionably on a chair and at the foot of the bed. It was pleasantly untidy.

'It's all very hugger-mugger,' Eve said a little impatiently. 'Has the poor thing been beaten? Why is she here?'

'Oh, why, why, why anything!' Ann retorted. 'She's here because I brought her here. I can't let Clem know she's here or he'll go berserk. That's the one thing he's absolutely determined about. I can't turn our home into a temporary refuge, he says. It's not fair on the children. Or on him. But never mind, never mind. That's my worry.' She waved her hands as if cobwebs of worry could be brushed aside. 'What that poor girl has been through! Oh, the evil. The evil. The wickedness of the world. Oh, the devils.'

'Is she badly hurt?' Eve asked.

'Hurt, hurt. Everywhere, inside, outside. The things that man did to her.'

Eve waited, silent.

'I can't say it. He and his friend tied her to the banisters. Raped her. Using, using, using ...' She burst into wild tears, sobbing with rage and grief. 'Oh, I must stop. A broom handle or something. She finds it hard to talk about. She won't go to a doctor. I can't persuade her. But he took the baby and she wants the baby back.'

'Oh, Christ,' Eve said and sat down on the bed. 'Shouldn't she go to the police? Catch this man? Did she see his face?'

'Of course she saw his face. He's her husband.'

'I don't understand.' Eve shook her head in bewilderment. 'Why would he do such a thing?'

'Why, why, why? There you go again. Do you know that you are always asking why? What does it matter why? It happens. That's all that matters. But he's not getting the baby. We're going to get the baby back, you and I, tonight.'

'Wouldn't that be kidnapping? Isn't that illegal or something?'

'Do you want to waste time running to some lawyer to find out? Look up your law books then. Let's all run to our lawyers and look up the proper reference to find out what is legal mutilation of woman in marriage or out of marriage, and what is legal kidnapping of your own children. I know you're too young for all this. I know I shouldn't have roped you into it. But I tried everyone else. The whole bloody committee is either out playing tennis, or down at the seaside, or changing nappies, or cooking the hubby's dinner, or fetching a child from some extra-curricular activity or other, or going to a bridge session. Could you believe it! Bridge. Golf. Tennis. And people are being tortured before their eyes.'

'Don't get so upset, Ann. I'm not too young to be roped in. I'm glad you called me. I'll do what I can.'

'Oh, darling Eve. You're such a pet. You're so good.'

A door banged downstairs and a man's voice called, 'Ann, Ann. I'm ho-me. We're ba-ck,' and a boy's voice yelled, 'Ma-mmy, Ma-mmy. Where's Mammy?'

Ann put a hand to her heart. 'Oh, my God. They're home early. Wait. You go into the bedroom and talk to her. Her name's Brenda. I forgot to tell you. I got so upset I don't know whether I'm coming or going. Just talk to her and comfort her. I'll be back in a few minutes.'

She ushered Eve back along the hall and into the bedroom that resembled a fairytale picture. The girl in the chair had not moved.

'I hope you'll feel better soon,' Eve said. 'I know that sounds stupid. But I do hope you will feel better soon. Don't worry. We'll get the baby back anyway.'

Then the girl covered her face with her hands and rocked to and fro on the chair. Eve timidly put a hand on her hair and stroked it as her own mother had often done to hers. 'Don't worry. Don't worry,' she said softly. 'It will all come right. You'll see. We'll sort everything out.'

Divine omniscience. The very saying of the words made her feel strong and powerful. No matter what happened, this poor bundle of uncomprehending misery would never suffer again. The face turned to Eve's like that of a despairing child, round and smooth where it was not blotched and out of shape. But the eyes were not the eyes of a child. They were dead.

From downstairs came the sound of a suddenly raised voice and then a hush. A door banged. Footsteps ran up the stairs. Ann came into the room wearing an anorak. A bright red spot burned on each cheek.

'Come on,' she said. 'Come on with me, Brenda.'

Ann's husband, Clem, was waiting at the front door. 'You're not to do it, Ann,' he said. 'I absolutely forbid it.'

'Forbid it!' Ann squeezed her eyes shut in a ferment of rage. 'Forbid!' she practically yelled. 'Don't be so bloody thick.'

'I warn you,' Clem said. 'I mean it. I don't want you to – '

'Don't threaten, Clem,' Ann said. 'Just don't threaten. You might have to follow it through.'

'I'm surprised at you, Eve,' Clem said. 'I'm sure Hugh wouldn't be pleased if he knew.'

The three women rushed out to the car in the drive.

'Thank God I have my own car,' Ann said as she screeched out of the drive. 'Thank God for Henry Ford. And for my mother, who left me this banger in her will. She taught me to drive, you know. She sat in the suicide seat and insisted I learn. Then I took driving lessons. Clem doesn't like me driving his car. He loves his car of course. Now I could love a horse that would carry me places. And I suppose I love my car too.'

Brenda and Eve sat completely silent, neither of them attempting to stem this monologue.

'I used to be nervous as a cat at first. There were very few women drivers then. Lorry drivers hated to see us on the road. There were letters in the papers, you know, about women drivers taking up road space. That they shouldn't be allowed out on weekdays, when real people were going about their business. I was always being hooted at and honked at. It's only recently I've realised no one does that any more. I don't think it's because I'm a better driver, but because there are more of us. I don't worry now if I stall at traffic lights. There's probably a woman driver behind me and she won't get impatient. Cars seem better too. They don't stall so much.'

'Where are we going?' Eve asked when Ann had stopped for breath.

'To Brenda's sister-in-law. Isn't that right, Brenda? That's where the baby is.'

'But where is Brenda going to stay?'

'I've got her a place. A place where she will be safe with the baby. I won't even tell you, in case you get into trouble. I just need you to sit at the wheel and be ready to drive away.'

'Oh God, Ann,' Eve said. 'I'll be terrified.'

'No, you won't. You can do it.'

'He won't be there now.' Brenda spoke for the first time, as if trying to reassure Eve. 'He has left the baby with his sister. But he's gone to the races somewhere with her husband. They have a stall there.'

'We have it all worked out,' Ann said. 'We'll go in. I'll say Brenda just wants to see if the baby is all right. Then we'll grab it and escape. You keep the engine running and the doors open and tear off as quickly as you can.'

The house was in a row at the edge of a great housing estate. They pulled up about twenty yards away. Ann got out and Eve slipped into her place behind the driving wheel. Brenda walked on wobbly high heels, trying to keep up with Ann's quick, determined walk. She'll never be able to run, Eve thought. She'll trip and fall.

She watched them walk up the cement path to a house with a green door. The door opened and there was some altercation. Ann was gesturing vehemently and then Brenda joined in, thrusting her bruised face forward. The woman who had opened the door looked out, apparently straight at Eve in the car, and the other two women rushed into the house. Eve started the car engine and kept it ticking over. I have thrown my hat in the ring with a vengeance, she thought. Her earlier fear had gone. She seemed to have been infected with Ann's excitement. It was Brenda's baby, after all. She had a right to it. But what if that awful man came back unexpectedly? Her heart was pitpatting. Her hands gripped the steering wheel.

A loud yell erupted in the house. The door burst open and Ann and Brenda came charging out, Ann carrying the baby. After them came two women, one older, the other in her twenties. Eve drove up to them and the kidnappers flung themselves in, baby and all.

'Drive off. Drive off.' Ann shouted and Eve put her foot down. She had to swerve past one of the women, who had leaped in front of the car.

'Don't knock her down,' Ann yelled and then burst out laughing.

Brenda began to chuckle in the back seat and the baby sucked at the bottle he had been clutching during the whole exercise.

'Turn up here,' Ann commanded and they took a narrow

road which brought them into an even narrower country lane.
'We can drive this way for a while. Even if she does send
someone after us, they'll never catch us now. Well, that's
done.' She sighed and settled back on her seat, closing her eyes.
'Oh, what a relief. You can drop me back at my place. Get your
own car and then go home.'

'What about Clem?'

'What about him?'

'Will he be angry?'

'Raging. Could you blame him? He's terrified. But I'll get
round him. And if he tells Hugh, there'll be a divorce.'

'It's not Hugh's affair.'

'That's right. You keep that up and you'll do. Mind you,
it won't be easy.' She began to laugh again and then went
pale and clutched her stomach. 'I think I'll have to lie down
when I get home,' she said. 'My stomach is giving me trouble
lately.'

Eve looked in alarm at her face. It was more than pale. It had
a dreadful, almost greenish tinge.

At Ann's house Eve said goodbye to Brenda and got into her
own car. Brenda and the baby stayed quietly in the back seat of
Ann's. Ann left the door ajar when she went inside. The sun
had gone behind a chestnut tree in the garden opposite. The
lawns deepened in the shade, the flowers glowed. Eve drove
away, thinking that something new and dramatic had happened in her life. She had taken a risk which would have been
unthinkable a few months earlier. She had become a conspirator. Whether it was for good or ill she could not tell.

Either way, nothing could ever be the same again. This
was another step, faltering but significant, in a particular
direction. She had not taken the step entirely on her own. In
fact, she supposed she had been pushed by Ann, dragged
almost, onto a highway of shared human suffering, of a special
female suffering. If she did not feel the same depth of rage
shown by Ann, or the pity expressed in her tears, it was because
she had come secondhand to the tragedy. The girl herself, the
object and subject of this terrible drama, was so much a part of
it that she was numbed and shocked. For Ann, the experience

had been immediate and intense. She seemed to feel what the girl was not capable of feeling just yet. Christ-like, she had wilfully taken the girl's burden on herself, the fear, the humiliation and the just and, again, Christ-like outrage.

As she drove back to her apartment, Eve recalled the scene like a series of camera shots click-clicking, bombarding her inner eye with scenes and images: the girl's face when she first saw her, bruised and swollen in Ann's glowing room, her hunched body, folded in on itself, the baby snatched from his terrible begetter, the crazy drive into the countryside from the sprawl of houses, and Ann's pale, stricken look as she clutched her stomach.

The cat had left its sun trap on the roof because the sun had dipped out of sight. Eve stripped and showered. The streets had seemed dirtier than usual as she drove into the city. The day's litter gathered on pavements and spilled out of its inadequate containers. The gaunt remains of partially demolished houses in the old part of town, the flaking paint on unoccupied shops were depressing signs of apathy. Could one go through life forever indifferent, without ever making a protest or committing oneself to action? The town looked ugly, seedy, uncaring. For a while she hated it.

12

Hugh felt particularly urbane when visiting his hospital patients. There was something about the cheerful deference of the nurses which soothed his soul. The childlike trust of patients inspired him with self-confidence. He had a great respect for nurses, although he could not regard the profession as being on an equal footing with his own. Their training could hardly be compared with the long period of study undergone by medical students. Nonetheless, their usefulness was unquestionable. Many times he had reason to be grateful to a nurse, even an unqualified junior probationer, for her skill in observation and her ability to diagnose. The fact that she was obliged by medical ethics to cloak her expertise under the guise of ignorance, only tentatively suggesting a diagnosis when reporting symptoms, made him more keenly aware of his power. He did not care much for male nurses, and he cared even less for women doctors. Both had stepped out of their traditional roles in a way that seemed to him uncomfortably challenging.

Yet he was occasionally reminded of the inconvenience of the hierarchical system when he himself was its victim. Although he had a reputation in the hospital for his integrity and caution, as well as for his kindness, he knew that the surgeons had all the prestige and power. Because a man had the temerity to open up a human body, grope inside it and remove an organ or tumour, he was endowed with unassailable mystique. Hugh referred to surgeons as 'the butchers'. Knowing his views, Eleanor once sent him a Hogarth print showing the ghastly

146

scene of an eighteenth-century operation, the victim's intestines spilling off a table onto the floor. Hugh, who remembered a surgeon of his student days flinging the patient's ribs on the floor during a resection, hung the print in his hallway, where it gave him macabre satisfaction. Medicine, he was fond of saying, had taken a wrong turning when it allowed entry to barber-school exponents.

He had learned from experience that confrontations with surgeons were to be avoided. Most patients were over-awed by cultivated arrogance and, since they were in no position to question the surgeons' judgement, having very little understanding of the workings of their own bodies, they blindly left themselves in the hands of the professionals. The worst victims, Hugh conceded, were women, and here he had a sneaking sympathy with Eleanor. A few of his own patients had been told by specialists that they were neurotic and should be out of the house interesting themselves in good works instead of conjuring up imaginary pains. One of his patients had been recommended to a psychiatrist and in despair had attended, believing herself to be mad to imagine pain so severe when all the experts assured her she had no pain. Her death a few years later was inevitable but she could have been spared the extra humiliation of believing herself insane. Hugh never forgot the disillusioned, almost cynical look she gave him when he went to see her after her first bout of major surgery.

He had reason to meditate on the whole medical ethos when, one morning, he was an observer in the theatre where a woman was to have a small tumour on the parathyroid gland removed. His friend Tom Rogers performed the operation. Watching the rhythmic movements of his hands, the co-ordination between himself and the theatre sister, Hugh admitted to a small feeling of envy. Here was a high priest, with great solemnity and panache challenging death, using the unconscious body of his patient like an ancient sacrificial offering. This theatre was an arena for drama where men gambled with other people's lives. Whether they were courageous or foolhardy made no difference. He almost forgave them their arrogance, their often crass disregard for feelings. He was brought sharply back to

147

reality when he discovered that the visiting surgeons who were watching this unusual operation with such interest had placed bets on the outcome. When Tom Rogers, with an air of triumph, held up the pea-sized tumour, a little cheer of congratulation rang out. The woman who had delivered herself up to this specialist was merely a mound of flesh under a green cloth.

Tom Rogers deposited the tumour in a specimen jar. 'Label it,' he told the junior nurse. 'And guard it with your life.'

'Well done,' Hugh said as he joined him. 'I hope that solves it.'

'Solves what?' Rogers looked blank. 'Good heavens, yes, of course. Have you no confidence in me? You saw it yourself. I'll send you the lab reports as soon as I have them.'

'It looks benign. But supposing it's not?'

'Come here and look at it.' They joined the queue of doctors peering in at the specimen jar. 'It's just a little cyst. Extra-ordinary thing. Who would have believed it? And after all you had tried everything else. You have to come to us in the end. Join me for lunch if you haven't anything better to do. Is it true you are getting married? About time too. You don't want to end up a loony old bachelor.' He grinned complacently, and Hugh, remembering his elegant, gracious wife, thought he had reason for complacency. He did not feel inclined to discuss his own engagement but fortunately Tom never expected answers to his questions. His conversation was mainly monologue with polite nods of interest but no real enthusiasm when dialogue entered in. Even the rejection of his invitation to dinner hardly registered. 'Fine, fine. Some other time. Keep in touch. Bye. Bye.' And he was gone, whisking his magical way through white corridors of power followed by his attendants. Hugh sighed and left, deflated.

It did not improve his ego when he bumped into Eleanor, as she came out of the X-ray department. He braced himself for a caustic salutation but for once she spared him. Her 'Well, Hugh' was almost friendly, almost placatory.

'Well, Eleanor,' he echoed.

'Were you up at the circus?'

'It wasn't really like that. Rogers is a fine surgeon. And a fine man.'

'Oh. So they say. Well, sooner him than me.'

'And me,' he agreed, forgetting the admiration and envy of a short while earlier.

'If you've a minute, Hugh, I could do with some advice.'

He was flattered. Never before had she asked him for advice.

'You're well in with the housing officer, aren't you? *Tá sibh mór le chéile.*'

Well, well, well, he thought. Adrian was having an influence in all kinds of ways.

'I've got a big problem with Miranda Connors,' she continued. 'She cannot go back to that house and her brute of a husband. And I can't keep her in hospital any longer. Could you use your influence on one of your friends to get a corporation house or flat for her?'

He was disappointed. 'I thought you wouldn't stoop to this sort of lobbying.'

'The woman needs help. I'd lick your boots if necessary. Is it?'

'What can I do?' he asked. 'Even if I had that kind of influence, which I haven't, there are hundreds of families on the housing lift, some waiting years for a house. Miranda Connors has a husband. Can't you talk sense to him? Get them to patch things up.'

'Sometimes I wonder about you,' she said and strode off. How terrible it is to be poor, she thought for the millionth time. Money would solve all Miranda's problems. But perhaps people like Miranda were born to be victims, too trusting, too pretty. Eleanor tried to remember if she had ever been so trusting. For a moment she was seared by a memory which she pushed aside. It left her, as she drove into the lunchtime traffic, Hugh's Granada forging ahead, with an unease, a sensation that seemed to be recurring too often lately. Only the week before she had woken after a nightmare in which she saw herself as an old woman saying, with her own unmistakable asperity, 'I am nothing but a bundle of rubbish, a bundle of rubbish.' It was something one of Eleanor's own patients had said as she lay dying in the city home and at the time it had hardly registered. But the nightmare left her fearful of the future. A recurring pain across her chest seemed to her to be triggered off by memories of her lost youth and lost love. Every now and again during her clinic that day she had paused to stare out of the window at the sky and clouds, trying to conjure up the intensity of first love. All morning she had felt that only an effort of will kept real sadness away. Never again to know the glory of being in love: it was a terrifying prospect. That pain in her chest was the reason she had been so eager to welcome Adrian into her bed. She smiled at the memory and glanced in the driving mirror to catch the smile. At the self-recognition, the smile flickered away, and two intense, wary, blue eyes stared back, revealing nothing, fending off everything. Like Hugh, she sighed for herself. Then, impulsively, she turned into the square and pulled up outside Eve's flat. When she rang the doorbell and heard Eve's voice calling, 'I'm coming,' she regretted the impulse and almost fled. But it was too late. Eve was standing at the open door, smiling, a little surprised, but still smiling.

'I've come to apologise,' Eleanor explained. 'I was particularly piggish yesterday.'

'I deserved it,' Eve said handsomely. 'And you weren't piggish. Just realistic. It is time I grew up.'

'Well, I don't know about that. Don't get hardboiled, whatever you do.'

'*You* aren't hardboiled,' Eve said, and Eleanor bit back the caustic 'Did I say I was?' 'But do come in. I have some news for you about Miranda. Can you stay for lunch?'

Interesting, Eleanor thought, now that *is* interesting. Most people she knew had a quick stand-up lunch, sloppy sandwiches and soup or saucerless mugs of coffee. But Eve had set the table with as much elegance as if she were expecting guests, even to the extent of a few tulips in a slender vase of embossed silver. 'It's only cold meat,' she was apologising, 'and some goo from the delicatessen. I don't eat until evening as a rule.'

Eleanor enjoyed it. When they had finished, Eve told her

that she had discovered it would be possible for Miranda to get a debarring order in the court.

'Sounds indecent,' Eleanor commented. 'What in hell is that?'

'It simply means that since a new bill was passed recently Miranda can now apply to the court for an order which will keep her husband out of the family home for three months.'

'What happens at the end of the three months? He comes back and kills her for keeping him out?'

'I know it isn't the perfect solution. But what is? She can't get a divorce so long as she lives in Ireland. If she went to England or some other country and got a divorce, her situation would be a little better. But that's not likely. He doesn't want a divorce. He wants a convenient doormat or punching bag. Did you know that in Irish law a woman's domicile is presumed to be that of her husband even if he lives in Timbuctoo and she lives in Ballydehob?'

'Yes, I did know. Doesn't everyone? You're getting the real legal jargon. Domicile!'

'It's precise. But anyway she has no money and no one in England, so she's stuck here. So we just have to make use of the laws we do have. At least this one gives her a breathing space.'

'That's assuming he takes the slightest bit of notice. What's to prevent him from ignoring the law and the courts and sneaking in some night and knocking her brains out?'

'Have you any better idea?'

'She could always kill him.'

'Be serious.'

'I am serious. Self-defence. Get in there first. I bet she'd kill him if he tried to kill one of her children. Is her own life not as valuable? Why shouldn't she call on the same reflex to protect herself?'

'It will probably never come to that.'

'I hope you're right. Anyway this barring order of yours will give some young solicitor his baptism of fire, no doubt. A chance to feel the singeing breath of old Dragon Teeth in court.'

'Who's old Dragon Teeth?'

151

'The bench, the bench. And what happens when the three months is up? Do you expect an intervening conversion. All of a sudden this psychopathic maniac is going to turn into a loving husband and father?'

'That will be up to the solicitor.'

'I hope he's good. I happen to know old Dragon Teeth. And his wife. I can just see him making a meal out of this. And of Miranda. Of you as well, if you happen to be in the vicinity. One thing he hates is officious amateurs, middle-class do-gooders in particular.'

'We are going to have a row and I don't want that.'

'Good God, are we? I thought we were just having a discussion and that I was giving you fair warning and sisterly advice.'

'I am not an officious amateur. I am – '

'A caring human being,' Eleanor intoned in sepulchral accents. 'The court's business is the business of the plain people of Ireland. Justice must be seen to be done. And a fat lot Dragon Teeth cares about justice or the plain people of Ireland, or caring human beings. His job is to interpret the law. That gives him power and he likes it. He likes making jokes at the expense of raw young solicitors. He likes cutting short the startled babbling of defendants. If you get him on a good day when his missus hasn't burnt his toast – which she is quite capable of doing, since she doesn't see herself as being his cook and attendant and he is too mean to hire domestic help – you may win. If you get him on a bad day, you may lose. It's as simple as that. Never forget the human element. It applies in law as in medicine. Never appear before Judge Mulligan the day after the races and never have your tonsils out after the August weekend.'

'It really is impossible to know when you're serious.'

'I am always serious. When you know me better you will realise I have absolutely no sense of humour. Did Hugh never mention that?'

'Hugh never talks about you.' Eve stopped, cut short by the lie.

'Well, hardly ever,' Eleanor added for her with amusement.

152

'But you're right. It *is* hard to know whether I am serious or not. Half the time I don't know myself. Perhaps I am heading for the menopause. Isn't that the answer to everything? Ah, the poor eejit, it must be the menopause, or pre-menstrual tension, or she's a frustrated bitch and needs a good – ' She stopped and Eve braced herself. 'No. I've never used that particular word. I don't know why. God knows, even convent schoolgirls use it nowadays. Even when I'm angry I can't use it. And for some reason I seem to be angry most of the time now. Do you think it can be the weather? Lunch was delicious. Thank you very much. I really appreciated it. I hope I haven't insulted you again.'

She was gone. The door closed quietly behind her. Eve stood there helplessly, overwhelmed by the vacuum created by her sudden absence.

Eleanor was like a hurricane. She left empty spaces in her wake. Ann was a sudden gust of wind, stirring things up quickly and then letting everything settle. In certain ways they were uncomfortable acquaintances. Even Ann, even Ann, thought Eve regretfully.

Ann called on Eve a few days after their adventure to tell her that Brenda was a little better. 'She went to her own doctor. I wanted her to go to your friend Eleanor, but she seems to trust this man. Did you tell Eleanor?'

'About what happened? No. It's hard to talk about it. You never know with Eleanor, how she will react. She's kind, but – '

'But but but. She's a doctor! How could she escape completely? She had a man's training. Do you know, I'm often thankful that I was educated by nuns. It was a totally female experience. We learned to rely on ourselves. Of course we were brainwashed into being ladylike. And Virgin Marys! But we had enough of a sense of humour to get over that. Do you think you could ever let yourself be raped?' Her eyes had a feverish look as she turned them on Eve. 'Wouldn't you fight back? What would you do?'

'I'm not very aggressive,' Eve said apologetically.

'Well, it's hard to learn. But it can be done. You have to get

153

over the psychological control. That's almost more important.'

'Did you have brothers?' Eve asked her.

'Ah. Funny you should ask that. Yes, I did. I do. And I love them all. I have three. And three sisters. We are a good Catholic family, you see. Rosary every night when I was a child.'

'I have only one brother, much younger, and a small sister. There is a big gap between us. I was an only child for years.'

'It helps to have brothers near your age. You learn to beat their brains out before they beat out yours. All good clean fun. I'm glad I was part of all that. I remember being furious when it ended. In fact I can remember the day when my father called my brother (the one next to me) to one side and told him the roughing and tumbling had to stop. I was "developing". Lucky for me I was a late developer. I had more fun than most girls of my age. Then there were games. Netball, camogie, hockey, badminton. I miss that now. I never seem to have time. When I have time, I don't have the energy.'

'Did Clem have a psychological advantage over you when you got married?' Eve asked, pursuing the interesting comment Ann had made.

'I've a feeling he tried,' Ann grinned. 'I think he's still trying. Only last week when I was reading that tome of Hans Kung's, *On Being a Christian*, which seems clear as daylight to me, and quite reasonable, he said, "Isn't that a bit deep for you?" But I got back at him. You know that poem "Was it my enemy or my friend I heard – What a big book for such a little – no, not bird – head!"? The American poet Edna St Vincent Millay. She should have changed her name. Well, I rushed to get it, learned it off by heart and quoted it to him at supper. "Come, I will show you now, my newest hat, And you may watch me purse my mouth and prink! Oh, I shall love you still, and all of that. I never again shall tell you what I think." (That's brilliant, isn't it? "I never again shall tell you what I think.") "I shall be sweet and crafty, soft and sly. You will not catch me reading any more. I shall be called a wife to pattern by. And some day when you knock and push the door, Some sane day, not too

154

bright and not too stormy, I shall be gone and you may whistle for me." I love that last bit. I shall be gone and you may whistle for me. The way it rhymes with stormy. Lovely, lovely, lovely.'

Eve laughed with her. 'But you and Clem get on marvellously well.'

'Heigh ho. Yes and no. Yes. Yes. We do love each other.'

'Did you make it up. After the other night?'

'I told him what happened to her. I didn't want to at all. It seemed a kind of treachery, talking about her after all she has been through. There is too much talk. Words can be so invasive, don't you think? They become predators, like vultures on the psyche. He was upset. I think he really doesn't believe it happened, that she exaggerated or something. That's another reason why I don't tell him so much any more. And that's hard for me. I used to keep him awake half the night, pouring out my rage. But not any more.'

'I suppose it is hard to have to be secretive with someone you love.'

'Secretive? Yes. We become conspirators, don't we?'

'But even married people must have a private part of themselves. You can't share everything.'

'I used to. I don't like being secretive. Or a conspirator. Perhaps it is because we don't have a political voice. The worst thing of all would be to become accomplices in our own oppression. To learn to enjoy being weak and passive and feminine. If we believed all that rubbish about how nasty it is to be "strident", we'd never do anything. It's a tough old station. But I've just thought. Do you know the worst thing that could happen to us?'

'We could get spots. Or go blind?'

'Very funny. No. We could become clowns. Be the entertaining sex. Do the tricks. Tell the jokes. Wear the funny noses.'

'We wear funny clothes sometimes,' Eve said. 'And very funny shoes.'

They both looked down at their feet.

'Crazy, isn't it?' Ann gave her wide grin. 'We're both wearing flip-flops. As a matter of fact I like telling jokes. Most

155

of them are bawdy and not fit for your delicate ears. When you are older, come to me for initiation.'

'I can't wait,' Eve said. 'You should come with Eleanor to Tower Hill some day. You'd make a great pair.'

'I don't much care for your friend Eleanor. That's one tough lady. Any time I meet her she seems to be glaring.'

'Poor old Eleanor,' Eve said.

'Poor old Eve,' Ann mocked. 'Poor old Ann. Poor old world.'

13

During the summer, Eve visited Tower Hill each Sunday with Hugh. It was easier to fall into a routine with him than to have to make any decisions about her feelings. At times she looked forward to the visits, but usually she went with some apprehension. Individually the sisters were charming and entertaining. Together they could be fearsome, uniting on some principle or point of view with a force and conviction which could not be shifted. Of the four, Florence, the second youngest, was the most intimidating. The others might take time to get to know, but their little foibles and prejudices would be allowed for eventually. Ruth's demure wit could suddenly be transformed into a rapier sharpness. Honora's little asides had to be considered before their real meaning could be discovered. Bridget, though more incisive, had nonetheless a habit of fixing her gaze at an imaginary object above her victim's head while delivering a delicate coupe de grâce.

Florence's conversation was unnerving. Talking to her was like treading on a minefield. Invariably one of the mines exploded. Eve was only beginning to learn how to weave her way through these verbal dangers. Now and again she rebelled and suffered the consequences. When Florence said, 'We were always such a close family,' the tilt of her chin or the twitch of her eyebrow, or even the peculiarly cold look which was her speciality, made the remark a challenge to be rebutted. (Hugh's sisters had such expressive faces it was a miracle that any of them ever won a game of poker. The reason they won, Eleanor explained, was because they were totally unpredictable.) Eve resisted the temptation to say, 'My family are close too, but not incestuously so.' They would scarcely have understood the word and she had so recently discovered the tragedy of its real meaning that she was able to refrain from using it as a counter-challenge.

'We expect you to encourage Hugh to take more rest, dear. He really should not be getting involved in politics.' The remark begged for the response 'I am not his keeper', but she knew that would lead to horror and disbelief that one so young should be so sharp, and that genuine concern for a brother's welfare should be so treated. Once, when Florence remarked that mother used to say you could always tell a lady by the condition of her lavatory, Eve thought she was expected to laugh and discovered she had blundered into another mine-field. When Grandmother lay on her deathbed, Florence boasted, she reprimanded the maid who brought her medicine for carrying the glass in her hand and not on the little silver salver, apparently specifically designed with that great task in mind. Ordinary courtesies which should have been common-place had become fetishes. Ignorance or dismissal of them was sacrilegious.

In spite of these differences, Eve was often seduced by an unexpectedly warm welcome, a demonstration of affection or just a smile of amazing sweetness. Then she basked in their good humour, their delight in her presence.

'Already,' Florence said, 'you are one of our own dear sisters.'

At such times, she could imagine nothing more pleasant than being in their company and she reproached herself for her failure to understand them and for not loving Hugh as he should be loved. It was all her fault and with patience she would be able to sort it out. But then, the sight of a possessive hand on Hugh's arm, an encircling of the five around some family treasure (effectively excluding her), a failure to intro-duce her to another guest except as an afterthought, followed (it seemed to her deliberately) by an effusive apology and explanation, threw her back into resentment and irritation.

One Sunday afternoon in July Florence burst in to the

sitting room with the news that a caravan was parked near their beach.

'Isn't it a public beach?' Eve asked.

They fixed her with scornful expressions.

'It is the beginning of the end,' Ruth sighed, clasping her hands in despair.

'Can't anything be done?' Bridget directed her question to Hugh.

'Probably,' he answered. 'There's always the question of hygiene. There is probably some by-law to cover it.'

'I expect they have portable toilets,' Eve suggested, trying to be helpful and consoling.

'Portable toilets!' Florence raged. 'And where, tell me, would they empty these portable toilets?'

'I suppose they'll dig a hole. I'm sure it would be good for the land.'

Florence and Ruth looked at each other and then at Eve. She turned away from their censorious gaze and continued, 'I saw them this morning. They were instructing their little girl not to leave litter on the beach. At least you won't have that to contend with.'

'We're bad enough off as it is. We get all those day trippers and they're not always too careful. I suppose we're lucky they don't live here the whole year round.'

'You may be getting more people,' Hugh said. 'I'm told McGrath's have outline planning permission for five bungalows.'

The sisters were distressed and Hugh tried to reassure them. Eve wondered at his tactlessness in telling them the bad news on top of their discovery of the caravan. Their little kingdom was being breached. They loved Tower Hill. When they were young they had travelled through Europe but never found anything to compare with it. On their occasional excursions to town they grudged the time spent away from their home and scurried back to it in haste, complaining about the tediousness of travel, the fumes and congestion of streets. Oh, thank God we're back, the relief of being able to breathe again, they cried as they inhaled the herb-laden air.

'All those people,' Honora sighed. 'Where do they come from? I sometimes feel we are about to be dispossessed again.'

'It's not so bad to be pushed out by your own people,' Bridget remarked. 'At least they are Irish.'

'I don't agree,' Honora replied with spirit. 'We can make allowances for the enemy because we know what they are. To be betrayed by your own is much harder.'

'Who is talking about being betrayed?' Bridget joined in.

'I suppose I mean let down. I think we have all been let down. The country isn't what we thought it was going to be. Everything has changed for the worse. Everything was so much nicer when we were young.'

'It's always nicer when you are young,' Florence said, unexpectedly wise.

'Young people nowadays complain a lot,' Ruth said. 'But what does it matter? Oafs and boors have taken over the country. I remember Great-aunt Honora saying it was always the same. People of refinement and talent are always destroyed by ruffians. I don't know how we have survived at all,' she added innocently. 'First those horrible Vikings, then the English with their bigotry and arrogance. And now look what we have! We know people who are millionaires today and their grandparents worked here. You know who I mean, Hugh. There must be many more like that. How did they do it? It must be dishonest. You couldn't make so much money by honest means.'

Ruth's remark about honest means reflected uncannily Hugh's train of thought just then. He had been reading yet another letter before he appeared for lunch that day and was thinking about it when Ruth spoke. It was addressed again to Pierce Creagh and was signed *Aine*, Turlogh's wife. It said:

I can tell you it was not by honest means that your sister, my friend and cousin, has been brought to this trouble or that we who sheltered her have been so used. Treachery is everywhere around us. She was a strong woman who could kill a man as well as any but she never spoke a bad word against you. You

*took her ruby and her letters. She prayed each night for ease
from pain as I cursed you each night and do curse you now. We
had riches, fine clothes and good food and house with
furnishings, cattle and horses on our land, honey and cream in
plenty, as you know. Now we are beggars in this wild place and
speak the garbh Béarla and kiss the arse of robbers. Lawyers
in plenty write deeds and sign names. We have made no
petitions and no promises and will die on the roadside. Long
winters stretch before us but ruin may reach you and force
your cold heart to pity for yourself. There are no priests left
here. The last was taken from us and hanged at Ennis. Christ's
mother be our guard.*

Such strength of feeling must have had grievous cause. Was it
possible, Hugh wondered, that he and his sisters were the
descendants of a man who had been a coward and a traitor to
his own family, a man who had turned his back on them for the
sake of his own gain? But the times had been terrible and the
power of the enemy immense. Was his behaviour cowardly or
merely expedient? It would have been common sense to have
lain low and acquiesced when the alternative was to be
landless, uprooted, forced into vagabondism. What good
would his intervention have done? No doubt he had his own
battle to fight, his immediate family to protect. And very
likely, thought Hugh, this Honora was a tough woman, well
able to fight for herself – maybe, for all he knew, a seventeenth-
century feminist. If that were the case, she was courting trouble
and she certainly got what she deserved. Some women did not
seem to know when the time to stay quiet had arrived. Eleanor
could never keep her mouth shut.

'Look at those women down on the beach,' Ruth said,
twitching the curtains angrily. 'Such young mothers, so
careless with their babies. They don't realise how dangerous
the sea is, and the tide going out. Look at that little baby and its
mother not taking a bit of notice.' She tapped futilely at the
window.

'I think I'll go for a walk,' Eve said. Hugh nodded vaguely at
her.

161

'You spend a great deal of your time walking, dear,' Ruth said. 'Of course I'm sure it's healthy exercise.'

Eve escaped thankfully. She followed the road to the headland and branched off into a narrow lane. Searching along the hedgerows she found some sorrel leaves and rolled up a bunch to eat. The sharp flavour was refreshing. The hedges were thick, in full bloom, rhododendrons hanging their splendid heads of purple and scarlet. At the edge of the promontory she came upon a small beach covered in seaweed. A donkey and cart hauled a load along the strand, attended by a man who waved cheerfully when he saw her. She waved back and scrambled down to talk to him, eager for some local news and innocent conversation.

'Are you bringing that to the factory?'

'I couldn't go that distance,' he said in an unmistakable London accent. 'The lorry will collect it when it's dried out.'

'Do the local people collect it as well?'

'I'm a local.' He smiled. 'I just can't get rid of this damn accent.'

'Oh, I'm sorry. I didn't know. How long are you living here?'

'Six years permanent. Twenty years coming and going. My wife comes from here.'

'Well, you've plenty of seaweed there.'

He shook his head. 'It's very scarce this year. The rough seas have torn it up too far out. It rots very quickly once it's off the rocks. And what's left and we can't get at, the winkles make short work of.'

'Periwinkles?'

'You call them peris. I call them winkles. That's right. Makes you think, don't it? Never imagine those little creatures could eat so much.'

'They're delicious. Do you like them?'

'Never could eat one of them, nor cockles, nor those other black things that stick on the rocks.'

'Oh, you mean limpets.'

'No. Long kind of shape. The Frenchies go mad for 'em.'

'Mussels?'

'That's right. Mussels. Wouldn't eat them neither.'

All his life spent in London and here he was not able to eat mussels.

'Do you like it here?' she asked, pitying him his exile.

'It's the best place in the world,' he replied with conviction. 'When I think of all the winters I spent driving a taxi in London, freezing, killing myself working.' He shook his head in amazement at the memory of his wasted years.

'Tourists don't bother you?'

He laughed gently. 'Why should they? I was one myself for too long to have any grudge against them.'

She watched him move along the beach, a small man, a man who had come to terms with his life, in his proper place at last, doing what he wanted. Suddenly, cynically, she wondered if he beat his wife, and she felt contaminated by the thought. Already the sordid world had touched her in a way it had probably never touched him, even as a London taxi driver. Was his contentment a reflection of innocence or immaturity or simply a lack of imagination?

Hugh was being brisk and practical when she returned to the house, every gesture and intonation an unsubtle attempt to reassure the sisters. She wished he could be more delicate, less obvious. But they didn't seem to mind. They didn't notice her when she stood in the doorway. After a few minutes Hugh nodded to her while he carried on talking. The sisters gave no sign that they had seen her and yet she knew they must have heard her footsteps outside and the creak the door made as she pushed it in. Perhaps, in spite of their protestations of sisterhood, they saw her merely as an adjunct to their lives. How did Hugh see her? An adjunct, a spare rib? Would he breathe life into her, his own life, suffocating at the same time her own? Eleanor had once referred to Eve's fragile ego in a warning tone and she had been angry at the implication. But perhaps her ego *was* fragile. If so, this house and Hugh and his sisters posed a threat. Eleanor had said, 'Your mother was very brave to call you Eve. Didn't you ever mind?' No, Eve had not minded. She had carried the name proudly, she remembered, even in her timid school days, perhaps instinctively acknowledging the lost ancient strength and innocence of scapegoat Eve.

Eve sat on the window seat pondering, drawing the curtain slightly around her to hide her thoughtfulness. It must have seemed like an act of rebellion, for in an instant Ruth was beside her.

'You know, dear,' Ruth placed a conciliatory hand on her knee, 'you looked quite sad just now. Quite lost. Are you feeling well?' The bright inquisitive eyes peered into her own as if trying to penetrate into the dark of her mind, to rummage in those secret recesses as Hugh rummaged in the attic. 'I sometimes feel,' Ruth added, 'as if you have put up a barrier between us.'

'I didn't mean to,' Eve said, blushing guiltily.

'There. I knew it.' Ruth clapped her hands. 'You can't fool us. The little pink in the cheeks betrays you. You find us all too much. And I don't blame you. I don't blame you at all.'

It's nice not to be blamed, Eve almost said. It's nice not to be blamed for being myself, for not being you, for not being like you, for being young and inexperienced and unsure.

But she did not say any of those things and was again amazed at her daring in even thinking them. And what, she asked herself, almost in the next thought, was so daring about such ordinary, unrevolutionary thoughts? Why did they make her feel guilty, remorseful, self-accusing?

Hugh had assumed his authoritative male air and the sisters were making passive, submissive noises. Eve wished that Ruth would leap up and rush to her accordion and blare her forceful music through the room – anything to challenge that complacent self-confidence. But action of that sort was unthinkable for the moment. Four timid, fearful women leaned on their protector and saviour as if they had never lived independent lives. Even their jealous comments and their polite savagery would have been better than this.

From her corner, Eve surprised them by contributing to the conversation. 'Don't you think it is up to yourselves to take whatever steps you need with the planning board? Why should they listen to Hugh any more than they listen to you?'

164

'What chance would four old women have? Besides, we wouldn't dream of lowering ourselves in such a vulgar commercial manner. In any case, Hugh is a man of good standing and of course he will be listened to. As poor Eleanor often says, and I must say it is one of the few occasions when I wholeheartedly agree with her, "It's a man's world."'

'That's only because you let it be that way. You lock yourselves up in your homes and gardens and never join in conquering the world; you battle against the weather and pests and the diseases that afflict your garden. Why can't you do battle outside as well?'

'Battle? Battle? Who wants to do battle with anything? What has come over the child?' Florence looked around at the others in appeal. 'We couldn't be so unfeminine.'

'What has that got to do with anything? What does it mean other than to have a uterus, ovaries, fallopian tubes –'

'You sound just like Eleanor now.' Bridget stood up, shaking her skirts as if they were contaminated. 'I do not know why we have to listen to such disgusting talk from anyone. Least of all from Hugh's intended bride.'

Hugh got up and left the room.

There was a silence so brittle and full of pain, of passions being held tightly in control, that Eve expected the moment to disintegrate in more accusation and reproach.

She hovered over a pit of destruction. One word, one syllable might hurl her into it. Recovering, she said, 'I'm sorry. I don't know what came over me. I've been feeling a little nervy lately.'

They were appeased. Nerves were feminine and under-standable. Nerves were to be pitied and coped with.

Yet she had a feeling of missed opportunity. If she *had* plunged into the pit, destruction might have led to resurrection. Her head began to ache and she accepted their offer of coffee laced with whiskey. It made her headache worse but it numbed the other, deeper pains. In bed that night she sobbed into the pillow as she had not done since she was a small child, lonely and afraid of the dark.

*   *   *

165

Lately Eve had become afraid of the night, whether driving through the silent countryside or walking back to her flat through shadowy side streets. She was afraid that the savagery of men might come upon her, that she would be leaped upon, dragged into an alleyway or car, humiliatingly assaulted and raped. Her flesh crawled when she read horror stories in the newspapers of women who had been brutally treated in this way and sometimes murdered. Girls in their teens, widows in their eighties, spinsters in their thirties, mature matrons in their forties: rich, poor, sophisticated, naive, black, white – their one common link was their sex. Mixed with her fear was a terrible rage, all the more terrible because it seemed to her an impotent rage, that she, like all women, was vulnerable, a permanent potential victim, that she relied for survival on the restraint, not of other women, but of all men. When popes and bishops and politicians spoke eloquently on behalf of the poor and oppressed, for peace and political stability, when they talked about the sanctity of marriage, the sacredness of the family, and most of all when they preached against contraception and abortion, their silence on violence against women was deafening. She struggled to hold to her faith, pushing aside Eleanor's contemptuous dismissal: 'A man's Church for a man's world. What has it to do with us? Nothing. Nothing. There is no God and men have proved that to me over and over again. That wretched, brave man Jesus did his best and look where it got him. Racked and crucified with a few women weeping by his feet. As well they might. And oh, it had to happen. Who comes along but convert Paul, leaping on the bandwagon, burying his own guilt for goodness knows what deeds of his past, the precursor of all the nuts to come, including that sex psychotic Freud, churning out his theories in true sausage-machine fashion. But the worst thing about all of this is the number of stupid, stupid women who trot along behind, too busy churning out their own sausages in the shape of babies to wonder about it all, to ask why or even how. God help us all, if there is a God.'

Eve always laughed when Eleanor said, 'God help us all, if there is a God,' and Eleanor always laughed back and said, 'I can't help it. I'll be a Catholic atheist till the day I die. And no doubt I'll shout, "Jesus help me," whenever I'm in agony. That's my culture. That's my conditioning. That's my indelible seal.'

Eve contemplated taking up karate, but that seemed another kind of betrayal, an acceptance of defeat, an acknowledgement that violence determined the winner and that the only way to survive was to become accomplished in one of the arts of violence, even if it was a disciplined one. Yet self-defence was surely not only necessary but admirable. To leave the defence of one's life in the hands of someone else was to be a parasite, a burden. It meant relinquishing the essential ingredient of an independent life. Arguments with Hugh on the topic were no help. He believed it was in a woman's nature to be gentle, persuasive, encouraging. He ignored her mention of Gandhi as the male protagonist of passive resistance. Women were by nature passive, men were not. All who denied it ignored the sacred essence of their sexual difference. He quoted the case of the alcoholic woman as proof and – it seemed to her with unnecessary relish – described the raucous, shrieking harridans they became simply because they had turned against their own natures. She was confused and bewildered by his lack of logic. Perhaps such women have smaller livers than average, she said. They get poisoned more quickly. Perhaps the restraints upon them had been so vicious that, when they escaped them under the influence of alcohol, they could only give utterance to their grievances in the wildest way. It is obvious that they have smaller livers, he agreed with impatience – but the liver has a tremendous capacity for regeneration. No. You cannot escape the biological factor – and, God knows, he added, I've had enough experience of dealing with *both* sexes to have learned something about this subject. Every psychiatrist knows the consequences of going against your nature.

14

Some nights when she was alone at home, Eve dreamed she was in the middle of an outburst of rage, shrieking at Hugh in despair and frustration. When she woke, sweating, her heart pounding, she could not understand how anyone could experience such unhappiness for no apparent reason. Then she would lie awake, going over her life in detail, particularly her relationship with Hugh, trying to recall some incident, some injury from the past, which might explain her dreams. But she could find none.

In spite of the tensions and arguments at the group meetings, she began to look forward to them. There was reassurance to be had from a common cause. Although there were many disagreements and viewpoints expressed, she felt hopeful that they would eventually be sorted out. After much debate and counter-argument the women had resolved to acquire a building to house the families who needed protection. Eve was at first against the idea. 'I thought we were trying to get away from institutions,' she said. 'Why can't the husbands be moved? It is easier to move one body than nine or ten.'

'Would you like to shift Christine Taylor's husband?' she was asked.

'Can't the police do it?'

'On what grounds? A family quarrel. You can't blame them for not wanting to interfere. They don't know what's going on.'

'And do we?'

'Look,' Ann said. 'I don't know about the rest of you but I

168

have seen enough bruises and heard enough sagas with the same theme. They can't all be lying. I believe something terrible is going on within the family. Maybe it has always gone on. But I'm not prepared to sit back and do nothing. These women need our help. Are we going to spend the rest of our lives arguing and debating about *how* to help them? Let's just do it.'

As it turned out, it was not too difficult. Quite by chance, a building owned by the Health Board was available. Eve and Ann were deputised to discuss the lease. Within a week the roof had been patched up temporarily. Within a month the house had been redecorated, mainly by voluntary help, and they had their first resident.

She was a woman who had been so terrorised by her husband that she had had herself admitted to a mental hospital. She came to the house shaking all over, constantly weeping, with her two small children. Listening to her account of the years of abuse, broken jaws, cracked ribs, bruises whose changes in colour she could accurately predict, so accustomed to them was she, Eve found it difficult to believe such brutality possible.

'It's as bad as the torture of prisoners,' she cried to Ann. 'Why don't we have amnesty for battered wives?'

'I suppose because up until now few people cared enough. You know the attitude. What happens behind the closed doors of the home is private. It's a little kingdom ruled by the stronger partner. If that stronger partner happens to be a paranoid male, well, there's going to be trouble. We know the trouble domineering mothers cause but somehow domineering fathers have been accepted.'

'You take it all so calmly,' Eve complained.

'No, I don't. But perhaps you are too young to be involved in all this. You should marry that nice doctor friend of yours. Leave this battle to old warhorses like myself.'

'I can't. It's all too unjust. I can't do nothing.'

'Well, I'm glad you're not leaving us yet. There are few enough to do the work. The women can't defend themselves in court and the judge gives me funny looks every time I appear.

He always clears the court now – he was pressurised into it – but he used to allow me to sit at the back. Last time, he said I had to leave. And he said there were too many of these cases taking up the court's time.' She made a comical face of disapproval.

'I suppose the refuge *is* more important than anything,' Eve admitted.

'We need the sanction of the court as well. The law should encourage justice and a change in attitudes. Eventually men may realise that society officially disapproves of their actions, even if they get approval from their public-house friends.'

'I sometimes think,' Eve said hesitantly, 'that it is all too much for me. It affects how I feel about people.'

Ann looked at her sympathetically. 'You *are* too young. You shouldn't be involved in this sort of thing at all. But I don't want you to leave. You're one of the few people here with a brain and we need that. When the others start dithering and arguing about procedures and what people will think of them, I could scream. There are too few who care at all, so I just have to put up with them. But it's a relief to have you there chipping in with a word of common sense.'

'I don't feel I'm much use.'

'You are. Believe me, you are,' Ann assured her. 'Of course what we really need is someone with a cool detached approach who could research why men/women relationships erupt into violence, and why there is such a rift between us when, after all, we do love each other. Right through history women have been treated scandalously, just because they were women. You know those witches in the Middle Ages who were tortured because they could cure people? They were the victims of professional jealousy. The Church and the medical men were afraid of their power and were greedy for the money they made.'

'I hadn't really thought about it,' Eve said.

'Well, ask your doctor friend what he thinks. The Church even went so far as to say that cures by women were not the result of skill but of an alliance with the devil. It's a wonder

170

women managed to hang on to any power at all. But, mind you, there's a fine effort going on in our own country to take away what little gains have been made. The minute there's an economic recession, women bite the dust and all the old arguments about their role in the home and the horrors of contraception and abortion are trotted out. Not that I'm for abortion. But it's the business of women and they should confront their own consciences on the matter. But will they? They're too stupid. They'll follow the men like sheep. I suppose it's love.'

'Sounds more like stupidity,' Eve said.

'I think you're getting fiery.' Ann put her arm around her. 'We'll make a woman of you yet.'

Ann's arm was a comfort, safe, undemanding, understanding. Why didn't Hugh's arm feel the same way? Perhaps it was because they did not share the same battlefield experience. Hugh might embrace his friend Adrian with similar ease. Perhaps it would change if they married and had a common life and common friends. But Hugh had already expressed misgivings about her friends and she had a nagging fear that she might not always be able to fight him to hold on to them. Why should she have to fight to hold on to her friends? As she sat in what Ann began to call the 'confession box', listening to her sisters in distress, she discovered that such fights were fairly frequent occurrences in some marriages.

'He doesn't like my friends. He called my best friend a whore. Not to her face, but to me,' or, 'He has forbidden me to go out with the girls. He goes out to the pub but I'm not allowed to go to the pictures with them. He says they're bad for me.'

Still, it was a mild enough grievance, a simple expression of jealousy. It was the truly shocking accounts of violent sexual intercourse or of the impotent attempts at intercourse followed by abuse and recrimination that horrified Eve. She had never imagined marriage could be so terrible.

As the stories unfolded – at first hesitantly, but later when the trust had been established, in an outburst of confidence, a flood of anguish that might overwhelm them – Eve and Ann felt physical shock. As Ann remarked, it was like being violated oneself.

So must people have felt who were forced to work with plague bearers. This might be too strong an analogy, but Eve was increasingly aware of a sharp sense of danger, made all the more painful because she could not identify precisely its source. Were all women in some way carriers of this plague, just as they carried in their bodies the seeds of mankind with all its troubles, a Pandora's box of misery? They were the bearers of life and therefore the bearers of death. Did they have to be punished because of that?

And yet, and yet . . . She proclaimed to herself her innocence. She resented the implication of taint. She was not and would not accept that she was corrupt. If she was not, who was? Guilt was everywhere. Accusation was rife. Were the accusers in reality the accused, pointing the finger away from themselves to avoid their own condemnation? Were men so unable to accept their sexual needs that they had to justify them or do penance for them? The lusty call of the flesh debased to the misery of sackcloth and ashes. Why had the ritual of mating been so perverted and abused that two people could be trapped in a relationship which was a living death to one or both?

At Ann's insistence they sought professional help for the refuge and were surprised by the frequently hostile responses from solicitors and doctors.

'You middle-class women don't understand how these women live. They're used to violence. They can't do without it.' When someone pointed out that violence occurred in middle-class homes too, it was shrugged aside with, 'Some women deserve it. They look for it.'

At first no one would defend a woman in court. They appealed for help to politicians, to clergymen, to the community care officers. It seemed to Eve that they spent more time on deputations than in actually helping the women. But she began to grow less confused and more angry. She knew Eleanor would approve. Eleanor had said, 'If you want a quiet life, don't take up a cause. Try flower arranging. It's not so dangerous.'

Eventually a solicitor was found who agreed to take a case, the first debarring order. Eve remembered Eleanor's caustic remarks as the solicitor warned her of the difficulties of proving a case of this kind. 'These bills,' he said, 'are drafted in too much of a hurry, the result of pressure from reform groups like yours. The language can be ambiguous, and it's grist to the mill of some judges who have a natural contempt for the great unwashed, and particularly for women, who are a nuisance, cluttering up the courts with marriage complaints. But our man is fair and you'll get a fair hearing.'

As it happened, it fell to Eve to accompany the woman to court. Marion was their second resident at the refuge. She had five children aged from seven years to six weeks. When her husband had first beaten her, she had been three months pregnant with their first child. Since then it had been a continuous series of assaults, but the most recent one had driven her to the refuge because he had attacked her when she was breastfeeding the new baby.

'I think he's mad,' she said sadly. 'I didn't realise it before, because you know some men are rough, but this is different.'

So, timidly, awed by the might of the court, she had agreed to present herself and plead her cause, or let the solicitor do it for her.

Her case was last to be called.

'How long will it take?' the judge asked crossly. 'I won't hear it today if it is defended. You know that.'

'It's fairly straightforward, justice,' the solicitor pleaded, 'and it is undefended.'

'After lunch. The court to be cleared,' the judge said, and rose.

'Have I to come back again? Your whole morning is wasted on me.' Marion nearly wept.

'It isn't wasted. I'll meet you here at two. Will someone collect the children for you if you aren't back in time?'

'A neighbour is minding the little ones. Carmel will mind the others. She's eight now and full of old sense. I don't know what I'd do without her. It's great to have a girl first after all. It's hard to believe I cried when I saw her because I knew Bennie

173

would be raging, he wanted a boy so much. It's funny the way you'd want to please a man so much you'd nearly deny your own baby.'

After lunch the judge was in better form, even sympathetic, patient with Marion's nervous, stumbling answers. Eve had been permitted to sit alone at the back of the court while the two guards stood with their arms folded near the door. Outside, people pressed their noses against the small glass panes, and occasionally pushed in, to be moved back by the guards. Eve thought their gaping curiosity unbearably callous. Was this a gathering place for the dregs of humanity or was it the building itself and its purpose that made them so soulless? She felt oppressed by the legal procedure and its unimaginative approach to problems. The institution had again taken over and seemed to be operating for its own sake. Its original purpose had long ago been forgotten. Justice was surely more than a matter of apportioning blame or assessing degrees of innocence and guilt, of giving petty officials power and the liberty to be gruff and insulting when the mood seized them. Perhaps a robot handing out forms would be more suitable in the clerk's office, a computer calculating the degree of injury and offering the appropriate remedy would be more efficient and no less human than the figure on the bench? The power then would lie with the statistician, the compiler of information, the framer of proper questions. A grenade in the machine would be the defendant's only means of answering back. Her thoughts returned to Marion's sad tale, the beatings, the miscarriages, the two retarded children whose condition she blamed on her husband's brutality. She wanted to leave him, but where could she go? For the sake of her health and her children, for the sake of her life, she must be protected from him. He was insanely jealous, accused her of having affairs with the milkman, the postman, the butcher. It was funny in a way. 'Look at me,' she said dramatically to the judge in a surprising burst of confidence. 'I'm no beauty, am I? Yet if I go to a shop for a few things he wants to know who I met, who I talked to.' If she could divorce him, she would.

'Well, that's another matter,' the judge said. 'What we are

dealing with here is a simple debarring order. Is he supporting you?'

'He's on the dole, your honour. I get split dole. He gets thirteen pounds and I get nine. I pay the rent and feed the children on mine. He drinks and gambles his.'

'I'll grant you the order,' the judge said, writing busily. 'I'll give him seven days to leave the house.'

Seven days? Marion was relieved and yet worried. How would she survive the days with him after the order was served? He'd be a raving lunatic. But she dared not query the decision. Her solicitor signalled her to get down from the stand and she did so, bobbing a curtsey of gratitude which neither man noticed. They were talking about the phrasing of the order.

Eve listened to her car radio as she drove to work after the court case. Three intelligent women were cheerfully broadcasting to the nation their taste for romantic literature. Marion, Eve remembered, loved romances. Amongst the bundle of treasures she had brought to the refuge was a pile of paperback novels in which passion and fantasy were partnered with few concessions to human love. Her marriage, as she had recounted it to Eve, was a sordid repetition of mechanical acts, which had nothing to do with romance or even with honest passion. And love? Marion laughed wryly at the word. 'Men don't know what it is to love. You do everything to please them and I think it makes them hate you. They don't want you to love them because no matter what you do it is never enough. You could stand on your head or lap the milk out of the cat's saucer because they wanted you to and they would still say you weren't doing it right. Maybe women love too much. Maybe men aren't worth it and they know it. But I shouldn't be talking to you like this. There are things I can say to the other women that I couldn't say to you. It's different when you are married.'

Was she ever, Eve wondered with irritation, going to shake off the label of innocence and be accepted as a part of that fellowship of vulgar human nature in which things might be said and secrets shared without fear of scandal?

Marion's legal victory had at first elated them. They had

been brought down to earth when the solicitor said as he walked with them to the forecourt, 'Let me know if he breaks the order, or if you have any trouble enforcing it.'

'He won't go easily,' Marion had said. 'I know that. I'll have to keep the children from school or he'll get them, maybe kidnap them. He knows I'll do anything for them. I'm pure foolish about them children.'

All afternoon Eve was haunted by the remark and the heavy resignation that accompanied it. Marion's life was already wrecked, and the lawmakers, for all their supposed wisdom, could not even provide the most basic of remedies. Eve had felt self-consciously female in the courtroom, because, apart from herself and Marion, there were only two other women present. Was an institution which, like the Church and the medical profession, had excluded women for so long incapable of making the leap across the great sex divide to comprehend this kind of injustice? Or was the bias more sinister, deliberate and calculated?

The same question occurred to her when she took part in a deputation of women appealing to the Health Board for funds to provide a social worker and to help with their food bills. A Labour councillor came with them, supposedly to give support, but he suddenly changed sides, used the occasion to score political points, and concluded by lecturing the group on the need for understanding fiscal difficulties.

When, after several meetings, expressions of concern were winkled out of the Health Board, they were guarded and qualified. There were knowing nods about provocation and references to morality and wives who were the responsibility of their husbands. Sometimes Eve wondered if Eleanor's irascible intolerance had infected her, or if it was righteous indignation that made her wish to leap up and yell at the cool faces across the polished mahogany table. Invariably, as Ann had said, the committee felt compelled to dress in their Sunday best, 'even down to their pearls'. Invariably, they were offered coffee in an insufferably patronising tone, which made allowances for their female emotionalism. Coffee for the ladies. A lady secretary, who was the only person present who could offer intelligent

176

suggestions, or who knew anything about leases or potential sites or buildings, was dispatched to provide this innocuous refreshment.

Thus, politely, but with devastating effect, they were reminded of their lowly status. At their most recent meeting they had been told that the state should not interfere in family life, that the Health Board had only a 'residual responsibility'. When Ann asked what this phrase meant, she was told it simply meant what it said, and the phrase was repeated. A residual responsibility. The group had just come from the refuge, which was crammed with mothers and children, including one infant of two weeks and one of seven weeks. It was suggested that they lobby the Department of Health in Dublin and their local TDs. The building was only temporary accommodation, they were reminded; they could not stay in it for ever. They should look for another place.

Eve had never felt such rage and frustration. Both she and Ann reacted with unveiled hostility which rebounded on them all, for they were denied further meetings. They were asked by the rest of the committee to be more tactful.

'We must win the men around to our side, not drive them away,' they were told. It was eminently sensible advice, but not easy to follow when one was caught up in tragedies of Greek proportions. Incest, rape, suicide, murder were no longer the safely controlled fantasies of fiction writers, but the undeniable profanities of everyday life. Each day that passed without action to alleviate at least some of the suffering seemed to Eve betrayal at its most foul.

They inspected sites, talked with auctioneers, the city planner, the city engineer. They looked at houses. They issued a report. The headlines in the local press were titillating. Council members were shocked at the mud being thrown at the good name of the city. Only one councillor was shocked that such things could happen, rather than by the fact that they had been revealed. And she was the sole woman on the council.

Eve hid this part of her life from Hugh as much as she could. She knew how he hated the headlines, her name associated with some sordid tale of family violence. She was caught in a web of conflicting loyalties and ethics. It was hard to protect the privacy of the families involved and at the same time expose the injustices and hardships. But, almost worse than that, her view of Hugh became more and more critical. He was no longer just Hugh, but a man, one of *them*. She had never before thought of people in stereotypical terms, sexual or otherwise, and it was a disconcerting, even painful, experience. She struggled to find a balance. She tried prayer. Meetings with the clergy and the bishop proved unsatisfactory. They were bland, careful, defensive. She began to question the structure of the Church, the role of women within it, the very God behind the structure. To whom could she pray? An almighty, all-knowing God who was undisguisedly male? A placid, female, virgin mother whose only power lay in her ability to intercede, to placate? Marion had spent her life placating, interceding. For the first time, Eve asked herself the question in terror: were men mortal enemies of women because they were born to them but were not of them?

15

All summer the country lived in expectation of the real summer. Occasional flashes of beneficence, days when the sun actually shone and the temperature rose above the mediocre, stirred new hopes. On those days the entire population blossomed into lightweight suits and lighter dresses. The countryside bloomed also, with weeds rampaging gloriously through pastures and gardens, to be hacked down like invading enemies.

'Why can't we use all this for food? When you consider the parched deserts of the world, where all this lushness would be luxury, it seems a sin to do this.'

Eleanor was forking a barrowful of grass cuttings and annual weeds on to her compost heap, watched by Eve, who lolled on a deck chair.

'You're a great conservationist. The deserts are what they are, partly because of lack of the kind of thought you're showing.'

'It's the moisture that makes all the difference. We grumble too much about our climate. Think what a fraction of the rain we despise would do for the Sahara. Think what a fraction of their sun would do for us.'

'As you say yourself, life isn't fair.'

Eleanor put down the shovel and stared coldly at Eve. 'Having my own maxims thrown back at me all the time is not my most favourite experience.'

Eve, feeling regal, was not disturbed. With a grunt Eleanor went into the house. Eve could hear the sound of the tap running, the slurp of soap on hands, then the clatter of cups on saucers, the friendly, forgiving sounds of tea being prepared. China tea, delightfully weak with a faint, musky fragrance, was a speciality of Eleanor's.

'You haven't told me about your liberated weekend,' she called from the kitchen.

'I don't know what you mean by liberated. It was simply a weekend with other members of the women's movement.'

'What a peculiar title that is.' Eleanor sat down on the steps leading to the lawn and looked quizzically at Eve. 'Women's movement. Sounds threatening. Or laxative. Or are you all on the march?'

'Since the day I was born. Aren't you?'

'Like the Salvation Army. No. I am not. And I can't imagine anything more appalling than a weekend hen-party.'

'If Ruth or Bridget said that, you would sneer at them.'

'If Ruth or Bridget said there are seven days in the week, I'd sneer at them.'

'You aren't very consistent.'

'Consistent about what? I don't belong to a group or a gang. I do my own thing. Does that make me inconsistent?'

'You do belong to a group or gang, human, female, Caucasian, Irish, and so on.'

'Animal, vegetable or mineral. I hate amateur anthropologists.'

'You should know all anthropologists are amateurs. It's the nature of the study.'

'If all anthropologists are amateurs, are all amateurs anthropologists? If all feminists are female, are all females feminists?'

'Lots of men are feminists. Do you want to hear about it or not?'

'Wait till I get the tea and we can relax. And don't mind me. Being facetious is second nature to me now. Like breathing out and breathing in,' she sang as she went for the tea trolley.

Eve moved the card table and two folding chairs into position. When Eleanor reappeared, rattling the trolley through the open french windows, she relaxed and waited to be served.

Marriage, she supposed, must be something like this: battling for position, saving face and then sipping China tea in the garden to gird one's loins again or to seduce one into thinking it might always be like this. One day of sunshine and they forgave all the grey cold wet days that went before. No one ever really grew up. No one came to terms with the realities of drought or flood or frostbitten toes or sunblistered skin. The perfect climate was somewhere, even if it brought midges or pollution or hippies in its wake. Like children, they lived in a state of insane optimism. No wonder we turn despair into the sin of the damned, she thought. Somewhere, around the corner, was the perfect marriage, the perfect home, the perfect job, the perfect children. It was a world of admen. Not even Hiroshima or the mutilated flesh of the world's victims could shake them. The despairing were the only honest people. Christ had despaired.

'You have that look on your face again,' Eleanor said as she poured tea.

Eve tasted the tea. 'Lovely,' she said.

'That look,' Eleanor continued, 'which the suicidal wear when they are just about to finally do it. I assure you the tea is not poisoned.'

'You asked about the weekend. The liberated weekend, you called it. What does it mean – to be liberated?'

'What does weekend mean?' Eleanor asked professorially.

'You look like that creature in *Alice* who sat on a large toadstool puffing smoke out of an excessively long pipe and deflating Alice repeatedly.'

'All Alices need deflation. It is my mission in life to deflate Alices. Like the biscuits? Try them.'

Eve sighed and reached for one. She nibbled delicately and gave her verdict. 'Very good.'

Eleanor smiled at some secret joke. 'Well! Were you attacked by a voracious lesbian?'

'There you go again. Scoffing. It wasn't a bit like that.'

It hadn't been a bit like anything else, either. Everyone had

181

worn a uniform of blue denim, trousers and shirts. Eve, for a reason she did not stop to analyse, wore a pink silk dress and high-heeled shoes. She found herself uneasy in the presence of the overweight. Their large breasts seemed too obtrusive and she blamed herself for a kind of treachery which made her view such essentially female characteristics with distaste. Very quickly her reservations were detected and challenged. She was not clever enough to hide her feelings or to refrain from expressing mild opinions about the unusually braless state of the company.

'You are a product of your society,' she was told.

'Aren't we all?' she countered feebly.

'We, as women, see ourselves through the eyes of men. We learn to hate our own bodies because we see them as the objects of male lust, the instruments we use to seduce the male. Why should we go around corseted and brassièred? Our mothers threw away their corsets. Our grandmothers stopped swadd-ling their babies' limbs. The Chinese have stopped binding little female feet into deformity. Women have been restricted and restrained mentally, physically and emotionally. We have been deprived of education, of the means for full artistic and religious expression, even of freedom of movement. You may say that is all in the past. But is it? How much has really changed under all the surface gestures of goodwill from politicians? They won't change attitudes by changing laws. We need to be ourselves, not to be cast into some acceptable mould ordained by the patriarchy. We need to accept the challenge of life for ourselves. We must make our own decisions and our own mistakes. We must get out of the uniform and into living.'

'But you're all wearing a new uniform. Do you expect me to wear blue denim to prove something? That's only exchanging one kind of servitude for another.'

'You can wear sackcloth for all we care. We just feel that this garb declares a revolution. It says, away with cosmetic disguise and away with scents and perfumes.'

'You can't discard the customs of civilised society just like that.'

She was greeted with hoots of derision. 'Afraid of your own

smells? Afraid of your own sweat and body odours. You've a lot to learn.'

It appeared she had. Someone said you weren't truly liberated until you could lick your own menstrual blood as you would a cut on your finger.

Yet she had felt relaxed and at home in a way she had never felt before. She could have run around naked there, thrown herself on the floor and kicked her clothes off, sprawling inelegantly, legs apart, and no one would notice or care. Everywhere women lolled and flopped and let go. For the first day, a euphoric sisterliness abounded. They were beginning to pick up rhythms from each other, ways of moving and talking which seemed to hark back to some forgotten past. Only later in the second day did the familiar touch of aggression creep in. The voices of dissent became louder, the calls to reform more insistent. But, in between, there were some wonderful moments of easy comradeship, perhaps similar to that felt by men on board a battleship in wartime. And there were no sexual undercurrents to stir things up. At least, not many.

Early on the first evening a young woman approached Eve tentatively and confided that she had been living with a friend but was now on her own. Eve, not certain how to react, remarked inconsequentially, 'That's interesting,' and the young woman wandered off. Eve saw her later, her pale face lit by excitement, talking and laughing with a heavy-set girl. Later again, arms around each other, the two kissed and murmured secrets to one another.

Few wore make-up. Its absence, Eve noticed, gave the women a new individuality which not even the uniform denim could hide. Cosmetics turned people into carbon copies of one another. Eyes shadowed in purple all assumed the same shape; mouths etched in colour became fashionably large or fashionably small. Hair dyed and permed changed the contours of a face. Here were real faces and real bodies, with lines of despair or laughter, sagging muscles or upright posture, for all to see.

There were exceptions. Eve noticed with disillusion that her pale, anonymous friend had yielded to convention and applied heavy face make-up. Occasionally they exchanged smiles when

183

they passed each other on corridors or in the lecture room, and Eve was sorry to see increasing signs of harassment on the other's face. Her partner adopted the regular proprietary air of one who is to be obeyed, and the tension between them became inescapable.

'My God,' a woman said to Eve, 'I thought we were here to escape all that. By the way, are you bi-, hetero- or mono-, or should I say homo? I don't want to tread on any more corns. I've trodden on quite a few already.'

'I suppose I'm hetero. I haven't really thought about it much.'

'Haven't you indeed? Where have you been all your life? In a nunnery?'

'I thought you said we were here to escape all that?'

'Wishful thinking,' the woman answered cheerfully. 'Copulate to populate. It's the name of the game. Otherwise we might as well drown ourselves.'

'Women are so illogical,' commented a neighbour, a tall unhappy-looking woman who kept running her fingers through her hair every time she spoke. By evening it stood up in spikes all over her head.

'Are you really?' Threateningly polite.

'Not me. Other women.'

'Oh. Them. The others,' the first woman said with supreme sarcasm and went away.

'See what I mean,' the unhappy-looking woman bemoaned. 'You can't make the simplest remark without being taken up in some completely different way. My husband doesn't know I'm here, of course. He'd kill me if he knew. Especially if he knew there were queers here. I never knew there were female queers, did you? People are so weird, aren't they?'

'I suppose we all have our problems,' Eve said, trying to be tactful.

'*You* don't, I'm quite sure. The minute I saw you I said to myself, there's the one normal one among us. I mean, all this denim. My friend who brought me here wouldn't let me wear anything else. I had to borrow some of hers. If my husband knew, he'd ...' She stopped.

184

'Kill you?' Eve suggested helpfully.

Offended, the woman got up and moved away.

Later, there was a long discussion on health. This included intimate revelations by individual women and accounts of their own, usually awful, experiences at the hands of others, usually men. One woman recounted a tragic incident where her sister had been diagnosed a hypochrondriac and sent from one psychiatrist to another before haemorrhaging dramatically at a concert and dying five hours later. 'If she were a man,' the woman said bitterly, 'she would have been listened to. But no. They said she should get married and have children. That she was unfulfilled. Can you believe that? A perfectly sane, well-adjusted woman of high intelligence who had cancer of the uterus and they told her she should get married and have children!' She began to weep at the memory and the women beside her stroked her hair and comforted her. Eve thought of Eleanor's tirade against Adrian. Other tales were told of neglect and bad treatment which they agreed among themselves was criminal. But what was the answer? Not more women doctors trained in the same way, viewing women with the same fear and lack of understanding. At first the pathos of the stories moved the group to pity and some cried in sympathy. But a girl of about eighteen leaped up in fury and cried passionately, 'You are only crying out of pity and self-pity. What you need is to be angry. Not pitying. Not bitter. But angry. You are only victims because you allow yourselves to be victims. Who in their senses would stay with a man who regularly beats her? Who would go to a doctor who treats her as if she were mentally retarded? They can't all be like that.'

The older women smiled at each other ruefully but compassionately. There was something about their resigned expressions which made Eve shut her eyes tightly to hold back tears of inexplicable grief. She grieved over some loss, some nameless terror.

At different times during the three days the women formed groups to discuss common problems and share experiences. The trouble was, Eve explained to Eleanor over China tea in the garden, the experiences all seemed to be problems. 'I know what you mean,' Eleanor said. 'If you haven't got a problem you've got a problem.'

'Exactly. That was exactly it. But why did I feel so foreign to it all, so removed?'

'I suppose it was because they were very special experiences.'

Yet that was not the reason. The experiences were believable, identifiable. The humiliation, the sense of being deprived of opportunity, of being limited and restricted, of being pushed into accepting roles which one rejected inwardly or even raged against – all of that was familiar. 'I can't bear it,' one woman had said, 'when some self-seeking woman boasts that, after all, she has made it in a man's world, so why are we complaining?' Why, indeed? It was all very puzzling. Perhaps it was simply too much to take in at one time. Yet the sisterhood was warm and comforting. It was relaxing to be a part of something in which there could be no interference from aggressive, authoritarian males with their bad jokes. If someone here tried to be bossy, you could, if you wished, kick her teeth in with a fair chance of victory. There was plenty of humour. But no sex jokes, no womb jokes, and certainly no penis jokes. In fact, when the subject of humour came up, one girl said plaintively that she believed she had a very good sense of humour but she didn't like being the butt of it. 'Mother-in-law jokes, or girlfriend jokes. Or the wife jokes. Do any of us think they're funny?'

'And penis jokes are so boring,' a voice of great resignation put in.

'So are boob jokes,' came a voice from a corner.

'I suppose,' a young, hitherto quiet but very earnest woman said, 'men make jokes of that sort because of their extraordinary attachment to their, their thing, you know.'

'Penis,' someone else offered, helpfully accurate.

'Yes. That.'

'Say it,' someone called. 'It won't bite.'

They roared with laughter.

'I'm not that liberated, if you don't mind. In fact, I'm not liberated at all. I'm only here –'

'For the queer,' a tall girl with a humorous nose shouted.

186

'It's getting out of hand. Let her speak.'

'I object to that last remark. I object to the use of the word queer.'

'Apologise.'

'We're just the same as men. No discipline. Can't we have a reasoned discussion on anything?'

'I only wanted to say,' the quiet girl insisted, 'that perhaps men make jokes like that because they have to. I mean it's such an inconvenient thing. Especially for young men. It must be really embarrassing at times. I should hate to have it. Getting in the way and being a general nuisance.'

'Like boobs,' a voice of muffled mirth said.

'But they are necessary after all. For babies.'

Three women in the back of the room collapsed in uncontrollable hilarity.

The quiet girl grew heated. 'I know the other thing is necessary too. I'm not a fool. I think it's very unfair to make fun of me. We are all entitled to have our say. I thought that's why we were here. It's why *I* came. I thought we could listen here. I've listened to everything. Even to that person who wanted to start a witches' coven where they could develop the evil eye and kill the men. Or the woman who said we should get rid of all the boy babies and have a sperm bank locked away on an island that we could use whenever we needed. It's crazy. But I listened and out of respect to her I didn't laugh.'

'She's right, you know. The trouble is, men make a skit out of everything serious and go out and kill one another over nothing. What are all the wars about? Nothing. Prestige and power, that's all. If they want to know about survival they should consult us. We know all about it.'

'But I like men,' the quiet girl said earnestly.

The three women in the back row collapsed again and were stared at with such hostility from all sides that they excused themselves and left the room.

It was strange that religion or the role of women in religion was the one area they had not touched during the week. The few cult-seekers in the group had been practically ignored. The woman who had wanted to start the witches' coven had been

187

dismissed as a crank. The other religions were accepted as being men's business. The fact that women swarmed to churches in their thousands, that as nuns they made up the vast bulk of the missionary church, was of no interest. There was a gap, an unthinking, inexcusable gap, in the logic of the whole weekend. She left, when it was over, feeling dissatisfied and frustrated.

She could not explain all of this to Eleanor. It would be like explaining the alphabet to someone who had learned to read without it. And she could not account for the irritation she had recently felt on reading a review of a woman's collection of poetry which the reviewer described as verse, the work of a minor poet – too self-absorbed, as was the work of so many women. Only two weeks earlier another critic had described a woman's first novel as lacking the obsessive voice. The weight of prejudice against women seemed at times beyond endurance, yet it was difficult to pin down and classify. Infuriating instances cropped up constantly. It would take a heroine of extraordinary stature to chart them and decode them and emerge emotionally unscathed at the end. She read the poems the critic had dismissed, and the same night, by coincidence, read a psalm when she went to the Bible for comfort. The psalm and the poem could have been written by the same hand.

Men did not see women as being born, she thought, only as giving birth. I shall never bear a child. In that promise to herself she totally excluded Hugh and did not even know it.

After she had confided in Eleanor, she regretted having revealed so much. She might have left herself too open and Eleanor would surely mock her. She stared into the wide delicate teacup and waited.

'It's not that simple,' Eleanor said. 'In some ways it's too easy to have a child. Much more difficult not to have one, unless you're my age, or we wouldn't be having all this fuss about contraceptives.'

'Children complicate things so.'

'Did you feel like a complication when you were a child? I didn't. We don't ask to be born, but when we do make it we have as many rights as our so-called adult parents. Do you love Hugh?'

The question, so typical in its suddenness, brought tears to Eve's eyes.

'I don't know. I just don't know.'

'If you loved him, you would know. I never interfere in people's lives, in spite of what Hugh seems to think, but I will this time. Don't marry him. For his sake as well as for yours. But I suppose I'm more on your side, so for your own sake don't. When a woman loves a man she dissolves into him, her flesh into his flesh, her spirit into his spirit. She loses herself in him. I don't know why it is like that but, believe me, it is. For such sacrifice there has to be a reckoning. Sooner or later it comes. Disillusion, the sad undeniable truth of the man's frailty, the mourning for the death of her own self. Then comes the desperate, despairing urge to rediscover self, to pull into some shape the dissolved bones, to build up again the disintegrated flesh. Think of the turmoil created. Divided and torn, not just by husband or lover but by the children who have come from their union, she has to be reborn while still giving birth. Her life is an endless contradiction. Mocked for her passivity, abused for her aggression, she embodies everyone's failures and guilts. She is the perennial scapegoat. God knows, you must have seen women like that, women you have despised because their faces are chewed up with hatred and despair, women who are beaten by the world and ten feet of make-up won't hide the defeat. There is only one supremely basic and primitive urge in woman which makes her run so terrible a risk and that is the urge to produce a child. Give her a test-tube baby and you give her freedom. So have a baby, rear it, but do it without making yourself a slave to two masters, the marriage bed and the crib, and all the other slaveries that go with them, the kitchen sink, the endless cleaning up. When all is said and done and when all the platitudes about the joys of motherhood and homemaking have been uttered, only one thing is certain: women are the skivvies of the world.'

'You don't hold out much hope.'

'I'm not a charlatan. Go to priests and churches if you want false hopes. I thought you wanted truth. Maybe you're too young to bear it.'

'You should be out there with Hugh. You'd make a great orator.'

'Politics,' Eleanor sneered. 'Politicians. Every one of them the same. Egomaniacs. Self-seekers. To think we trust our destiny to such people. Well, I never expect anything from them but bumbling arrogance. Unveiling plaques to themselves. We muddle along in spite of them.'

'Perhaps you're an anarchist at heart.'

'An anarchist!' Eleanor sneered twice as viciously. 'You're getting worse. You dish out labels like workhouse soup. A spoonful for every open mouth. I'd better keep mine shut.'

'I don't know why I bother ever trying to talk to you,' Eve said angrily. 'You seem to feel you have to lecture or hector or abuse me. I don't have to take it from you.'

'No, you don't. Why do you? Ever ask yourself that?'

'I like you. I can't make myself not like you. I wish I could.'

'That's not a reason, that's another excuse.'

'Maybe it is. But what if it is? Why shouldn't I make excuses?'

'Because there's no need. You have everything because you have youth and looks and education and good health. I'm old enough to be your mother. Perhaps that's why I'm so hard on you.'

'I have a mother and I don't need two. And she doesn't carry on the way you do. She is remarkably tolerant.'

'Maybe it's just Limerick apathy or brain damage caused by the lack of oxygen in our polluted town.'

'Now you're attacking my mother and you haven't even met her! I think Hugh must be right. I think you are sick.'

'Oh, brotherly loverly Hugh. Comforter of the afflicted. He should know.'

Eve stood up abruptly, knocking over the delicate teacup as she did so and spilling out the last of the brew onto the embroidered tablecloth. The rooftops of the high Georgian houses behind the garden shimmered in the heat of the afternoon sun. Down in the far corner a peony rose showed itself, flauntingly crimson.

'I must go,' said Eve as she ran from the garden.

16

'Everyone to their own trouble,' the Clare woman who tidied Hugh's flat and surgery said, whether her Yorkshire terrier was in heat or her neighbour had a gangrenous toe. Hugh might have agreed. Honora Creagh's voice from the past, insistent and nagging, goaded him into continual reassessment of himself. So powerful had the effect of the letters been that by late summer he found himself reluctant to venture up to the attic. Two further items had turned up and he was not certain of their significance, apart from the fact that someone had actually taken the trouble to copy out what were transplanters' certificates.

The first was headed simply *James Bonfield, of the City of Limerick*, and it read:

We, the said Commissioners, do hereby certify that James Bonfield, of the city of Limerick, Burgess, hath upon the 20th day of December, 1653, in pursuance of a Declaration of the Commissioners of the Parliament of the Commonwealth of England for the affairs of Ireland, bearing date the 14th day of October, 1653, delivered unto us in writing the names of himself and of such other persons as are to remove with him, with the quantities and qualities of their stocks and tillage, the contents whereof are as followeth: viz. – the said James Bonfield, *of the city aforesaid, aged thirty-eight years, tall stature, browne flaxen haire.* Catherine Bonfield, *his wife, aged thirty-eight years, red haire.* John Hynane, *aged twenty years, middle stature, black haire.* Gabriel Creagh, Gennett*

Creagh, Anthony Creagh, *and* James Creagh, *small children under the ages of eight years.* Ellen ny Cahill, *maidservant, aged forty years, middle stature, browne haire.* Mary ny Lyddy, *aged forty years, black haire, middle stature. His substance, foure cows, foure garrans, and desires the benefit of his claim. The substance whereof we believe to be true. In witness whereof we have hereunto set our hands and seals the 20th day of December, 1653.*

Why these apparently orphaned children should have been included in this list he could not tell, he could not even begin to guess at the reason, and the other copy was of no help. It referred to a Margaret Healy, alias Creagh, the relict of John Healy, Esq., deceased, and she had, apparently, as the document put it:

... delivered unto us in writing the names of herself and of such other persons as are to remove with her, with the quantities and qualities of their stocks and tillage, the contents of which are as followeth, viz. – the said Margaret, *aged thirty years, flaxen haire, full face, middle size. Her substance, two cows, three ploughs of garrans, and two acres of barley and wheate sowen.* John Neal, *her servant, adged twenty-eight years, red haire, middle stature, full face.* Gennet Comyn, *one of her servants, adged twenty-four years, brown haire, slender face, of middle stature.* John Keane, *servant, adged thurtie-six years, brown haire, middle size, full face, and her little daughter, adged six years. Out of the above substance she payeth contribution. In witness whereof we have hereunto set our hands and seals, the 19th day of December, 1653.*

Defeated or law-abiding, they had at least attempted to conform to the new regime. Dragging their goods and chattels, their children and servants in the middle of winter to unknown territory, their experience must have been far removed from the dry tones of the legal document which was the only record of their journey. If it had not been for Honora Creagh's letters, thought Hugh bitterly, he would have been able to look at the transplanters' copies as merely the dull stuff of history.

Damn, he thought, damn. Women and their complaints. They force you to feel pain in spite of yourself. When he and Adrian were discussing Hugh's political future, Hugh confided a little of this to his friend. Adrian merely warned him against pandering to the collective mediocrity and when Hugh said he knew the danger Adrian remarked, 'You're full of surprises lately.'

Hugh felt rebuffed. Even when they had been students, he had never found it possible to confide fully in Adrian. 'Everyone has an axe to grind,' Adrian would say, before retiring to churn out the agonised secrets of his soul in verse. An obsession with words, Hugh decided, was as bad as any other obsession.

He said as much to Eve. 'Men are so peculiar,' she replied. He was as stunned as if she had hit him with a strong left. 'You worry about such trivial things,' she continued. 'And you're always talking about your souls or your bodies in capital letters. And they are always men's souls or men's bodies. Unless you actually specify women. Of course, you all think that to be human is to be male. Female is separate, apart, like being black. God knows what it must be like to be black and female.'

He was about to retaliate in anger when he wondered if she might be suffering from pre-menstrual tension. He stared at her chin, trying to detect the little spot that appeared at regular monthly intervals, the harbinger of hormonal storms.

'You needn't look at me in that funny way, Hugh. I honestly think you're all crazy. No wonder women have created their own world, their world within a world. It must be self-preservation, a way of escaping the hypocrisies, the sordid conventions of men. I'm sure that's why women don't write great tomes of philosophy and theology. They don't have to sort out a mess because they haven't *made* a mess, because they aren't *in* a mess, at least not until they get tied up with – ' She stopped. She had been thinking about Marion in particular, but the temptation to generalise became too strong. 'I don't mean all men, of course, and I don't mean you. You're too intelligent and kind and decent, in spite of what Eleanor said.'

193

She stopped again, horrified at the path along which her stumbling words had taken her.

At the time, they were standing in the hallway of her flat and she was buttoning up a long cardigan with knitted knobbles for buttons. She resembled a comical rabbit, he thought tenderly, his anger vanishing. You couldn't be cross with a comical rabbit.

They were on their way to Adrian's tower house for his long-promised poetry reading. Eleanor had left earlier. She wouldn't let anyone else drive her. Neither would Hugh. Eve was relieved. Eleanor at the wheel was a late-night horror movie. The worst seemed inevitable. No one was impressed by her assertion that she had remarkably quick reflexes or by her boast of twenty years of accident-free driving – she didn't count the times she had been towed or dug out of ditches. If no one was hurt, it wasn't an accident. Hugh said that relying on good brakes and good reflexes left too much to chance. One thing you could say about Hugh, Eve thought, he never left anything to chance. It was all the more surprising then to hear him talk about an encounter he'd had with Tom Rogers. Tom had wanted him to forsake his political ambition.

'Does he think it's beneath your dignity or something stupid like that?' she asked.

'No. At least I don't think so. Well, he may think so, but that isn't the reason, and I'm afraid I can't tell you just now what the reason was.'

'Well, I think you were perfectly right. He had a nerve, trying to talk you out of it. It isn't any of his business. Honestly, there isn't much to choose between medical and church hierarchies. However much you cover up and pretend it's all in the name of service to others, or to God, you're just obsessed with power.'

'I don't think I'm like that. But we do have to have authority. We can't have chaos and anarchy. We all have our roles and we must fit them as best we can.'

'Roles.' She sighed with discontent.

He patted her knee. 'Don't worry. I'm not going to preach.

And I'm not going to argue. We are on the same team, you and I. Remember?'

'The important thing is, you made it, in spite of old Uncle Tom.'

'Some cabin he lives in,' Hugh laughed. 'I wish I had it. Cost eighty-five thousand several years ago, when money was money.'

'Sounds like a palace.'

'They have great taste, Patricia and Tom. They entertain a bit. But they aren't ostentatious. It's you women and your babies turn them into millionaires.'

'His wife is always beautifully dressed. Never a hair out of place. I always feel scruffy when I meet her, just as I always feel retarded when I meet Eleanor.'

'What nonsense,' Hugh said. 'You always look very nice. As for Eleanor, I hope you don't set any store by her opinions.' He thought he had slipped it in very well. When she did not respond, he took it as a cue for his next remark. 'She isn't really a suitable companion for you. She has weird ideas. Way-out ideas.'

'I don't think they are way-out. I think she is just honest and she doesn't suffer fools gladly. That makes people wary of her. But I'm not wary. I like her. She just makes me feel inferior, but then maybe I *am* inferior. To her.'

'What you need is a little more self-confidence. I shouldn't love you if I thought you were inferior. Doesn't that prove something?'

'It could prove *you're* inferior too.'

She meant it as a joke, he knew. So why did it sting? He blundered on. 'I think you're seeing too much of her. She's nearly twenty years older than you.'

'So are you. You don't think you are too old for me, do you?'

'It's different for a man,' Hugh said. 'And I'm young for my age. Eleanor is old and bitter. She was old and bitter ten years ago. I know it isn't all her fault. But a lot of it is. Other people suffer disappointment and betrayal, and there are two sides to every story.'

'I don't think she's bitter. I don't think she's old. And I wish you would stop treating me as if I were a piece of fragile merchandise that you have to protect and cherish. You don't *own* me, you know.'

He took the next corner too fast and they drove on for a few miles before he answered. 'We can't talk while I'm driving. But really, Eve. Lately you've changed. You aren't the girl I met a year ago at all. What has happened? If it's something I have done, please tell me. I want to know. You know how I feel about you. You're the only one in the world for me. When you go on like that, you make me miserable.'

Why couldn't she have fallen for a Ginger Man, she thought, watching the country flash by. A lecherous charlatan would have been easy to kick. 'I don't want to make you miserable. Maybe I'm just not ready for marriage.'

He had half expected it, but when it came it was too sudden. It took his breath away. She did not help him, but retreated into the woolly collar of her cardigan.

'Most young women of your age are married or engaged. What makes you feel you aren't ready? Do you mean you aren't ready for marriage with me?'

'I don't know what it is. Please let's not talk about it now.'

'We have to talk about it some time. What's wrong with now? I like to know where I stand,' he said grimly.

'We can't discuss anything as serious as this while we're driving. Can't we just leave it for a while? Forget all about it until the weekend is over.'

'No, it can't wait until the weekend is over,' he said furiously. 'And don't worry about my driving. I'm perfectly in control. Are you, or are you not, having doubts about marriage?'

'I've always had doubts. You know that. You've always known it.'

'Yes. You're right. I *have* always known it. But I never took them seriously before. I thought you were just being female or something. Playing hard to get.'

'It's hopeless,' she said. 'That's the very kind of remark that makes me see how hopeless it all is. You have such a peculiar

196

idea about women, Hugh. I don't know why. Maybe all men think the way you do. I suppose they must, judging by the extraordinary references to women one comes across throughout literature. I find it insulting. And I have found you very insulting at times, but I know you didn't mean to be. I *have* loved you. But perhaps I can't love any man who could say the kind of things you say, because, even though they are half in joke, underneath they are in earnest. I'm not the type to take up cudgels and do battle to change attitudes. I want to live in peace.'

'What about placards and marches? And knocking around with Eleanor? It's an odd way of looking for peace.'

'I don't knock around with her. I hardly ever see her. And she doesn't make me half as angry as you do.'

'I thought I only bored you.'

'You never bore me. You just make me unhappy.'

She linked her hands tightly together when she said it, trying to lock out both the pain she knew he felt and her own reflected pain.

'Well, that's straight enough. I know where I stand now. What I cannot understand is why you didn't say it before.'

'It didn't happen before. I didn't really know how I felt. I was confused. You are very persuasive, and it was so easy to love you. I did try to tell you, or warn you, but you never listened. I just got swept along. Anyway, there's your family. I don't think they approve of me.'

'They have nothing to do with it. You can leave them out of it. This is entirely between you and me.'

'I can't leave them out of it. When I saw you at home with them and realised how close you all were, I knew I could never fit in. In a way that's what happened to Eleanor too. You couldn't accept her difference. You never learned to live with it.'

'She never learned to live with ours.'

'I think she did. But there was only one of her and so many of you.'

'You make us sound like the Mafia.'

'In a way, you are. You are still a tribe. I may be quiet, but I

197

am very independent and I won't allow myself to be swallowed up in someone else's life. I won't end up like Eleanor, soul-destroyed. If I can't fight the system, and I don't think I can, then I won't live in it.'

'You've got the real trendy jargon. What system? Don't let Eleanor condition you. She's warped and twisted and if you look at things her way you'll never be happy. This is all her fault. Bloody bitch. She's like a malevolent witch. She should be burned at the stake, and everyone like her.'

Eve had never seen him in such a state. Full of grief for him, she said, '*I'd* rather be burned at the stake than make you suffer.'

'That's very melodramatic, and it's not necessary. I'll get over you. You aren't the first woman to make a fool of a man, and I don't suppose you'll be the last.'

She sank back into the seat, closing her eyes, delivering up her life to him. He could crash the car at any moment and kill them both and she didn't care. But he drove with his usual caution, with a restraint of the kind trained athletes might use when marshalling their energies for some testing event.

A dozen or so cars were parked in the courtyard when they arrived at Adrian's place.

'What a fabulous setting,' Eve said, marvelling at the mixture of late summer green in the hedges and trees, the brilliance of little fields newly mown and the magnificence of the sea.

'If you like that sort of thing,' Hugh replied. 'Very romantic of course. Suitable for the young and foolish.'

He seemed ponderously middle-aged as he levered himself up out of the car. She stood back, watching him lock it, smoothing his hair, glancing into the side mirror and brushing off loose hairs or dust with his gloved hands. He had always been ponderous and pompous, probably even as a baby. It had nothing to do with age and it should have been fitting, but somehow it wasn't. It was just Hugh. Stuffy, kind, loving, unlovable Hugh. She felt cruel assessing him, and she did it deliberately so that all links between them might be severed. Perhaps not tonight, but one by one and little by little, the chain they had forged to hold them together had to be destroyed.

A small crowd had already assembled in the hall. Eleanor, dressed in a long tweed skirt and cape-like top, was ladling out glasses of punch from a large soup tureen. Adrian was busy handing around paper plates with unidentified objects of food on them.

'Good God,' Hugh commented crankily, 'not squares of brown bread and smoked salmon yet again. I couldn't bear it.'

'Mackerel,' Eve said, sampling one tentatively. 'And quite tasty.'

'I'm sorry for being so gruff on the way down. It wasn't the time or place for that kind of conversation,' Hugh said to her privately.

'Never mind. We're here now. We might as well enjoy ourselves.'

'A challenging thought for a philistine like myself. But I'll do my best.'

They moved from the hall, which was heated by a gas fire. into a long narrow room. At one end a kind of dais had been placed, and on it a chair, a table with some books and two wine bottles with candles stuck in their necks. Along the unplastered walls hung rugs and tapestries of varying shades and degrees of wear. They looked as if they had been hung up just before people arrived, without any concession to harmony of colour or shape. Between the narrow slit windows iron brackets held more candles, all of them lit and flickering in the movements of air caused by the guests settling themselves in the chairs around the room. With relief Hugh saw that some of the chairs were upholstered and those with wooden seats had cushions. In the centre of the room burned a charcoal fire in an iron basket.

'I hope there's sufficient ventilation,' Hugh whispered to Eve as they made for the two most comfortable-looking chairs. 'Where's the smoke from the fire going?'

'Straight through the hole in the roof, I think. It's quite early, this tower. Certainly pre-fireplace.'

'Adrian's mad. I've only been here in the summer and it's

199

always freezing. How does he stick it in the winter? Has he central heating?'

'I doubt it. Eleanor mentioned gas heaters. And apparently there's electricity in the flat annexe. I think it's lovely. Full of character.'

'Bad character,' Hugh said sourly. 'It's neither original nor beautiful, and it has no purpose in today's world, unless he's going to be attacked by arrow-shooting neighbours.'

'Maybe that's what he's hoping for. Perhaps he has boiling tar ready to pour on top of them.'

'Oh well, the punch is good.'

They sipped from their glasses, savouring the spicy warmth.

Adrian stood at the table, reading his poetry by the light of the candles, while Eleanor sat on a cushion on the floor, literally at his feet. The candles cast shadows on the wall, and the great stones behind emitted a forcefulness, a thrusting power, hardly softened by the shabby rugs. Adrian's husky voice recited ideas and images Eve would never have believed him capable of conceiving. Every now and again she glanced at Eleanor's rapt face as she sat drinking in each syllable, each phrase. The candlelight softened her profile and gave a sheen to her hair.

The audience clapped with enthusiasm and uttered encouraging words – 'Sound man', 'You have it, boy, you have it' – in much the same way as the black American congregations joined in the exultation of their preachers. Adrian looked the part, with his long, cream-coloured *báinín* coat and his hair brushed smoothly behind his ears. He might have been a druid or a bard. Such grace and style were a pleasure to observe. For once, an unselfconscious revelation had been permitted and accepted. His face seemed different, not so much soft as gentle. Eve had never noticed his hair before, and now observed it following the line of his brow, the curve of his cheekbone. He must have been a beautiful young man. When he turned his back to bend over his papers on the table behind him, she was astonished to feel a pang of tenderness at the glimpse of the thin patch on his crown and the shimmer of skin showing through the grey.

He held his audience, never once losing them by a faltering line or a flat phrase. His theme was the landscape around him, the rock, sea, birds, thundering ocean and the godly loneliness. He was in his element, and Eleanor looked as if she had found her final resting place. Entranced was the word to describe her. Ravished, seduced, entranced.

Afterwards, the congratulations seemed unnecessary. It would have been more appropriate for the audience to have slipped away quietly, leaving its aura behind, still basking in the beneficence of its sun god. When they did leave, some of the magic had been dissipated and at Eve's side Hugh made a hearty remark which angered her. Had he been only embarrassed rather than moved?

'What are you scowling at?' he asked her.

'Didn't you think Adrian was fantastic?'

'Fantastic? Yes. I suppose I did. He certainly held the audience.'

'He looked like a druid. I felt transported a thousand years back in time.'

Women and their imagination, he thought. They get carried away by poets. Even Eleanor.

'He did have something of the priest about him,' he admitted, trying to be fair, 'or, more accurately, the prophet.'

'What makes you say that?'

'Adrian is too much of an individual to be a priest. The priest is bound to the sanctuary, slave to tradition, the guardian and inheritor of rites. The prophet and the poet must speak only out of their own inspiration. They may call it the voice of God or their muse, but it is their own, and they know it. It is what gives them their untouchable air. It's what makes them most vulnerable. The prophets and poets are first to be burned in the market place, with their paraphernalia, books and the like.'

'I always thought women were first. All those witches.'

'Same thing. Same thing.'

He got up as he spoke, as if his words were a dismissal, as if he already recognised that she had left him in spirit and he could salvage some of his pride by marking her departure. The way he turned from her, the deliberately unconcerned air with

201

which he shrugged himself into his coat, added to the effect. *Nunc dimittis*, she murmured. *Et absolvo te*. There had to be ritual words for such release. Some recognisable ceremony by which the severance could be made easier. The familiar words of an incantation. It hurt that in one of the few moments when he had shown some sensitivity, some insight which she could share, in that moment, just as she was drawn towards him, he rejected her and withdrew.

Eleanor joined Adrian. They stood reading something from the same page, heads touching, each illuminated by the candlelight. They turned, it seemed on the same pivot, to smile at Hugh as he approached them. Eve, watching from her shadowed corner, could see that each smile had a similar quality, reminiscent of indulgent parents receiving the polite thank-you of children leaving a birthday party. One of the candles guttered and went out. Adrian reached into the drawer of the table and brought out a flash lamp.

'We'll have to go back to modern aids,' he said and quenched the other candle near him. The cold battery light found the familiar lines and grooves in his face, even the pouches under his eyes. For a fanciful moment Eve expected him to collapse at a touch or explode like a paper bag from which all air has suddenly been excluded. Eleanor did touch him lightly on the arm, but he did not explode, nor even collapse. He only shrank back a little, as if folding in on himself for an instant to draw some energising force before responding to her. 'It went well, I think.'

'It was wonderful,' Eleanor said.

'It was a very successful evening,' Hugh agreed. 'You must do it again.'

Adrian looked alarmed at the prospect but said nothing, and Eve, thinking of Hugh's observations a few minutes earlier, was silent too. Hugh gave the impression that he considered it an entertainment which could be repeated like a coffee morning or a beer evening. Did he not understand, in spite of what he had said, that they had all been part of an evening which could never be repeated, like youth, or first love, or the first drawn breath after birth?

'I have your rooms ready,' Adrian said. 'But first we'll have a cup of hot milk, for the sake of all our ulcers.'

'Speak for yourself,' Eleanor told him, brisk again. 'I've never had one and I don't intend ever to get one.'

'Don't get them, give them, I suppose,' Hugh said sarcastically.

'I'm glad to see we are all back to healthy acerbity,' Adrian commented. 'I thought for a moment you were going to kiss my feet.'

'I was tempted,' Eleanor said lovingly, 'until I saw your socks.'

Even Hugh smiled. 'I'll have a whiskey in my milk. If you don't mind.'

'I do mind. It's dear bloody stuff.'

'Why don't you keep a cow?'

'For whiskey?'

'That's a thought. All we need is the right fodder, the right chemical combination, and an extra stomach in the cow for long-term fermentation.'

'The cow has an extra stomach. Didn't you know?'

Eve trailed behind them to the kitchen, excluded from their middle-aged humour but not caring too much. Eventually she would be reduced to the same repartee, the last defence against pot bellies and jowls. She paused for a moment outside the kitchen door, waiting for Eleanor to call cheerily, 'Come on slow coach,' but Eleanor was fetching the carton of milk from the fridge and Adrian was turning on the gas cooker and Hugh was lounging in the most comfortable chair. Probably, if she went home, they would hardly notice she had gone.

'Milk and water?' Adrian asked as she entered. For a moment she was shocked by this implied comment on her own character.

'Milk and whiskey,' Hugh said.

'Get up, Toad of Toad Hall,' Eleanor said severely to him, 'and fix your own. I'm not your servant.'

'Ah, for one blissful second I thought domesticity had finally got to you.'

203

'That'll be the day,' Eleanor replied, but not as firmly as Eve expected.

'She's nobody's fool, our Eleanor. No apron strings, kitchen sink and bawling babies,' Adrian said from the stove, tying his own apron around his middle and then carefully measuring the milk into the saucepan.

'Other people's babies, that's my life,' Eleanor sang cheerfully.

'We're all in the same boat,' Hugh said.

'It doesn't mean the same to you. After all, you can't have a baby, but I . . . ' They rushed to fill the silence, Adrian, Eleanor and Eve, with busy little actions. Eve clattered mugs onto the table. Hugh ignored it. 'I can't say it ever struck me as a deprivation,' he said. 'Nine months of pregnancy, morning sickness, and afterwards the stink of nappies, sleepless nights, first teeth, whooping cough and teenage spots and sex experimentation. It's all a great bore.'

'Well, that cuts you out of the father list.'

'I've already been cut out. Or haven't you noticed? I should have thought you would have been the first to know, Eleanor.'

'What *is* the man talking about?' She turned to Adrian.

'I think it has something to do with Eve.'

'Oh.'

'As if you didn't know,' Hugh said with venom. 'I've never known you to be lost for words before. I suppose you're feeling guilty.'

'Guilty? Why the hell should I feel guilty? It's nothing to do with me.'

'Isn't it? All those little hen-parties. All that nit-picking, soul-searching, exchange of confidences.'

'A neat mixture of metaphor and cliché,' Adrian murmured into his hot milk.

'What a literary hack you are after all,' Hugh said. 'You turn every emotion into verbal acrobatics.'

'Nobody's perfect,' Adrian replied complacently.

'I have never looked for perfection in humanity,' Hugh said, 'only a little decency, a little honour.'

'Wowee! The man bleeds,' Eleanor crowed.

'We both have fed as well,' chanted Adrian.

Hugh leaped up from the chair and clenched his fists in rage.

'Hey,' Adrian exclaimed in astonishment. 'Don't get mad.'

Hugh sat down and reached for the whiskey bottle. 'I like my milk well diluted,' he said as he deliberately filled the glass to the brim.

Eve said, 'Goodnight, all,' and turned to leave.

'I'll escort you upstairs, modom, in just one moment,' Adrian said, and winked behind her back at Eleanor before following Eve from the room.

'Goodnight, Eve,' Eleanor called.

Hugh took a large swallow of the whiskey-diluted milk. It was revolting.

'God, what a face,' Eleanor said. 'How can you drink the stuff if it tastes the way you look?'

'Everything tastes the way I look,' Hugh replied grandly. 'Usually porridgy, suet puddingly, bland. Tonight everything tastes curdled.'

'You poor old fellow,' Eleanor commiserated. 'But I could have told you. It wouldn't have worked. Better to know now than later.'

'No, it isn't better to know now than later. Later I would have had something apart from a broken heart, a past, even a bitter one, a child, maybe a son.'

'You can always find someone else if all you want is to retire to stud.'

'You are so coarse, Eleanor.'

'I beg your pardon. I thought that's what you were saying.'

'You know what I was saying. You're a bit of a prig, Eleanor, for all your bravado. You're so full of your own problems. You think no one but you ever had a broken marriage or ever suffered. We all suffer.'

'Oh, pardon me, sir. When were you last raped?'

'Jesus, you should see a psychiatrist. I really mean that. Next thing you'll be going around with scissors castrating every poor guy who looks crooked at you.'

'Ah! The castration complex! All the familiar symptoms. I'll go if you'll go. Can you recommend a good woman psychiatrist

205

who won't dish up the same formula: Oedipal complex, penis envy, smother-mother.'

'There aren't any *good* women psychiatrists. They haven't the brains for it.'

'I don't know why we even try to communicate. I've never liked you. I've never even pretended to like you. And you've never liked me. I don't know what you have against me. Apart from an instinctive distaste for your personal qualities, which are not really your fault but the unfortunate result of inherited genes, I've never done you any harm.'

'You ruined Donogh.'

'I ruined Donogh?'

'He was too much of a man for you and you couldn't take it. If it weren't for you, he could be at home here with his family, maybe in practice with me. You drove him out of the country with your lies and your complaints.'

'I don't remember ever complaining to you.'

'No. But you came running to Mother. Telling poor Mother all those terrible things. I've never said this to you before, but in a way you were responsible for her death. It broke her heart when Donogh had to leave.'

'I never knew she had a heart. She hid it very well. I didn't complain to her. I was twenty years old and frightened. The bruises took ages to fade that time. I trusted your family. I left the baby with them. I trusted her. I never dreamed she'd let Donogh take her away. I never dreamed she would go that far.'

'You shouldn't have gone running to Adrian. Dragging him into it. Donogh's friend and my friend. It was just like you. You never cared about anyone but yourself. Selfish, selfish, selfish. That's all you ever were. And you wanted to wear the trousers. He was too good for you, a fine strong man, full of fun and energy. You tried to emasculate him and he wouldn't let you. I'm not saying he should have beaten you. You know I don't approve of violence. But I know you must have provoked him.'

'The perfect non sequitur. I was beaten, therefore I must have provoked. You're improving, Hugh. Mellowing with age. I'll admit I provoke you! I spend my life doing to you what I should have done to your brother. Pricking your pompous balloon.'

'And you ask me what harm you have done me?'

'Purely rhetorical. I don't think I put it that way. And I'm amazed to learn that you actually miss my ex-husband or would ever have considered sharing a practice with him.'

'We always got on very well together. I don't know why you should be amazed.'

'You were always in awe of him. A little jealous too, I think.'

'Nonsense. Men don't feel jealous of one another. That's for the bum-tit brigade.'

He had never said such a thing before. He had never made Eleanor flinch before. She winced as if in pain and he was glad. A delightful satisfaction set his veins throbbing and his heart thumping. He reached for the whiskey bottle again.

'Re-fuelling?' Adrian said behind him. 'What's wrong with you, Eleanor?'

'I think I have just been paid in kind,' Eleanor said. 'And Hugh wants to get drunk.'

'Well, the sooner the better, if that's the case. But you and I had better retire before he forces us to join him.'

'I wouldn't force you to do anything. I believe in free speech, civil rights for all, equal pay for equal work. I believe in all the goodies. I just don't go around being martyred for it or preaching about it or waving placards. We are all entitled to do our own thing, as the young so pithily put it.' He held the whiskey bottle with affection and looked with already blurring vision into his glass of curdled toddy.

'Who waves placards?'

'Little Eve. Innocent little Eve. Martyred, preaching, placard-waving Eve.'

'I see he has a bad case of the let-downs. Better now than later. Always better to find out before. Think what a life of misery you have just spared yourself.'

'I didn't ask to be spared. Did I ask your advice? My miserable life is my own affair. Toddle off to your lecherous bed and leave me to my nightmares.'

They left him, arm in arm, he was sure, although he did not

207

glance around, just as he was sure they smiled conspiratorially at one another, the way lovers exchange looks across crowded rooms.

'Some enchanted evening,' Hugh hummed drunkenly to himself on his fifth whiskey. They were upstairs. They had closed the door of the bedroom, they were climbing into bed, they were wrapped around each other, legs, arms and mouths in places where they shouldn't be. Or were they too middle-aged for that? By his seventh whiskey he didn't care.

At ten to three he woke, his neck stiff from lying in the twisted position across his arm on the table. When he raised his head he began to retch. He reached the sink just in time and vomited up the total contents of his stomach and his upper dentures. He knew as he heard the set rattle in the cold delft of Adrian's ancient sink that he had reached the nadir of his life. 'Sweet Jesus,' he groaned in genuine prayer, 'sweet agonised crucified Jesus, was Your betrayal worse than mine?' He gargled with a glass of water but the insipid taste made him feel even more sick. He rooted in the cupboard over the sink and found two bottles of beer hidden behind the washing-up liquid and the detergents. His hand shook while he poured the two into one pint glass. Into the depths of the fireside armchair Hugh lowered himself, carefully arranging his camel-hair overcoat on his knees. He leaned his head thankfully against the upholstered back of the chair and, mouth slightly open, slightly snoring, he slept.

17

Dawn did not wake him, nor did the chattering of birds, nor the bawling of hungry calves, nor the clank of buckets as Eleanor helped Adrian feed his backyard animals, the two calves, the sow with her bonhams, six hens and one arrogant bantam cock. But Eve, filling the kettle to make the morning tea, woke him, not by the gentle sound of her movements but by her presence. Her expression of pity changed to one of distaste when he opened his eyes and stared at her.

'What time is it?'

'Time you had a wash and shave,' she said.

'Ah,' he said humorously. 'The lecturer has now taken over from the do-gooder. By noon I suppose we will have the feminist, by sundown the lesbian.'

'You're talking nonsense. Why don't you wash and shave?'

'Because I do not choose to. This smell, this odour now emanating from me, is not sweat or grime, not the product of honest toil. It is merely the remnants of an emptied stomach now putrefying in my nostrils and on my skin. Of such corruption are we all. Even you, Eve. It is a reminder of our last end, a foretaste of our fatal decomposition, the slimy, maggoty grand finale of our lives.'

'I have never heard you so lyrical.'

'I have never been so drunk. I have never been drunk in any degree, now that I think of it. There's a lot more to me than meets the eye. And now your eye won't see it. Isn't that sad?'

'Very sad,' she said.

Adrian came rushing through and started pulling bottles

209

out of a small cupboard. 'Scour,' he complained. 'Bloody scour. And I nurse them like babies. There's no justice.' He grabbed a container and vanished.

'Hey presto,' Hugh said. 'The vanishing-poet trick. The mystery of the malingering medic. Soon we may expect to see little lyrical articles about how the west was won appearing in prestigious magazines and papers. How I managed to escape from the terrors of petrol fumes and faced the simple hardships of real life. Every twenty years or so the back-to-the-land syndrome appears. And the land either devours them all or pukes them up. But if it gets him out of medicine it will be worth it. He was never much good anyway.'

'As far as I can see,' Eve commented, 'you're the only one puking around here.'

'I puke. The land pukes. You puke. He, she or it pukes. *Nous pukons, vous pukez. Ils pukent go léir.*'

She managed not to laugh.

'There is also of course that other linguistic incantation which we need not go into now since it would undoubtedly corrupt the morals of the young – to wit, *amo, amas, amat, amamus, amatis, amant.* Or better still, *non amo,* because non capable of amoing. Because there is too much of the latent lesbian about the non-amo-er.'

She did not have to try to avoid laughter then. 'That's the second time in the past few minutes you have used that word in reference to me.'

'What word?' He looked around, searching for witnesses to his innocence. 'What word? Oh, *that* word. *Lesbian.*' He said it in a tone that managed to convey hatred, bitterness and pain all at once. She reached across the table and hit him hard on the cheek.

'That stung,' he said calmly.

'It was meant to.' She was shaking a little, he saw with pleasure.

'I don't mean the slap. You aren't even able to hit properly. I mean the word. You were stung. And I'm sure there is some significance in that.'

'The only significance lies in the fact that you were insulting

210

because you meant to be insulting. I'm sorry I hit you.'

'Don't apologise, please. It's all right for women to hit men. Didn't you know? It's when it's the other way around it's wrong.'

'You can hit much harder.'

'Luckily we can defend ourselves.'

'I forgot men were such helpless, hard-done-by creatures. I forgot you needed to be protected from wicked women, especially wicked lesbians who might put magic spells on you, poison you, cook your food whilst menstruating, give you nightmares. I forgot you had all those refuges for battered husbands.'

'We don't need them. We have public houses. We cry into our beer.'

Eleanor came rushing in and began to search in the cupboard.

'Having a nice time?' Hugh said.

'The white goat has mastitis,' she said. 'Anyone know where Adrian keeps his vet stuff? Oh good, this looks like it. It's lovely out. Make us a cup of tea while you're at it. Back in a minute.'

'Busy, busy, busy bee. Haven't the time for a cup of tea,' Hugh sang.

'I've never seen you like this,' Eve told him.

'Lots of ways and places you've never seen me. On the loo, in the bath, with my teeth out. I nearly lost them last night.'

'Oh, Hugh.' She had to laugh. She ran to him and put her arms around him.

He pushed her away. 'It's too late for that.'

'Why is it too late?'

'Because you should have taken me at face value first. The analysis should come much later, when we have time for it. Love should be spontaneous. Especially when you have youth on your side. If you can't give that, what else can you give?'

'I never expected to be taken at face value.'

'With your face you didn't need anything else.'

'You mean *you* didn't need anything else. I'm not just a pretty face, you know.'

He clapped his hands to his ears. 'I didn't hear that. I'll pretend you didn't say that.'

'There you go again,' she said. 'It's hopeless. You're all the same – you, Eleanor and Adrian. You go cliché-hunting, you're word predators. The rest of us fall into traps we don't even know are there. Can't you just accept things for what they are? Babbling words included – they are just a desperate effort to explain.'

'That's your trouble. You seem to feel it necessary to explain everything. It's your generation's disease. Usually everything as it relates to yourselves. I think you have been over-educated.'

'How can one possibly be over-educated? It's a contradiction in terms.'

'Here we go again,' he sighed. 'Round and round the merry go round.'

Throughout the morning Eleanor and Adrian joked with one another, gazing into each other's eyes as if by slipping one glance sideways they risked losing each other for ever. They sucked the honey of each other's speech as if their lips were glued together in an unending kiss. It would have been unthinkable to have come between them, unforgivable to have begrudged them their pleasure.

At lunchtime Hugh said, 'You don't know how disgusting you have both become.'

'Jealous?' Eleanor asked.

'Of course not. But you must admit it's all a bit ridiculous. Middle-aged passion.'

'At least we are both middle-aged. We share the same torpid decline. Some comfort in that, don't you think?'

'Comfort, yes. If that's all you're looking for.'

'What were you looking for with little Miss Muffet?' Adrian chimed in.

'Leave her out of it,' Hugh said angrily as Eve got up quickly and left.

'A neat trick that,' Adrian mused. 'She slips away with the greatest of ease, her little tail wagging behind in the breeze.'

'Funny how derogatory that word "little" can sound,'

Eleanor said. 'Almost always applied to the female. The little woman. The little man, on the other hand, is a literary device. Large heroism in a small parcel. David against Goliath. The righteous oppressed against the world.'

'No one could call *you* little,' Adrian said fondly, chewing on a piece of cold cod.

'I should hope not,' Eleanor said devoutly.

'My God, you're disgusting,' Hugh yelled in fury. 'Disgusting and cruel and complacent. You should see yourselves.'

'O wad some power the giftie gie us to see oursels as others see us,' Adrian chanted.

'Is that pure Scots or pure pidgin?' Eleanor asked.

'You go too far. You go much too far,' Hugh replied bitterly. He was filled to the top of his head, it seemed, with suffering, with humiliation, grief and loss. He was powerless to describe the variety of his emotions. He wanted to burst into wild sobbing, like a woman, weak and feeble-minded, or he would lift up the chair and smash it over the heads of the lovers before breaking everything in the room. He would get drunk again. But his stomach revolted against the last, and years of tradition and restraint kept him from the first. He did as Eve did. He left the room.

'What about a little rhyme for that exit?' Eleanor asked Adrian.

'Poor old Hugh,' he said. 'Perhaps we were too hard on him.'

'And not hard on Eve?'

'She's young,' he said sourly. 'She can take it.'

'That's another convenient myth. When you're young you *can't* take it. You can't even forget. You just become – ' She paused, and then said coolly, 'Like you, Adrian. Sour. Like you.'

He stood up and began to clear away the dishes. She made no effort to help him.

'Let's get out of here,' he said. 'We'll drive to the top of the hill and I'll show you the kingdoms of the world spread below you.'

Eve heard them go. Lying on her bed in the gloomy stonewalled cell that Adrian called the guest room, she knew it was Adrian's car by its loud roar. Exhaust pipes never lasted in the salty air of the Atlantic coast, he said. Around here no one cares. The seas roar, the asses roar, the cars roar.

The weekend had become a nightmare. It was even worse than the days with Hugh's family. There, at least, good manners prevented small animosities from turning into large hatreds. There was much to be said for the traditional courtesies, the silences, even the half-hinted truths. The veneer, so carefully cultivated and however thin, kept everything from boiling over. She had been too young, too gauche, to understand that. There was nothing left now between herself and Hugh, not even good manners or friendship. Yet, she could hardly blame herself that she had at last been forced to acknowledge her own uncertainty, even her own fear of what had begun to seem like a life sentence. Was it too much to expect from him some understanding and consideration instead of the anger and maudlin self-pity he had shown? She had been ashamed of him and for him, and lying on the bed even the pity she had felt now began to dissolve. It was wonderful to be loved, but when you saw the other side – the bullying, the possessiveness – it was a relief not to be loved. It would be better if he could hate her for a while. He might then learn only to dislike her and he might finally become indifferent. She doubted if she would ever be totally indifferent to him. He would be a part of her past, an entry in a diary, a love letter, a memory of a certain summer. Since she already cherished childhood memories because they symbolised the steps on her way to adulthood, she knew that some day this episode would be a vital part of her final maturing. The fact that it was painful made it all the more effective. She did not know what value it might have for Hugh. Perhaps it would prove destructive. But she could not be held responsible. He was older than she, more experienced, and she had not seduced him.

She packed her overnight bag and brought it down to the hall. Hugh was sitting under a wall-hanging depicting Cuchulain and Ferdia's fight at the Ford.

'Are you ready to leave now?' he asked. 'I intended going for a walk. Have you any idea what their plans are?'

'No, Hugh. I'm sorry, Hugh.'

'Stop saying that,' he said. 'It means nothing. I don't blame you. You're just too easily influenced by other people. But not by me apparently. Never by me.'

She wandered out through the arched doorway into a little fuchsia-fringed field. A few hens picked in a nettle patch. Clouds of lavender and pearl moved across the skies. She lay down on the grass to observe them. Her eyes grew tired and she dozed.

She woke cramped and chilled and returned to the tower. The hall was empty. In the kitchen the sink was piled with dirty dishes. She heated water in the electric kettle and washed them. She could hear the calves bawling in the yard and went out to see them. They pushed their heads through the bars of the stall and frantically nuzzled at her skirt. In a little paddock beside the yard Adrian's white goats grazed.

'All he ever does is play at everything.' Hugh's voice came from behind her. 'He's not a real doctor, or a real farmer. He just dabbles. A bit of this, a bit of that. And he won't make a real husband. He hasn't got stamina.'

'Perhaps Eleanor doesn't want a husband.'

'Every woman of Eleanor's age wants a husband. She wants love. She knows that it can't last. It's a flash in the pan, a few moments of indulgence.'

'Aren't you talking about lust?'

'Miss Semantics. And no, I'm not.'

'Words mean things. If they don't, why use them at all? Even the clichés you sneer at mean things to some people. All we have to do is learn the right words to express the right feelings and forget about the others.'

'Language is dialogue. The other person has to understand the language.'

'So what,' she said impatiently. 'We have to make the effort to get out of bed in the morning; we might as well make the effort to communicate properly.'

'It's all borrowed,' he said. 'That's what I object to.

215

Everything has become a jargon. Medicine has one jargon and I understand it because I have to. Poetry has another and they call it art. Your obsession with rights and status is another. One cannot understand them all.'

'It's just a code. If you want to grasp the ideas you have to learn the code. If it's worth it, you make the effort. You made it for medicine. Why not for me?'

She shouldn't have said it. She knew it was a mistake as soon as the words left her mouth. He turned eagerly to her. 'I can learn. I am sure I can learn if you have the patience to teach me.'

'Oh, Hugh,' she said hopelessly. 'It's more than that.'

His face closed up again and he turned away. He began to talk about Adrian's poetry. He said he wasn't a judge, but then who was? People who set themselves up as judges merely formed another elite to make more rules. Eleanor criticised medicine for the very vices she accepted in poetry. And poets, he said, were the worst chauvinists of all, probably because they were not men in the traditional sense. They used women as tools to their trade. Muses. Surprisingly, he revealed that he had enjoyed the work of women poets. He thought they were less pretentious, more honest than men.

'Perhaps I am not a proper judge,' he said. 'I only judge by integrity, by good faith, by the honest use of the craft. Adrian's poetry moves me, but I think it is because he writes it in Irish and that has haunting memories for me. I don't know if he is really a good poet. He's not a good doctor. He is careless and unpredictable. He may well be a careless poet. He is a good performer. But then, so are circus clowns.'

'Bring in the clowns,' she said wistfully and he hummed the tune to himself as he moved away again. He met Eleanor in the driveway. Adrian had dropped her off and gone on to the village for some supplies.

'I have news for you both,' Eleanor sang. 'Adrian and I have decided to take the plunge.'

'Congratulations,' Hugh growled and strode off.

'Let him go. I need a more cheerful face near me.' She was so cheery herself that it was, to use Hugh's phrase, almost indecent – especially, thought Eve, somewhat dishonestly, given that Eleanor had practically made the funeral arrangements for her and Hugh's affair. Where were the bodeful looks, the dark hints, to threaten the future of this happy couple? Apart from Hugh, any bad fairies at the christening?

'I suppose you know what you're doing.' Eve felt a little triumph at her mastery of the occasion.

'Ooooh. 'Ark at 'er.' Eleanor's cockney imitation was always bad. 'Wot abaht congratulations then?'

'I hope you both have all the happiness you deserve,' Eve said, still masterful.

Eleanor threw her arms around her and laughed. 'Cheese. Say cheese, and I'll add you to the fossils in my album. You're making it fast into the big bad world.'

'Whilst you gallop off into fairyland?'

'I hope there's no sinister implication there. I have a brilliant idea. Hugh's family live only fifteen miles from here. Let's zip over and tell them the news.'

'What about Hugh?'

'I'll leave him a note. I couldn't be bothered looking for him now. He's going to sulk for weeks. Anyway, he never visits them in September and he has always put me off. It's some ancient family taboo. Maybe their father's anniversary or something. You know the way they are. I can't wait to see their faces. Ruth will probably swoon.'

Eve allowed herself to be persuaded. Hugh's family did not like uninvited guests. They liked to be well prepared. But the drive along the coast was a pleasant one. There was nothing more interesting to do. Eleanor wrote a note to Hugh and left it pinned to the milk carton on the kitchen table.

18

The drive took half an hour. Throughout, Eleanor talked without pause. Afterwards, Eve remembered the journey as a revelatory experience, similar to the evening of poetry, but with a deeper and sadder significance. The sunshine, the brilliant blues and greens of sky, sea and land imposed a multi-dimensional quality on Eleanor's monologue. Her story, as it unfolded, seemed so much a part of the landscape in spite of, or perhaps because of, its tragic undercurrents that she could never afterwards travel the same road without hearing Eleanor's voice, its rhythms changing with remembered grief and anger and then joy at being able to love again and be loved. Her happiness at her present state was surely childish, and yet so full of hope, so full of gratitude, that it seemed at times like a canticle, her own Magnificat. For that half-hour she shed the skin of asperity and showed in full what she had only shown in glimpses before: the loving, warm, generous, humorous person she once was and should still have been.

She had been pregnant when she married Donogh, halfway through medical school, supported by an ageing aunt who could not forgive her for making so terrible a mistake. 'I remember my fury,' Eleanor said, 'when she called my poor unborn child a mistake. There was a terrible scene. Then she cried, and I cried, and she said of course she would help me. But she never really forgave me. She thought I had let her down. And of course, so I had. Donogh did the noble thing. I didn't realise he was being noble. I just thought we were both in it together and I felt very vulnerable and very responsible at the

218

same time. I knew that such a passionate affair as ours could hardly last but I did think it would settle down into comfortable acceptance.' She had had to give up medicine but kept up her reading in the expectation that she would be able to renew her studies.

For a while everything was fine, although now and again Donogh accused her of chaining him down. When she reminded him that she was chained too, he said that wasn't his fault, after all he hadn't had the baby. One evening, in a fit of rage, he said how did he *know* the baby was his anyway? She screamed at him, called him a bastard and he hit her. 'It was the first time,' Eleanor said, 'I had used bad language and it was the first time anyone had ever used force on me. I felt doubly violated. I hated him for saying what he did and for hitting me but I felt I deserved it because I had called him a foul name. It was like taking the first step down to hell.'

He began to stay out late, or not come home at all, and to drink more and more. Several times he was called out on emergencies and he was too drunk to turn up. The nurses at the hospital covered up for him and she made excuses. She turned into a drudge. The baby was teething and fretful at night. Donogh became increasingly violent and she began to fear him. One evening Adrian called to see her and when he saw her bruised face he insisted on her going to his flat. She knew Donogh was having affairs and she thought he would be glad to be rid of her. Instead he nearly beat down Adrian's door and in the end Adrian had to call the guards. It was all so humiliating.

'The funny thing was,' Eleanor said, 'I never thought of sleeping with Adrian. I never thought of him like that. He and Hugh and Donogh were such great friends. I was just part of the little gang. In a way, I thought I was privileged. Adrian had an old dinghy and we used to sail a bit. We played tennis together, badminton in the winter, even went on hikes through Kerry. We were very fit and outdoorish. I always love being out of doors. It's a penance to be inside.'

She had not wanted to involve Adrian on his own so she confided in Hugh. 'For ages afterwards,' she said, 'he wore a particularly martyred expression whenever we met, as if I had irreparably damaged the family escutcheon and crucified him in the process. Poor old Hugh. He's such an old stodge.' But he suggested that she and the baby spend a while in Tower Hill and give everyone a chance to cool down. The family were kind and welcoming, but to spare their feelings were told nothing of what was going on. She left the baby with them and went back to Donogh to try and sort things out. She said she wanted a divorce. He got into a rage and when she tried to run out of the room he caught her and flung her against the wall. He then kicked her while she lay on the ground, until she passed out. She had fractured ribs, a fractured collarbone, and clumps of her hair were torn out. Two weeks later, when she went back to Tower Hill, the baby was gone with Donogh.

'I suppose they told the truth,' she said, 'that they didn't know where he was. I was frantic. I tried every possible contact, every possible legal device. I once traced him to Camden Town but when I got there he had left. After about a year I gave up and went back to medical school. I knew he was seeking a church annulment because I kept getting letters and documents from ecclesiastical lawyers. I refused to sign. We knew what we were doing when we got married. If *I* couldn't get a divorce, why should *he* get a church annulment? One day some prissy priest telephoned me to say that my husband had been given an annulment on the grounds of his immaturity at the time of marriage. I hear he has married a good little Irish Catholic since then. Probably a native speaker to boot.' It was a marvellous kind of justice, she said, that she was able to love Adrian and he her after all those years. If one could believe in miracles that was surely a miracle.

'It must seem very inconsistent of me, maybe even dishonest after what I've said to you about marriage. But one can't reason about these things. I don't really want to reason. I just know the feeling is good and I want to hold on to it while I can. I'm sure Adrian feels something the same. Perhaps I shouldn't have warned you off Hugh, confirmed you in your worst fears. But you know as well as I do that, if you want to do something badly enough, nothing, nobody will stop you. I'm quite fond of

Hugh and his family but I wouldn't advise my worst enemy to marry one of them. There's a kind of a wild unreason lurking somewhere there. I've never told Hugh but some of my tinker patients are Creaghs and they don't come much wilder. It's different with Adrian. We use the same rules when we fight. That is very important. We fight without hatred. I'm comfortable with him. I can relax and be my real self. I can be dotty and motherly if I want to. It's a crazy thing, but I even see myself ironing his shirts and putting them away in a linen cupboard. I'm sure there's something symbolic in that! Putting away the baby's clothes in the linen cupboard had a rhythm to it which gave me a little security in a cruelly uncertain situation. For years afterwards, when I had finally given up hope of ever seeing her again, I used to have a flash of memory when I went to my own linen cupboard and I'd bury my head in a clean neatly folded towel and want to cry. Only I never could. I never could cry.'

'I don't know how you ever got over it,' Eve said, so full of pity and admiration her voice sounded choked to her own ears.

'I don't think I really did get over it until now. Do you know another crazy thing? I'm over forty and my chances are nil and the risks enormous, but I've even begun to think about a baby. It must be hormonal changes because of bloody love. Or is it the other way around? It's autumn and the oestrus is rising. Nest-making instincts. Babies. Jeez, I'm out of my mind.'

They were laughing in delight when they reached the entrance to Tower Hill. The house seemed to sleep in the afternoon sun. A few late summer trippers dotted the beach below them. The air was warm and scented and good to breathe. When they got out of the car Eve stretched her arms high above her head, while Eleanor attacked the front door in her usual imperious manner. There was a long silence after she rang and knocked. '"Is there anybody here?' said the traveller, knocking at the moonlit door."' She put on a deep dramatic voice. 'I'll try again. I know they're in. The side gate is open. They always close it when they leave the house empty.'

Eve began to feel nervous. She sensed curious, apprehensive eyes twitching around curtains upstairs. Her heart pounded as if they were about to commit some misdemeanour for which they would both be punished. Or, worse, as if they were poised to commit a crime against innocent and unsuspecting Sunday afternoon sleepers. Was Eleanor really so insensitive? Eve imagined the caustic remarks intermingled with the polite salutations. 'Oh! You're unexpected visitors. What a funny time to call. I do wish you had told us you were coming.' And the unspoken dread that these uncivilised callers might expect to be given refreshments, in the shape of tea and cake. Somewhere in the depths of the basement kitchen an unfortunate pair of female hands would have to whisk up a sponge or the ancient laws of hospitality might be seen to be broken. A creamy confection would make its casual appearance on the table with the hastily dusted best china and the silver teaspoons newly rescued from their wrappings of tissue paper. What desperate scurryings there would be to the bathroom to freshen up a tired face or pull a comb across straggling hair, what scutterings across bedroom floors to replace ragged and comfortable wool with clean respectability in the shape of matching skirt and jacket or Sunday dress.

'I don't think they're in,' Eve said, 'or it may be an inconvenient time to call.'

'Nonsense,' Eleanor replied. 'You're too sensitive. They know I don't stand on ceremony. And *I* know they're in. I can feel it. They're bloody well going to hear my good news if I have to stand here all night banging this door. The back kitchen window never closes properly. I could push you through and you could open the door. We'll catch them snoring their sherry off.'

She banged again. The door pulled back suddenly and Eleanor tripped over the doorstep, still hanging onto the knocker. Ruth stood inside. 'There's no one home. They are all gone out,' she said.

During the drive Eleanor had remarked how being in love heightened one's perceptions and Eve, standing behind her, wondered at her obtuseness in persisting with her unwelcome visit. Ruth, having opened the door wide as if deliberately to cause Eleanor to fall inwards, now closed it across so that her

222

tiny body was placed between the doorpost and the door itself.
Acutely embarrassed, Eve said that they had been passing by
and of course had no wish to intrude on Sunday privacy.

'Eleanor knows very well that we close the house to visitors
in September. There's no one here but myself and I'm busy
practising. That's why I didn't hear you knock for so long. I'm
sorry to have kept you. Come back next month. We'll all be
here then and it will be more convenient.'

'Have they gone on holiday?' Eve said, trying to extricate
Ruth from the situation, she looked so cross and confused.

'We never discuss our private affairs. Not even with
someone who will soon be one of the family. Not that you will
ever be quite family, of course. You must understand that.
Eleanor knows and she has accepted it. Eleanor is sensible.'

'But I'm giving up my place in the family, Ruthy dear,'
Eleanor announced sarcastically. 'If Eve wants it, she can have
it. Will that double her chances of belonging?'

'Don't be silly,' Ruth replied. 'It doesn't work like that. How
can you possibly give up your place? You were married to my
brother. Your daughter –' She clapped a hand over her mouth
and stopped.

'Don't worry, Ruth. I've got over all that. I've come to tell
you I'm getting married to Adrian and I hope you will wish me
luck. Let me in, for heaven's sake, so that I can talk to the
others.'

'Nonsense,' Ruth said. 'You can't get married. You can't get
a divorce. The Church doesn't allow it. Even if it did, the
family would never consider it. You live in Ireland, you know,
not in some other heathen country.'

'Look, Ruth.' Eleanor was getting angry. 'I haven't time to
explain the intricacies, ambiguities, hypocrisies of the law, civil
and religious, as it relates to marriage, and particularly as it
relates to women, and I have no intention of even attempting it
while I'm standing here on your doorstep. Believe me, I *am*
getting married. I thought you would wish me luck, or
happiness at least. Don't you think I deserve that?'

'Oh, indeed, I don't know what you deserve. You must
examine your own conscience. I wouldn't dream of interfering.

Wouldn't dream of it. None of us would. You always went your own way. Poor Donogh had to make the best of things. And he has a heart of gold, Donogh has, a heart of gold.'

Eleanor, whose face was getting red with temper, pushed her foot firmly against the door as Ruth tried to close it. 'You're getting nuttier by the year, Ruth. I want to talk to Bridget or Florence.'

'They don't want to talk to you,' Ruth hissed triumphantly. 'I mean, they wouldn't want to talk to you if they were here. They left me express instructions that I wasn't to talk to you either. If you don't pull your foot away, I'll squash it with this heavy door. It's solid oak.'

'Aunt Ruthy.' A girl's horrified voice came from behind Eve, who caught, just as she turned in its direction, the look of terror on Ruth's face. 'She's not usually rude, dear old thing,' the girl said apologetically. 'It must be the heat. Are you looking for someone? I got locked in the bathroom. I could hear the knocking and I kept shouting but no one heard. I climbed out the window and down the ivy onto the flat roof at the back.'

She had creamy skin with a flush of tan, brown hair falling from a centre parting, hazel eyes under dark arched brows. She was a younger, taller, beautiful version of Eleanor. She looked about seventeen or eighteen. But surely Eleanor could never have looked like that, confident yet wistful, loving yet withdrawn, courteous and sensitive, with a touch of laughter, a touch of sadness. A perfectly beautiful girl.

'Auntie Ruth,' she continued. 'How could you? Are they selling something?' She turned to look at them again with sympathy. 'Did you want to see someone from the house?'

Ruth closed her eyes.

'I'm – ' Eleanor said, and they were all poised in the centre of the silence that followed, waiting to be sucked down into a terrible maelstrom which would surely destroy each of them. 'I'm only a stranger,' Eleanor said, 'looking for directions.'

She made for the car and as Eve followed she saw Ruth beckon the girl to come inside. Before closing the door she looked straight into Eve's face, showing relief and something else. Eve thought it might be triumph.

They drove out the avenue gate, turned left, leaving the sea behind them, along the peaceful estuary glistening in the afternoon sun. On the far side Kerry and west Limerick blended together in a mixture of bog and heavy green pasture. Here Clare flung off the bitterness of the sea with its incessant demands and, celebrating its freedom, became flamboyant, lush. They drove along narrow leafy roads, bowers of green sycamore, chestnut and oak thrusting out of the hedgerows, small fields sheltering behind them, and always the innocent estuary glimmering to their right. They drove in a silence so cold that it hurt, the hum of the engine, the changes of gear, the sudden cry of brakes too fiercely applied only a background to their pain. Eve, who hated noise, leaned for comfort towards the engine sounds.

The car stopped to allow a herd of cattle to pass. Their drover whistled cheerfully to himself as they ambled along, stopping occasionally to pull at the hedges or the long grasses. Eleanor pulled into the verge to give them more room and switched off the ignition. It was only then that Eve saw that she was crying. The tears poured down her cheeks without any sign of upheaval, an overflow of despair.

'I'm so terribly sorry,' Eve said. 'I don't know what to say to comfort you.'

'That's a relief,' Eleanor answered, as if she wasn't crying, and with barely a shake to her voice. 'They always protested they didn't know where she was. I didn't really believe them. A family like that would never let one of its members go without a struggle. But what could I do? At first I kept in touch with them, thinking they might lead me to her, maybe drop a hint, give me a clue. Then it just became a habit, I suppose. I used to wonder about that September business but they are so adept at telling lies they make everything sound so reasonable, even funny at times. It's strange how people get into the habit of telling lies. You begin to accept their lies as normal and even make excuses for them. Perhaps they didn't know. Perhaps it was just a coincidence. Bridget is always on about coincidences.'

'I think they're wicked,' Eve said.

225

'Don't moralise. I'm simply their victim because they have always had the power to hurt me. I shouldn't have given them that power. That's why they were always able to wear the mask of good manners so well. They never had any need to rage.'

'I can remember Florence in a rage at intruders on the beach.'

'That wasn't rage. That was hysteria. They have lived so long together they must erupt sometimes. I understand why they are what they are. It's part of my affliction that I even understand their cruelty over my child.'

'You surely won't let them get away with it? I don't know how you can sit here being so calmly analytical when I know what you must be suffering.'

Eleanor wasn't listening. She was remembering the year she had spent in London in a miserable bedsitter, carrying on her futile search, working part-time in a dress shop. Every Sunday she walked a portion of Hyde Park or Regent's Park and occasionally Hampstead Heath watching for Donogh's tall figure and the giveaway blond hair. But there was never anyone even remotely like him. She peered into prams and chatted to toddlers. In the end it had become merely a routine exercise and she herself almost a zombie. If her Aunt Teresa had not died and left her enough money to see her through medical school, she might have become a drunken derelict – she had already taken to alcohol for relief. Back in Ireland, the year in London was like a bad dream. She had never been so near to taking her own life and yet she could never summon up quite enough courage. Often, as she stood on the shore or on a headland casting for bass or mackerel, she would marvel at her escape. There was a particular spot on the high road across the hills of Clare where the land stretched to the horizon, and only a passage grave showed the human presence, that invariably reminded her of her near disaster. The contrast between its emptiness and peace and the turmoil of her year of search in crowded streets and parks was so great that it helped to heal a little the bitterness of her betrayal. She could not begin to explain any of that to Eve. She could not even explain it to Adrian, and she hoped she would not have to try.

It was a pity that Eve had been there to witness the meeting and, worse, to witness her grief. She could say nothing more and still she would be the victim of Eve's pity. She might even strengthen the younger woman's burgeoning zeal for reform. What a waste if young Eve became an earnest, humourless missionary dropping leaflets through doorways, preaching and proselytising, spreading her particular propaganda on every possible occasion. Over the past year Eleanor had found herself becoming motherly and had to restrain herself – though Eve would never have guessed it – from an affection which she presumed was maternal. It was one thing being a kind of mentor – although she did not wish for that role either, there being too many dangers inherent in it – but it was quite another to inflict her own frustrated maternal instincts on her friend. Eve had had the sense to warn her off but the danger was there. Seeing her daughter had not aroused any great feelings of thwarted love. It was like meeting a stranger. Yet this was the baby she had carried in her body and born and nourished. She had fed her with her own milk. At that memory the tears welled up again and she cursed herself for her weakness. For years she had carefully protected herself from the tangle of emotions so much a part of love and friendship, and here she was embroiled in the worst of them. All that contempt, all that perverse wit crumbled away and there were no barriers left. Jeez, she said to herself in an effort to build up her defences, I've been caught with my knickers down.

For Eve, the silence was stifling. Her urge to comfort, her pity and love for her friend, her outrage at this most appalling injustice, were cemented into a prison from which only the rarest and most delicate words could rescue them. Perhaps Adrian could have found such words, he could have selected with the fastidious care of a mandarin a language which might be elegant and effective. She could not summon a suitable phrase which did not sound hackneyed, clichéd. She was imprisoned as much by her own perverse need for truth as by Eleanor's equally perverse practicality. I wish I were dumb, she thought. If I could utter no words I would touch her with my hand, and she could not shake my hand off.

They drove to Labasheeda, where Eleanor pulled up. 'I need a drink,' she said. 'I'm lousy company just now. But then, I'm a lousy bitch, as you always knew, and I'd probably have been a lousy mother.'

Eve got angry. 'What a liar you are. You're just as bad as they are. Why don't you simply hate them and be done with it? Why don't you raise hell, cause trouble, yell, do all the things you've been advising the rest of us to do?'

'You never listen, do you? You're even younger than I thought. When will you grow up? Didn't you see her face? Whatever lies the bastard told her, they must have been good ones. Probably that I'm dead. What do you think a resurrected mother would do to her?'

'She's not a baby. The truth is always best in the end.'

'Truth,' Eleanor declared, banging the car door. 'I don't know why I put up with you!'

'Leave me the key,' Eve said. 'I'll listen to the radio while you're inside swilling.'

When the pub door closed behind Eleanor, Eve slipped into the driver's seat and drove back to Tower Hill. Let Eleanor do what she liked; *she* was not going to be a party to more stupid deception.

Hugh's car was in the drive ahead of her. He came out to meet her. 'Don't say anything,' he said. 'I didn't know either. I swear. They kept it to themselves. I've had it out with them and I've told Eleanor's daughter that she has just met her mother. She's a very bewildered young woman at the moment but I think she understands. And she wants to meet Eleanor.'

'Eleanor will kill you. She didn't want that to happen.'

'Eleanor is a fool.'

'Aren't we all,' Eve said sadly.

When Adrian's car came screeching up the drive she felt like laughing, she didn't know why. Perhaps it was his outraged face as he emerged, grumbling about the variety of notes flying around his home and how his bantam cock had inexplicably attacked one of the hens and nearly killed her and why wasn't anyone there to keep an eye on things and why had they all rushed off here without explanation? And where was Eleanor and was someone dead and when was the funeral?

'Eleanor is getting drunk,' Hugh said. 'Her daughter has just turned up.'

'Sweet loving Christ.'

Bridget appeared at the front door and welcomed them in. 'Such a pity it had to happen this way,' she said. 'We had to give Donogh our word or he would never let us have the child here. What could we do? He never comes himself. Just sends her.'

'How could you have done that to Eleanor?' Eve asked. 'How could you have been so cruel?'

'Eleanor doesn't have feelings like the rest of us,' Bridget replied. 'She's very tough. We had given our word. We couldn't break that.'

'Don't argue about it,' Hugh said. 'What's done is done.'

'The poor bloody bitch,' Adrian said and scattered the gravel under his tyres as he chased after her to Labasheeda.

'Come in and have tea,' Bridget invited. 'We're simply exhausted with all this emotion. Poor Ruth is upstairs playing her accordion. Honora is crying and has just given young Honora the ruby to cheer her up, and Florence is in the kitchen helping Rosie to make a chocolate soufflé. What a funny old world it is.'

The evening tailed off somehow, incredibly without suicide or murder. Eve thought that either act would have been more fitting than the meal of cold beef and salad and the soufflé, which had collapsed because Rosie breathed on it. Hugh took her back to collect her things from Adrian's house and then he drove her to Limerick.

It was, surprisingly, quite a comfortable journey. Their discussions were cheerfully abstract. Even when they touched on freedom, injustice, systems, they steered carefully into harmless theories. Not once was Hugh able to say to her, 'You take everything too personally.' She obeyed all the rules, even discussing the fear of freedom without any reference to women. She knew she was learning something, although she was not sure what, and she didn't have Eleanor there to tell her.

19

'"There are," ' Eleanor quoted, ' "necessary treasons." Eve will learn that if she ever marries; although if she keeps on with these speeches, I can't see any true-blue Irish patriot taking her on. Positively undermining the comely maiden image.'

'Your reference, I assume, is to a certain brand of patriotism,' Adrian said. 'Otherwise I don't understand a word you're saying. "Necessary treasons." Whoever heard of such a thing!' He bestowed on her the tolerant, amused look she had often intercepted from expectant fathers.

'Look up your Greeks,' she said. 'And I am only pregnant. You're beginning to look at me as if I were slightly dotty. A fond and foolish expression was never what I expected from you.'

'Too bad,' he replied callously. 'It's too late to back out now.'

They had honeymooned in Rome as planned and were married a month later in a registry office. Adrian would have preferred a church wedding, but Eleanor said it was against her principles. She didn't seem to take seriously his objection that the registry office smacked of English Protestantism. She reminded him of his grandmother lying in her lonely grave overlooking the Shannon. 'I'm sure she'd approve. Poetic justice and all that. The wheel turns full circle. And life's little ironies, to boot. She must be chuckling to herself, across the road from her new neighbours in the old Williamite cottages. All a mere cannon ball roll away from the breached walls.'

'Why don't you pause for breath?' Adrian asked. 'You'll give yourself emphysema.'

He thought it a pity that she objected to his fond and foolish expression. It seemed to him to reflect, indeed to encourage, a comfortable tenderness. It had the soporific effect of a grain of phenobarbitone without the addictive side-effects.

They were ten months married. Eleanor was in her seventh month of pregnancy. Apart from one or two early alarms, he thought they had both weathered the pregnancy rather well. She bore his fussing and anxiety over an early threatened miscarriage with remarkable patience. As she wrote to Eve:

The poor fellow, I'm his last dab at immortality. He seems to have given up on the poetry for the time being. That saddens me. But I suppose it is rather a peculiar calling for a grown man. And fatherhood is creative enough at the moment. Perhaps it is just the novelty that's distracting him. No doubt, when nappy time comes, he'll discover inspirational sources afresh and he'll be able to retire with a good conscience, to compose some brilliant commentary on the human condition in three lines.

Such compassion from Eleanor was frightening, Eve thought, but then everything had changed so fast it was hard to keep up with events. The meeting on the doorstep of Hugh's house had consequences far removed from the collapsed soufflé. Eve herself ran away to visit a friend in the States for six months. Luxuriating in Santa Monica, Adrian remarked dismissively, as if indulgence in the pleasures of a good climate was sinful. She wrote to congratulate Eleanor on her pregnancy: *That is good news. I hope everything goes well.* Then went on to describe her meetings with women's groups in the US:

Here you realise what you can do with money. I wish we had more. It would solve so much. I have become quite material-istic. I am ashamed to say I even wish I had managed Hugh better. He would be useful later on. He seems to be getting places. Saying and doing all the right things. There is something to be said for manipulation. After all, it's what politics is all about.

'One visit to the fleshpots,' Adrian sneered, 'and all the high ideals fly out the window.'

'She is simply learning a bit faster than we did. Young people today understand about money and material things. We didn't. All that spirituality.' Eleanor's mouth drooped at the corners.

'I can't recall you being particularly spiritual,' Adrian laughed.

'You didn't know me very well,' she said and looked at him coldly.

There were many letters from Eve and all with a single obsession. Women. In trade unions, in religion, in revolution and reform, across continents and across the centuries. She commented on poets and painters, saints and sinners, the great foundresses of religious houses, the mesdames of the brothels, the patient Griseldas, the Joans of Arc, the earth mothers. It was as if at twenty-four she had had some unusual revelation about what it was to be female.

'Madame Butterfly,' Adrian said contemptuously.

Even Eleanor began to find it too much. Besides, when she visited her obstetrician and was able to see through the scanner the developing baby inside her own body, ideas, dreams and passions became commonplace when compared with the extraordinary miracle being shaped within her flesh. She wrote twice to her daughter Honora, painful, tear-stained letters which she tore up, and posted in their place carefully worded prose, confirming their relationship but making no demands or accusations. In reply, she had two dutiful letters, equally undemanding.

At one time Eleanor had hoped for a daughter to replace the child she had lost, but Honora in the flesh altered everything. A boy would be different but, best of all, with him there could be no comparisons, no indulgence in wistful might-have-beens. He would be just himself.

They called to see Hugh's family when Hugh himself was on one of his rare visits there.

'He hardly ever comes now,' Bridget said. 'And he never stays for the rosary.'

232

'Mother would be very upset if she knew,' Florence nodded.

'One good thing,' Ruth remarked. 'He has given up poking in the past. It can't have been healthy.'

'Another good thing,' Florence said. 'He doesn't believe in women politicians. He'll keep them in their place.'

'Quite right too,' Honora said. 'But fortunately most women have too much sense to be bothered.'

They stood delicately back to allow Eleanor's extra girth more room, but they never mentioned the expected baby. They asked after her health and congratulated her on looking so fit and well. Several times during the evening, Adrian referred in an oblique way to the fact that they would soon be parents but they ignored him.

'It's a pity you are so busy now, Hugh,' Ruth said, at the same time shooting a black look at Eleanor. 'I wanted to ask your advice. But I have decided anyway. I'm going to give the bundle of letters to Donogh's daughter.'

'She is my daughter too,' Eleanor said mildly.

'Of course dear. We know that. It's not always easy to remember. She is like poor dear mother in so many ways. Apart from the hair colour.'

'As I remember her, she seemed very like her own mother,' Adrian said stiffly.

'Well, never mind,' Florence said. 'It doesn't matter who she is like. And after all, she is nothing to you, Adrian,' she said deliberately, staring at him.

Eleanor kicked him under the table when he bent his head to hide his rage.

'I thought I had put all the letters in my safe,' Hugh said coldly.

'Oh, these are different. I've had these for years. Didn't I mention them to you? Grandmother gave them to me herself.'

Hugh leaped to his feet. 'I wish you wouldn't be so secretive,' he cried. 'You know how much time I have spent sorting out those papers. And now you tell me you have more. Where are they?'

'Oh, for goodness sake, sit down and finish your meal.

You'll give us all indigestion. Patience. Patience,' Ruth said and reached for the jam sauce.

Hugh got up and left the room.

'Tsk ...' Bridget said. 'He's getting very touchy. I'm afraid his poor heart is broken. We always felt it was a mistake, you know. But you can't advise people. They will go their own way. Everyone learns the hard way. Go after him, Ruth. Give him the letters if he wants them. He has a greater claim to them than Honora.'

'It's very rude to leave the table in the middle of a meal,' Ruth complained. 'Especially when we have guests. Would you like another glass of blackberry wine, Adrian? The elderberry is quite good too. A little too joli beau for me.' She laughed at her joke.

'I'm sure he'd prefer a glass of whiskey, and when you're on your feet get the letters for Hugh or he'll sulk all night. You mustn't think we are always like this.' Bridget turned to Adrian. 'But we have had some little upsets lately. Poor Hugh. What an escape! We've heard her on the wireless. Always going on about something. Always giving out.'

'Anything for peace,' Ruth said and left the room also.

'Isn't it lovely to have the natural light for late dinner?' Honora beamed. 'It must be my age or something but I find the winters harder and harder to bear.'

'There you go again,' Florence frowned. 'You'll have us all in the grave the way you go on.'

Across the table from Eleanor, Adrian emitted a great sigh of despair. Eleanor winked at him and Bridget rose, saying haughtily, 'We'll leave you two love birds to share your little secrets while we clear up. Poor Rosie is quite beyond it.'

'Christ,' Adrian groaned after they had left bearing dishes and pushing the tea trolley. He and Eleanor sat in splendour, gazing at each other across the expanse of polished mahogany and the centrepiece of dried flowers and leaves. 'I hope you don't intend to do this too often. You'll have to come on your own next time.'

'It's great fun,' Eleanor said. 'Relax and enjoy it.'

From upstairs loud angry voices were heard and then a

thumping as if something heavy was being dragged across a floor.

'That's the body,' Eleanor explained solemnly, 'being pushed into the wardrobe. I wonder is it Hugh's or Ruth's.'

'Perhaps it is Rosie's,' Adrian suggested, and they giggled callously.

A flushed Hugh opened the door, said, 'Oh, there you are,' and closed it quickly without coming in. A wailing sound of piano-accordion wind being squeezed out floated down from a room above.

'Herewith the dying moans of a dinosaur,' Adrian chanted.

'Ruth tunes up before burning the house down,' Eleanor contributed, and as Hugh came back, 'Enter Hugh.'

'What?' asked Hugh, not caring. 'I got the letters. Nothing important after all. But I do like to have all the family papers together. Saves confusion.'

'That would be useful,' Eleanor said.

'There's something I've been meaning to say to you. Well, to give you both. Well, for the baby. Some investments I didn't expect to do well have provided me with a windfall. I'd like you both to accept it.'

Ignoring their embarrassed protests, he gave Eleanor a cheque for £5,000.

'I wish you wouldn't,' Eleanor said, looking for support from Adrian, who just shrugged and laughed.

'In some ways I feel responsible for what happened, about young Honora. Although it wasn't my fault. And I knew nothing about it. Still, they are my family.' He stared for a moment at the wall opposite, where all the photographs hung, and then blurted out, 'I want you to know that I don't hold anything against you about that other business. It wouldn't have worked anyway. And I wish you both all the happiness in the world.'

'Don't, Hugh. You'll unwoman me or something,' Eleanor said shakily.

'You've plenty of guts, Eleanor. I've always admired that in you, though you can be difficult at times. But you're a fine

235

doctor. I'd better go and tell Ruth it's all right about the letters. I'm afraid I upset her.'

The silence he left behind was heavy with guilt and remorse. Adrian reached across the table, pushing aside the flowers, and patted Eleanor's hand.

'The terrible thing is, I'm fond of him, but I don't really like him, if you know what I mean,' she said.

'No, I don't. I don't want to unravel any more complexities. It's too taxing for my simple mind.'

'I suppose it's tied up with Donogh,' Eleanor mused. 'Though Hugh isn't really like him. But they are bound together in some way. And, although I hate Donogh for what he did to me, there probably is a touch of love somewhere there.'

Adrian cupped his face in his hands and said, 'I won't play second fiddle to an old romance, so don't try that on.'

As they said goodbye at the door, Florence beckoned to Bridget, who was digging in the garden. 'Hurry up,' she called. 'They're going.'

'I've something for Eleanor's garden,' Bridget explained when she climbed the steps, panting a little. 'I know you have always liked the ceanothus. Blue is such a good colour in the garden. I started this one from a cutting two years ago and it is quite strong and healthy now.'

'What about the agapanthus?' Florence apparently did not wish to be outdone in generosity. 'Give me the trowel and I'll get a root.'

'Very kind of you,' Eleanor said, surfeited with gifts, and waited while they fetched paper bags and placed soil in them, followed by the plants. Ruth and Honora joined them, smiling.

'I think the weather is going to pick up,' Ruth said, gazing benignly at the sky.

'We're due a good summer,' Eleanor agreed. 'Bye-bye. Bye.' She was still waving and craning her neck to catch a last glimpse of them as the car turned out of the drive. At the last moment Hugh's dark shape joined them but she couldn't see if he waved.

'Next time,' Adrian promised loudly, 'you can go on your

own. Thank God I was an only child and, as far as I know, I have no cousins.'

Eleanor didn't answer but patted the mound of her stomach thoughtfully.

'Women are quite remarkable for treachery,' Adrian continued musingly. 'It always amazes me. I suppose it's a kind of survival.'

'There are necessary treasons,' Eleanor reminded him.

'Your trouble,' Adrian remarked as they drove through Labasheeda, 'is that you feel guilty about Eve. You led her into temptation and now you are afraid you may have to deliver her from evil.'

'Now it's my turn to pretend I don't know what you're talking about. But I think I'll give her Hugh's cheque. For the cause. That's if you don't mind.'

'It's your money, although it was meant for our son. But if it will assuage your guilt, by all means do it. Don't you think it smacks of thirty pieces of silver?'

'Is it my fault she turned into a zealot?' Eleanor asked crankily. 'I tried to warn her. Everyone does their own thing.'

'A convenient philosophy. Next time someone is drowning and you are standing beside the lifebelt, I must remind you of it.'

'Shut up,' she retorted. 'I'm getting labour pains. Do you want a premature baby?'

'Blackmailer,' he said, shutting up.

'She seems to have pinned her hopes on the American women,' Eleanor relented. 'But she shouldn't count her chickens before they're hatched. They can bite the dust in true pioneer spirit too.'

'Yiz don't know when yiz are well off,' Adrian mocked and laughed because he knew Eleanor was gritting her teeth.

Eve returned from the States to find Ann ill and the refuge in a sorry state of disrepair, pigeons nesting over the ceilings and a smell of damp and stale urine everywhere. Children tumbled over each other and the mothers struggled to keep control. Upstairs in the icy bedrooms, small babies coughed. The lavatories were blocked. The committee drank coffee and complained that there was nothing they could do. She rushed to visit Ann in hospital and found her retching dryly and continuously.

'Why didn't you write?' she asked. 'Why didn't someone tell me you were ill?'

'I hadn't been feeling well for a long time,' Ann explained. 'I kind of got used to it. But it got worse after you left. I had different check-ups, you know. But you *know* what doctors are like. This was the first one to take notice. He said he heard "bowel sounds" if you don't mind, so he took me in. It's nearly a fortnight since the operation but I feel pretty lousy still.'

'Oh, Ann darling,' Eve said piteously and held her hand.

'Don't cry, or I'll cry too. Tell me a funny story. But not too funny. I don't want to laugh either.'

'I've just been to the refuge.'

'Don't tell me. I don't want to know. I want to forget about all of that. I just want to feel well again.'

'You will, you'll see, you will,' Eve promised.

She lied many times during the next few weeks when she visited Ann and watched her shrink and fade. She lied to herself, to Ann's husband, to Ann. They all lied, watching Ann die. The tumour had not been benign. It had been discovered too late. The surgeon had opened Ann up and then closed her again. That was the truth. It had been explained in medical jargon, but it was the truth. There was nothing anyone could do but sit and comfort her and love her.

'It's easy to love Ann,' Eve confided in Eleanor. 'She is the most marvellous, heroic person I have ever met.'

'Oh! Isn't that a bit extreme?'

'You don't know her. I wish I hadn't gone away when I did. I'm sure I should have noticed she was ill.'

'Well, it's too late now for reproaches.'

'Don't you have any compassion at all?'

'Not much. I've been puking all morning. I've got varicose veins. I'm carrying two-ton Tessie in my inside. It doesn't leave much room for compassion.'

238

'Well, I suppose that's what you get for being pregnant,' Eve said tartly.

'Oh, touché, touché.' Eleanor grinned and Eve apologised.

'Why do you ruin everything by apologising?' Eleanor asked. 'You're just coming along nicely and you go and spoil everything.'

'I'm a slow learner,' Eve said grimly and left.

Eleanor was in labour when Miranda Connors's husband stabbed his wife. He was newly out of prison, having served a six-month prison sentence for contempt of court when he broke the debarring order. She was in hospital and her husband on remand when Eleanor was delivered of an eight pound two and a half ounce baby boy by caesarean section.

'I was in trouble,' she admitted to Adrian. 'I had forgotten what it was like. But everyone was marvellous.'

She lay in bed looking bruised, her lips purple, her damp hair stuck to her forehead. It seemed as if all her vigour had been drained out or transferred to the new little lump of humanity in the cot beside the bed. Adrian looked at the wrinkled red face of his son and wondered if he would be stirred to write a poem about him. He tried a few phrases, considered a few words and wished he had brought his dictionary with him. New life. There was surely something new to be said about that and the mother, the vessel. He looked with interest at her, conscious of the irony of it. That would make a poem.

'How do you feel?' he asked.

'I inhabit the wax image of myself. I am a dartboard for witches.'

He was astonished. Did giving birth do that to her, release some creative energy long dormant? A dartboard for witches. He loved it.

'It's not mine,' she said wearily. 'Eve gave me a book of poems by Sylvia Plath.' He bent his head to hide his resentment. For the first time he observed the body of the baby, its forehead, the little blob of its nose. He stared intently and, as if aware of his gaze, the baby grimaced. Adrian smiled

239

and touched the tiny fist. When he turned around to look at Eleanor, she had drifted into sleep. He crept out of the room.

Along the corridor, white-clad nurses moved briskly. Through open doors he had glimpses of reclining bodies in pastel colours, pale pinks, baby blues. At the head of the stairs a long room housed many more. A technician tinkered at a machine, a carpenter repaired a cupboard. Out of doors on each side of the gravel paths, the flowerbeds were carefully blooming while a gardener hoed between them. As Adrian was leaving, an ambulance swerved to a jolting stop at the front door. Everything was very well organised. He felt enormously contented.